RENDER

THE RESISTANCE TRILOGY, BOOK TWO

K. A. RILEY

To my spouse, my partner, my best friend, my lover, my rock, and my wings: thank you for being so many magnificent people all in one!

"We don't even know how strong we are until we are forced to bring that hidden strength forward. In times of tragedy, of war, of necessity, people do amazing things. The human capacity for survival and renewal is awesome."

— Isabel Allende

"The croaking raven doth bellow for revenge."

— Shakespeare, *Hamlet* (Act 3, scene 2)

A NOTE FROM THE AUTHOR

Dearest Fellow Conspirator,

What you have in your hands is one-ninth of what's called an *ennealogy*, a rare and hard-to-pronounce word meaning "a nine-part series." It's basically three sequential, interlocking trilogies. (Think *Star Wars* or *Planet of the Apes*)

Here is the Reading Order for the *Conspiracy Ennealogy*…

#1: **Resistance Trilogy**
> *Recruitment*
> *Render*
> *Rebellion*

#2: **Emergents Trilogy**
> *Survival*
> *Sacrifice (Coming in November 2019)*
> *Synthesis (Coming in early 2020)*

#3: **Transcendent Trilogy**

Travelers
Transfigured
Terminus

I'm glad you chose to join in the Conspiracy! Enjoy the revolution!

— KAR

PROLOGUE

I don't really know how long it's been since the six of us escaped from the Processor.

We've been on the run from Hiller's soldiers for three or four weeks. Maybe more. It's hard to say, since the sun seems to come and go at will. We get our bearings by shadows and daylight when we can, and we go by our guts when we can't.

When we first discovered that the Eastern Order was a phantom, an intricate fabrication created to scare us into compliance, we lost all sense of purpose and our very reason for being. In the space of a few minutes, we went from lives of certainty to lives of pure chaos.

It wasn't only the revelation about the Order that hit hard, though.

Before Hiller took her own life, Amaranthine, Brohn and I listened, breath trapped in our chests, as she told us, "You're the ones whose abilities were beyond our control. Amaranthine's techno-sensitivity. Kress's telepathy…and you, Brohn…well, you haven't even begun to discover your power yet."

You'd think that being on the run for weeks would give someone a lot of time to contemplate what it all means. But not me. I'm still too freaked out to accept that I might really be some kind of telepathic raven-whisperer.

Brohn says he doesn't feel any different from before, although I suspect he's just masking his fear of what's coming, trying to be strong for all our sakes. Amaranthine, or Manthy, as we call her, barely talks to us on her best days. So it's as difficult as ever to know what's going on inside her head.

When we first escaped, the three of us agreed not to say anything about our "powers" to Cardyn, Kella, or Rain. Over time, though, we slowly broke down and told them everything we'd discovered up in the Halo, everything Hiller had told us about ourselves. We're a family after all, and families aren't supposed to keep things from each other.

Once we revealed our secret, Cardyn told us he was impressed. Rain seemed jealous. Kella didn't care one way or the other. She doesn't care about much these days.

Those were difficult conversations. How do you tell someone you've known all your life that you might have some kind of super power, and that your potential abilities are the reason the government kidnapped you and pretty much everyone you've ever known?

The worst part, though, was realizing that our abilities are the reason two of our best friends are dead. There used to be eight of us. We lost Terk and Karmine to the very people we thought we were being trained to help. Losing them carved a massive hole in each of us. A void nothing can fill.

Even when we didn't have anything, we always had each other. Now our Conspiracy of eight is down to six—seven, if you count Render, the jet-black raven who's been my friend and constant companion since I was a young girl.

Thanks to our time in the Processor, any shred of innocence we had left is gone. Every trace of trust has been ripped away. Without Terk and Karmine, we can never go back to what we used to be. We've lost too much.

Life on the run has meant a constant feeling of dread about what happens if we're caught and recaptured—and just as much dread about what happens if we aren't. We stay out of sight as much as we can. Every once in a while, when we need a respite from the woods, we're forced to follow the endless abandoned highway that takes us through an oppressive red desert. We keep going, hoping we can find a friendly town before we starve to death or, even worse, Hiller's soldiers track us down and kill us themselves.

But until we get our bearings, we can't hope to get any more answers. And without answers, we don't have any hope.

We're heading west. That's about all we know. We're pretty sure it's the direction of the Valta, the direction we came from.

The direction of home.

OVER THE LAST SEVERAL WEEKS, WE'VE PASSED A FEW SMALL TOWNS. At least, what used to be towns. Now, they're nothing but smoldering, heartbreaking lumps of fused black carbon.

In the single bombed-out town that's not too hot to approach, we do our best to wander through the cluttered and cratered laneways that are all that remain of the roads. We kick aside smoking debris of buildings and businesses. There are no supplies and nothing lying around we can make use of. The damage here is devastating. It is also complete. We're not sure who did this, but whoever it was, they weren't looking to send a message or win a war. This was total and uncompromising annihilation.

While the others wander off, I find myself frozen in place, staring at the wreckage as Render soars overhead, appraising the totality of the ruins. I close my eyes to study the scene below through the raven's mind. My gut clenches when all I take in is the horror of nothingness. Molten steel. Remnants of homes. Contorted skeletal remains of human beings burnt beyond all recognition.

"We'd better move on," I announce to the others in a quivering voice when I've seen all I can stand. "There's nothing for us here."

"You okay?" Brohn asks, sidling up next to me and laying a gentle hand on the small of my back. I look up into his eyes to see the same emotions that are eating away at me. Fear. Hopelessness. Sadness. He may not have looked through Render's eyes, but he knows what's out there just as well as I do.

I'm grateful for him. Grateful that he keeps me warm at night. That he checks in on me when he sees me go into silent moments of mourning. Grateful that he understands when I need space and when I need companionship. He's not my boyfriend, not exactly. I can't even imagine that such a word exists in a world like this. But he's my shelter. He's my protector. He's the most important person in the world to me right now, because he's one of the few people who understands me.

"I'll be fine," I tell him. "There's just so much...nothing. It's hard to take."

"I know," he replies, his voice barely more than a whisper. I know what's going through his mind right now, because it's the same thing that's in mine.

"The good news," I sigh, "is that I don't feel totally lost. Not as long as we have a general sense of direction and a specific sense of purpose. There are only two things I really care about right now."

Brohn nods. "Getting home and getting revenge," he says. "If we can just find the right road to the right mountain, and actually find our way back to the Valta..." he adds, but he doesn't finish the thought. We all know the chances of finding our way are low. But the stakes are high. We need to warn the friends we left behind about the danger they're in.

If it's not already too late, that is.

"Let's go," I say, taking his hand and squeezing before letting it go. I try not to flaunt our tenuous relationship in front of the others. It seems cruel, given that everyone in our group is alone.

The last thing I want is to be a cause of more pain for anyone in our Conspiracy.

"Where is everyone?" Rain asks as we climb our way out of the black and blistered crater of a town and return to our endless march. "I don't get it. If there's no enemy, where are all the people? What happened here?"

"Just because there's no enemy doesn't mean there's no war," I remind her. "Besides, we don't *know* there's no enemy. All we know is what Hiller told us, and she's not—I mean wasn't—the most reliable source of information."

Rain knows all this. Still, she's right to ask. Growing up, all we knew of the outside world was that our nation was engaged in a desperate fight against the invading Eastern Order, a ruthless army of cold-blooded killers. Now it turns out the world is empty, the enemy we thought we knew is an invention, and the war itself might be a lie.

But there is more going on here than Hiller admitted to. Every trail, road, and highway we walk is abandoned. There are no civilian mag-transports. No rumble of military convoys. There aren't even any spy-and-assault drones flying overhead.

Nothing.

"No one around means no one to attack us," Manthy mutters, nodding in quiet agreement with herself.

"No one around also means no help," Rain replies.

"Great," Cardyn adds with a dramatic eye-roll. "Lost and alone. Probably the two worst things anyone can be."

Brohn shakes his head. "I can think of a few things worse than that." We all know he's talking about Terk and Karmine.

Brohn and Karmine were rivals. But they were also friends who had come to rely on each other as we endured months of intense military and psychological training at the hands of the Recruiters. Brohn also had a special relationship with Terk, our gentle giant of a friend. From the day we were loaded into the back of the Recruiters' truck, Brohn's natural leadership abilities and Terk's intimidating size combined to form a wall around the rest of us, a wall we figured would keep us all safe for a long time.

Three months later, Karmine and Terk were both dead, and the rest of us were on the run from an enemy we never saw coming.

I watch from behind as Brohn lays a hand on Cardyn's shoulder. "Besides, we're not alone. We have each other."

"He's right," I say. "We're all we have left, but at least that's something to be grateful for." Then again, we're all we've ever had. Whether we were secluded in the Valta or locked away in the Processor, we always found a way to survive as a group.

For the past ten years, the Recruiters showed up in the Valta every November 1st like clockwork. They gathered up the new Seventeens, leaving everyone else to wait and wonder for another year. We spent every one of those years terrified about what the war and the outside world looked like. The viz-screens showed us cities on fire and our military in motion. We saw the enemy, the dreaded "Eastern Order," commit every atrocity imaginable. They flew bomb-carrying drones into buildings, shot up schools, ransacked cities, attacked women and children on the streets, and spread through our nation like the worst kind of virus. They were ruthless, evil, and completely unstoppable.

As it turns out, they may have also been non-existent.

When it was my Cohort's turn to be recruited, things went slanted, and we found answers to many of our questions and to a host of others we'd never even thought to ask. Now, the big dilemma is whether it was better being tricked or being disillusioned.

With no answer to that one yet, our only goal is to get back home, share what we've learned with those who still live in the Valta, and strategize about how to survive going forward.

As we trudge along, Rain says, "I wonder what we'll find if we ever make it home."

It's a question we've speculated about a few times, and one

that fills us with dread. I find myself looking over at Brohn, whose body tightens under the weight of the possibilities. He's the one with the most at stake in this journey of ours. My father and brother both disappeared ages ago, so I have no family left back home. No one does except for Brohn, whose sister Wisp had to stay behind when we were taken.

As we walk along, we debate the possibilities, partly as a way to pass the time, partly as a way to remind ourselves of everything that used to be, back in the days before the Recruitment.

"It'll probably look exactly like it did when we left," Cardyn says. "Shoshone High with its leaky roof. A bunch of caved-in buildings for the kids to run around in."

"Gardens," I add, recalling our attempts to cultivate vegetables. I miss the things that grew. I miss the greenness of the mountainside, the freshness of the air. Right now, it feels like we're in a wasteland, like the home we once knew is little more than a dream, a figment of our collective imagination.

As if listening in and agreeing with me, Render lets out a loud *kraa!* from somewhere overhead, which makes a few of us chuckle. There's something reassuring about his presence. Having a flying sentinel along on our trek makes us feel protected. We know he'll warn us of any potential trouble. He might even find a way to guide us in the right direction if we stray from the path.

As we walk and speculate about our uncertain future, we veer from joyful optimism to moments of total terror with a bunch of uncertainty sprinkled in. We talk about old times, the war, and about our months of being trained, tortured, and tricked by Hiller and her army of evil liars. It's an embarrassing and infuriating subject, but it's one we can't seem to avoid talking about. Anything to take our minds off our blistered feet and empty bellies.

Since our escape, we've come close to exhausting the meager supplies we were able to find back in the Eta Cube of the Processor. We've been stretching everything out as long as we can. The three small meal-replacement bars lasted nearly a week, but that was only after we split them up into pieces not much bigger than crumbs. A bag of protein flakes got us through another week. The salt tablets went fast, along with the iodine pills Rain said might help with water purification along the way. We divided up four palm-sized packages of crackers and spread out three bottles of a meal-replacement drink over a period of another week.

Brohn's expertise in hunting and trapping has saved us from crippling hunger a few times. Using one of the knives he swiped from our old training facility, he was able to rig a small trap that caught two skimpy squirrels, which he skinned and then cooked over a homemade fire. We supplemented that with anything remotely edible we could scavenge in the thin stretches of desolate woods scattered between expanses of dried-out land. At one point, we got lucky and stumbled across a trove of wax currants and holly grapes, which I remembered were safe to eat, even though Rain had her doubts.

"I'm sure there was something toxic in those," she said.

"It's called 'berberine,'" I reminded her. "It's only dangerous to newborns and pregnant women. I think we'll be okay."

"I don't know how you remember that," she said with a sideways glance in my direction. "Ria taught us those lessons about edible plants years ago. We couldn't have been more than nine or ten at the time."

"I don't know how I know either," I replied. "I just do."

Rain relented, and we wound up getting a nice energy boost, enough to keep us going for one more day.

When I told her I wasn't sure how I remembered the stuff about the berries, I wasn't lying. The truth is, I still don't quite understand what's happened to my memory over the past few months. It's like my brain took a video-capture of every moment of my life, and I'm only now learning how to press play, zoom in, and have a look around.

I didn't mention to Rain that I could remember everything about Ria, the Sixteen who taught us about the vegetation around the Valta. And I do mean that I remembered *everything*: Every item of clothing she ever wore. The way she moved. The spectrum of browns—chestnut, auburn, copper—in her hair. The cadence of her voice. The scar on her temple. The unevenness of her eyebrows. The sparkle of green in the irises of her eyes. Even the pattern of lines on the palms of her hands. Ria took us on a whole bunch of field trips in the woods around our isolated mountain town. She showed us Kinnikinnick, Rabbitbrush, Holly Grape, and a dozen other plants, and explained all about their uses and chemical compositions. Her mother was a botanist and one of the last adults to die in the drone attacks.

All this I remember now, even though if someone had asked me about it a few months ago, I couldn't have begun to tell them any of it.

I haven't been able to bring myself to tell Rain or the others what's happening to me. I already feel like a freak because of what Hiller said about my telepathic connection with Render. I'd always attributed our link to the implants—the "tattoos" as everyone calls them—that my father gave me when I was younger.

It sounds silly in my own head given everything that's happened, but part of me also feels protective of the little tidbit about my super-charged memory. After all, if my newly-enhanced power comes from my link to Render, it's his secret as much as mine, and I don't feel right betraying his trust. I don't think we'd have made it anywhere close to this far without him.

Like me, he seems to be getting smarter and more resourceful by the day. In a nearly lifeless world, he's brought us back remnants of field mice and once led us to the carcass of a mule deer. Of course, a black bear the size of an army jeep had already staked its claim, and we weren't quite desperate or crazy enough to challenge it.

With clicks and *kraas!* and even the occasional human-sounding holler, Render has alerted us to the presence of rogue, rabid wolves, which we've given a wide berth. He's even given us advance notice about radical temperature fluctuations by screeching and shepherding us under trees or rocky outcroppings to get us out of the sun when the reddish rays of midday are burning their hottest.

Overall, it's been an exhausting slog, one foot in front of the other, as we rely on our wits and our will-power to keep pushing forward and to keep from going insane along the way.

FOR THE PAST FEW DAYS, Render has been leading us along the dried-up river bed. The steep banks on either side give us some protection from the heat. Sometimes the bed disappears completely, and we find ourselves tromping along through clusters of crusted gray reeds and over fields of jagged red rocks. Every once in a while, the river bed returns, and Render leads us to small pockets in the earth where brownish water gurgles in shallow pools.

We drink when Render does, and we don't when he doesn't.

We keep trudging on, weighed down by knowledge and experience. When the parched ravine finally fades, we stumble upon yet another deserted highway, wide, overgrown with parasitic weeds, and sticky from the desert heat. Abandoned hydro-cell transports, burned nearly beyond recognition, sit like charred metal tombstones along the shoulders of the road. Deep craters pock-mark the highway in places where the pavement has been fused into glass by thermal plasma-bombs. Except for the eerie absence of other people, this is the world we witnessed from the viz-screens. It's the world we thought we were being trained to save. It's a depressing sight, and I find myself hoping for any sign of life. Right now, anything would do: a roving band of thugs, looters, a rogue militia, army deserters. Anything to reassure us that we aren't the last people on earth.

As we continue our march, Cardyn does his best to keep our spirits up by regaling us with tales of our young lives back in the Valta. Of course, they're stories we already know. After all, we lived them. But they're nice to hear anyway.

His timing is uncanny. Just when I'm thinking I can't take another step, just when I'm wondering if this next bend in the road is where I'll finally need to sit down and surrender to this relentless emotional and physical fatigue, Cardyn's voice rings out in the open expanse of the desolate highway.

His stories all start the same way: "Remember the time...?" and finish with any number of old memories:

"...when Terk lifted that giant cross-beam off Spence's leg and when Spence complained and called Terk a 'big clumsy idiot,' Terk dropped it on his other leg?"

Or "...when the Colson girls spent the whole day bragging about all those sacks of wild onions they'd gathered for Final Feast a few years back, and one of the Sixteens had to tell them it was actually Death Camas, and it was all poisonous?"

Or "...when Kress told that one Neo that if he didn't start helping out with the Clean-up Crew she was going to have Render peck his lips off in the middle of the night?"

And just like that, Cardyn has us laughing, transported back to the Valta. Back to uncertain but safer times. Back to when all we had to worry about was survival, instead of survival *and* betrayal *and* the distinct possibility of being hunted down and executed like the thirteen boys and girls we saw back in the clearing behind the Processor.

Despite the welcome distraction of Cardyn's stories, I can't shake the image of those thirteen bodies, their heads sagging as blood pooled around them. We don't know who they were or why they were butchered like that. They were kids. Probably Seventeens, like us. They could have *been* us if we hadn't gotten out of there when we did. Now, every step we take reminds me that we're a step farther away from a horrible tragedy that could have been. I keep reminding myself we're alive. We survived when others didn't. We escaped what could have been a terrible end.

It's small comfort, though, since I'm also reminded about my friends who didn't make it...and about how little I know about what's to come.

As we push on, I look back to see that Rain is walking next to Brohn, listening absently to Cardyn, trying to stay positive by taking in his half-hearted promises that our safe haven is just over the next hill or around the next bend in the road.

Little pangs of jealousy still assault me from time to time when I see Brohn and Rain together. I know it's selfish, but I want to be the one walking with Brohn, talking about home as we try to keep each other's spirits up. But Rain has a way about her, a kind of confidence and magnetism that draws people in. I can see why Brohn would feel strengthened around her. Besides, I remind myself, he's not mine. The important thing is that we all support each other and that we survive to see another day. Petty jealousy seems like too trivial an emotion to focus on in times like these.

Somehow, I keep winding up in the lead with Manthy walking just a half-step behind me. Every once in a while, after I forget she's still with us, I catch a glimpse of her shaggy-haired shadowy figure out of the corner of my eye. It's like she's decided that the back of the line isn't for her anymore. Instead, she's content to pad along at my side. We don't talk, but it's oddly comforting to know she's there.

It used to be that Manthy consistently brought up the rear, but that's Kella's position now. Kella barely says a word to anyone anymore. Her once tidy blond hair has become an unkempt tangle. Her smooth, flawless skin has grown rough from our journey. Her big blue eyes have gone a sad, sunken gray. She walks with her head low. Sometimes, she looks back the way we came, no doubt with Karmine on her mind. They were two of a kind. Gung-ho. High-energy. Heroic. Eager to finish our training so they could do their part to win our country back from the dreaded Eastern Order.

For Kella, all of that ambition died with Karmine.

Cardyn tries to talk to her sometimes, but her eyes remain empty with no desire to be filled. She barely seems to have any desire at all. She doesn't eat or drink. Her already thin frame has gone nearly skeletal. Her ribs push through her shirt like brittle twigs under a pile of dry leaves. It's like watching a slow suicide from the vantage point of a helpless onlooker.

I know she feels alone now. I try to tell her she's not, that we're still in this together, that everything will be okay. But even as I say it, the lies feel like acid in my mouth. Nothing is okay. I lost my family. Kella lost Karmine. We've all lost Terk, our home, and our innocent belief that we knew our enemy and understood the nature of the war raging around us.

At some point during our long trek, I stopped trying to reach out to Kella. Not because I was giving up on her, but because I was convinced she'd already given up on herself. And nothing I could say or do was going to bring her back.

"What's that?" Cardyn asks, snapping me out of the trance I feel like I've been in for days now.

I put my hand over my eyes to shield them from the sun, and I follow to where Cardyn is pointing.

"Not sure."

Brohn and Rain step up to stand on either side of me. "What is it?" Brohn asks, his hand on my shoulder in a quiet gesture of intimacy.

"Look there."

I point off into the distance with Brohn leaning down just

above my arm to follow my finger with his eyes. Up ahead, the foothills to a range of mountains appear through a shimmering wall of heat rising up from the broiling highway.

"Well," Rain sighs. "Should we head that way?"

"If there are mountains, it's just as good as any way," I say. "It might just be the safe haven we've been looking for."

Cardyn squints in the direction of the distant peaks. "Why do I get the feeling those might be famous last words?"

I assure him we'll be fine and begin to lead our group toward the patches of green at the foot of the remote mountain range.

After a while, my tired eyes make out a thin column of smoke rising up from a cluster of trees about halfway up the nearest mountain. At first I think it must be an optical illusion or a mirage, like the image of an oasis that fills your heart and then crushes it when you rub your eyes and it disappears.

But the others see it, too.

Rain suggests we head toward it. "Could be others like us," she says. "Runaways. Sixteens or even Seventeens who escaped like we did. People who can help."

Urging caution, Cardyn warns it could be a trap. "Or the Eastern Order."

"The Eastern Order isn't what we thought it was, remember?" I remind him. "Our own government's been lying to us for probably our entire lives. I need to know why. If there are people in those woods, I'm pretty sure they're not the government. They're probably on the run like us, which means they might have something to offer us other than torture and lies."

Cardyn must sense the fury and determination in my voice, because he doesn't push back. Brohn says he agrees with me. Kella and Manthy don't say anything.

"So I guess that means we go for it," I say.

"It's not exactly going to be easy getting over there," Rain points out.

She's right. In between us and the forest-speckled mountain is a blazing desert of deep fissures, razor-sharp rocks, and a massive expanse of hot red sand. It's how I imagine Mars must look. Only this place is scorching hot instead of icy cold.

After consulting with the others, I send Render out on a scouting mission and move away from the group. Connecting my mind silently to the raven's, I sit down on the hard ground and let the world in front of me go hazy white. The world around me disappears, replaced by flashes of the charred earth sweeping by far below, then by tangles of a half-dead forest, and finally by the column of smoke rising from the mountainside.

Render's memory and attention to detail are uncanny. His eyes and mind soak up visual information the way the dry earth soaks up rain. My eyes and mind don't always line up perfectly with his, so I can't sort through it all yet, but I'm learning.

He returns from his reconnaissance now, dropping down from the big looping circles he's been making with his winged, glistening black body cutting through the blood-red sky. Everything he's seen—plus his instincts and emotions—fills my mind in an overwhelming rush of sensation. The images are fuzzy, but the feelings are clear.

"There's risk up ahead," I tell the others. "There's danger in the mountains on the other side of this desert. There are people over there who know we're here, and they're preparing for us. It's not a welcome. It's an attack. An ambush."

"Then maybe we shouldn't…" Cardyn begins, but I stop him.

"But there's also hope," I say. "Render can sense it. I can, too." I look at Brohn, who nods his head slightly in a gesture of understanding.

With Render gliding ahead and the others close behind, I take a step into the forbidding desert. I head toward the slender plume of smoke snaking out above the distant foothills, leading our Conspiracy into the next unknown.

2

THINKING WE MAY HAVE FINALLY STUMBLED UPON THE POSSIBILITY of salvation, we step off the buckled and pock-marked highway and into an expansive red desert leading to an outcropping of trees and foothills to a mountain range on the far side. Better to take our chances with fellow runaways in the woods than risk getting dragged back to the Processor, a thought that haunts our memories like some fanged, demonic creature from a collective nightmare.

On the night we escaped, Granden—one of the men who trained us, lied to us, and may have been planning to kill us—pulled me aside as the soldiers from the Processor advanced. Before disappearing, he gave me one last instruction: "Follow Render."

So that's exactly what I do. And for reasons I can't explain, the other Seventeens follow me. I may be in the lead, but I'm no leader. I'm the kind of person who'll jump in when I'm needed. I answer when called upon. But I'm not one of those brimming-with-confidence alpha types who delegates responsibility, barks out orders, and inspires the troops.

All this time, I've been trying to call on Brohn and Rain to help me with decisions. They're the natural leaders, the ones over-flowing with talent and confidence. Through the woods and all along the paths and highways, I've asked them for advice. How far along this side road should we go? Which way should we turn at this crossroads? Should we cut through this wooded area or try to find a way around? Should we stop to rest before it gets too dark?

Every time, I've been greeted with doubt and deference.

"Whatever you think is best," Rain always says.

"We trust you," Brohn tells me with reassuring smiles.

Kella's been too far gone in sorrow, too deep in her own head to be of any help. Manthy wouldn't give me advice even if I pinned her down and tried to force it out of her. It's just not her way.

Only Cardyn is willing or brave enough to chime in from time to time. But even his advice has been reduced to tepid, wishy-washy suggestions. Maybe we should do this or that. Or maybe not. Maybe we should go left. On the other hand, maybe right is better. It all ends the same way: "Whatever you think is best, Kress."

So here I am, in the lead with my fellow Seventeens—no, my *friends*—looking to me for guidance. So I follow Render, and they follow me.

As we march along, the thick, solid-packed sand and jagged rocks make for an exhausting trek. With Render gliding ahead, we weave and navigate our route down treacherous red embank-ments and around large columns of dusty red stones. Everything is hot to the touch. Even the air feels like fiery dust in my lungs. Brohn drags a hand over a series of spiky rocks and speculates that they're casualties of the war. "Nuclear fall-out's my guess," he says as he takes a whiff of the powdery red dirt on his fingertips. He gestures with a flick of his thumb back toward the way we came. "Same thing that took out those towns we passed. Maybe the boosted fission bombs we learned about in training? Microwave pulse-blasts?"

Rain's not so sure. "From what I've read about radiation, we'd all be sick or dead by now."

"It depends on the amount of radiation and how long we've been exposed," I say. "That is, if this really is the result of nuclear fall-out at all."

"Well," Card chimes in, "something sure turned the world into a wasteland. Looks like someone put it in an oven and set it on char-broil. We know it wasn't the Eastern Order. That means either our own government did this to itself or else there's another enemy out there no one's talking about."

The thought of that sends a shiver through my body.

Having lived nearly our entire lives in the Valta, our knowledge of the world has been limited to viz-screens and to the last batches of paper books we were able to scrounge from our burned-out town. I have faint memories from when I was five years old, when I lived back East with Micah and our parents. The memories are mostly just flashes of green from a wooded area behind our house and images of my father's back as I watched him hunched over his white synth-steel worktable in his pristine, glass-walled lab up on the third floor. His office teemed with wide bands of soft white light, the kind where you can see tiny particles of dust dancing happily in the sunbeams. It felt like peace. It felt like a world brimming with life.

If that clean, bright, and verdant world has an opposite, I'm standing in it now.

There is some vegetation out here, mostly lethal-looking purple vines with long translucent spikes sticking out like the fangs of a snake, ready to kill us. If the heat and exhaustion don't bring us down first, that is. Otherwise, this is about as lifeless as it gets.

Our food is all but gone along with most of our water. The little bit of water we do have left in the clear aluminum bottle is brownish and filled with debris and ominous-looking cultures of microorganisms. Brohn figures we've got two days left. Three, tops. "After that," he says, "we're going to be in a bit of trouble."

And the award for Understatement of the Year goes to...

Rain calls out for me to slow down, which I do. I look back, only to realize how far ahead I've gotten from my friends. Render waits, too, hopping up onto one of the smoother stones to preen the red dust from his black feathers. The heat is oppressive. Up until now, we've been able to avoid the worst of it by traveling in the morning and evening hours and winding our way through half-dead forests and through gullies that at least provided some cover from the afternoon sun.

I wipe the sweat from my forehead with my sleeve. When the others catch up, Rain says, "Thanks," and I get us moving again.

What we need right now is to find someone out here, a friendly face to guide us in the right direction. Someone to help us to get home. We've been gone for...four months now? Five? It's easy to lose track of time when you can barely keep track of yourself and your own sanity.

So we keep hiking along, one foot after the other.

I may be following Render, but I know perfectly well that technically, trudging through the desert is my call. I really hope I don't get us all killed.

When I ask half-jokingly how I got to be in charge, Rain pats my shoulder. "Some are born great, some achieve greatness, and some have greatness thrust upon 'em."

"*Twelfth Night*," I say. "Act two, scene five."

"Your knowledge of Shakespeare is…"

"Pointless?"

Rain squints at me under the hot sun. "I was going to say 'amazing.'"

"Dad said all of life's mysteries can be found in the works of Shakespeare. Besides, you know Shakespeare as well as I do.

You're the one who helped me teach a bunch of his plays to the Juvens."

"Sure. But I didn't memorize every line, act, scene, stage direction, and punctuation mark." Despite her obvious fatigue, Rain seems to have gotten a second wind and manages a little laugh. "Did Shakespeare ever say anything about being on the run?"

I nod. "Now bid me run, and I will strive with things impossible. *Julius Caesar*. Act two, scene one."

"Now that's impressive," Brohn says as he skips across a four-foot wide fissure in the ground and strides up next to me. His lips are chapped, and the sun has darkened his forehead and cheeks to a half-red, half-brown medium-rare. But he still manages to look handsome and even succeeds in offering up a bright grin.

I give him a withering smile. The truth is, it scares me to recall things with so much clarity—even the most trivial details about stuff I never thought I particularly cared about. All I can guess is that it's my strengthening link to Render that's enhancing this particular skill. The closer I get to him, it seems, the closer I get to some weird, hyper-talented part of myself.

"It's nothing," I say to Brohn with a dismissive wave, trying my best to shrug it off.

"Sure," Cardyn pants. "If by 'nothing,' you mean 'the most amazing thing ever!' And I thought Manthy was the one with the real super power."

"I don't have a super power," Manthy whines, clearly annoyed.

"Well, you sure talked to the tech pretty good back in the Processor."

"Are you accusing me of being a traitor or some kind of Modified?"

"I'm not accusing you of anything. I'm just saying."

"Well, you can cram your 'just saying' up your—"

"Manthy!" I snap. "Cardyn! Let's focus on getting to that rock formation up ahead before it gets too dark out here. I promise, you can snipe at each other all day tomorrow if it makes you happy. We need to get through tonight. We can make it to the wooded area where we saw the smoke by mid-day tomorrow if the sun doesn't kill us and if the two of you don't murder each other first."

Card mumbles, "Okay, fine," and hangs his head like I've just whacked him on the rump with a rolled-up newspaper. He apologizes to Manthy, but she balls up her fists and glares at him until he looks away. I can't help but chuckle to myself. Manthy may not talk much, but when she does, it's usually to bicker like this with Cardyn. They're slowly devolving into squabbling little kids, and I'm turning into the exasperated mom, arms stretched out between them, trying to keep them from slap-fighting with each other as we struggle to survive the daily ordeal of our exodus. Brohn seems to enjoy my dilemma and grins every time he sees that I'm fed up and ready to push Cardyn and Manthy down the nearest steep embankment.

"Good thing they have you," he tells me quietly. "Otherwise, they really *might* kill each other."

"They'll need to stand in line behind me," I grumble. "I've got enough on my mind without having to worry about their pointless bickering."

"I don't know what they'd do without you," he laughs, reaching for my hand, which I offer gladly. "Actually, I'm not sure what any of us would do without you."

"Let's hope we don't have to find out." I'm trying to sound stoic, but the combination of Brohn's touch and knowing that he worries about the possibility of life without me gives me tingles of pleasure and a smile that I can't quite suppress.

When Cardyn turns his attention from Manthy to me, I pull my hand free of Brohn's.

"Hey, Kress," Cardyn says, "do you really think Granden was a…what do you call it…double agent?" He's asked me this before. I think he's waiting for me to change my answer. It's like he can't

19

get his mind around the possibility that a person doesn't have to be one thing or another, good or bad, innocent or corrupt, a prison guard or a helping hand. He can be all of the above.

"Actually, yes," I tell Card. "I still think there was more to him all along than we realized. Why else would he help us? And did you notice how he was the only one who ever really pulled us aside and talked with us one-on-one?"

Brohn says casually that he didn't really notice that. "But then again," he adds, "I was too busy trying to earn points and not get shot."

"Ugh," Rain half-groans, half-growls. "I still can't believe they tricked us into performing like circus monkeys. Racking up points just to help them determine who to keep and who to kill."

"It's embarrassing," Card agrees. "I wish I could've been there with you when Hiller blew her brains out. Might have made it all worth it."

"It didn't," I say. "All it did was keep us from learning the whole truth. All Hiller did was give us a teaser. She made sure the rest of the secrets died with her."

"It was her last act of torture," Manthy says, mostly to herself. We all nod in quiet agreement.

"There are others out there," I say at last, breaking the glum silence and pointing to the rising column of smoke that has become our magnetic North.

"What kind of others, do you think?" Rain asks.

"Not sure. I couldn't tell from what Render saw. Maybe others like us. Other escaped Seventeens. Maybe even Juvens and Neos. We need to get to them. We need to organize. We need to fight. After all, it's what we've been trained for."

"No," Brohn says. "We were being set up to get killed."

Rain shakes her head and begs to differ. "No. From what you told us Hiller said, we were being developed as weapons by our own government. They were going to train us, brainwash us like they did to Terk, and turn us loose on our own people."

"You're both right," I say. "About every bit of it. But the bottom line is that we *were* trained. Let's not forget that. We know more now than we did before. We can do more than we ever could. They didn't expect us to get to use our training, especially not against them. They figured we'd be dead or else totally under their control by now. It doesn't matter why we learned to fight. It's up to us to decide what to do with what we learned. Just getting away isn't good enough. We can't be the only ones who know what's going on. There've got to be others out there who know what the Order really is. Or, rather, what it isn't."

"And if not?" Kella asks. Her voice is weak, barely a whisper. I think it's the first thing she's said in three days. "If no one else knows? If no one else is out here?"

"If no one else knows," I say, "then it's our job to expose what's happened. The people, our people, need to know the government is also our enemy. That they're trying to infiltrate us at our most vulnerable, going after kids in isolated towns, and that they've been doing it for ten years now."

"At least ten," Cardyn says.

"That's true," Rain agrees. "We may have solved one mystery, but there are a lot more out there we need to figure out."

Cardyn plops his freckled hand onto Rain's shoulder. "Mysteries are your specialty." Normally, he'd say this in a teasing way, but it comes out like a compliment. Back in the Processor, Rain got us through most of the puzzles in the Escape Rooms and pretty much saved our lives a dozen times along the way. She's a born problem-solver with a mind made to figure things out.

"Either way," I add, "we can't do this alone. We need help."

I tip my head in the direction of the smoke rising above the treetops, still far in the distance. "Dad used to say, 'Where there's smoke, there's fire.'"

"Did your dad happen to mention anything about how going toward fire is good way to get burned?"

I give Cardyn a hard glare over my shoulder, and he holds up his hands in surrender. I hate to admit it, but he's right. I'm just hoping that this time, where's there's smoke, there's also salvation.

Card is right about something else, too. I also feel embarrassed about the Recruitment. For so long I wanted to be a member of Special Ops, to rise through the ranks, win the war, and be celebrated as part of the Cohort that finally expelled the Eastern Order and restored our democracy. Instead, I got tricked. We all did. It's like one of those experiments we learned about from a psychology textbook in the Valta. We thought we were the scientists. Instead, we were the rats in the maze, scrambling around on a greedy hunt for a piece of cheese that didn't even exist. The fact that the embarrassment is shared with my fellow Seventeens doesn't make the whole experience any less humiliating.

We keep walking for another hour until we finally reach the outcropping I'd spotted earlier.

The temperature has dropped off a cliff, and we go from sweat-soaked to chilled-to-the-bone in what feels like just a few minutes. It's too late and too cold to keep going. Kella is in bad shape, physically and emotionally. She's been letting us help her along for weeks now, but I know she wouldn't complain if we left her behind. Not that we'd ever do that. In her mind, I don't think she sees the point in going on. I can't totally blame her. I get those pangs of doubt in my mind, too. I've got two voices in my head. One asks, "Why bother? There's nothing out here but more pain and more loss." It tells me that every step could be bringing us that much closer to death.

The other voice disagrees. It says that every step could be getting us all that much closer to life.

Then there's the third voice in my head. The one everyone else hears as a demonic *kraa!* That voice soars up ahead and calls on me to trust myself and to be the leader our Conspiracy needs right now.

Guided by only the thinnest slivers of moonlight, we find a decent place to stop, and set up camp in a cave under an inviting rock formation. Fortunately, the cave is empty and not too deep, and the temperature inside is stable, comfortable even. We kick small rocks to the side to clear an area of the floor suitable for sleeping. A natural shelf running along one side of the cave makes a perfect perch for Render, who struts along the narrow ledge, his head lightly bobbing until he finds just the right spot. He tucks his head against his wing and, like us, settles in for what we hope is our last night on the run for a while. If we can get to that smoke, we can get to people. It's a risk, but chances are that anyone out in the woods will either help us or else point us in the direction of safety. At least they're not likely to be soldiers. Not out here.

For right now, my brain is a baked and muddled mess. If I don't get some sleep, I'm going to be beyond useless.

While we've been on the run, we've been sleeping in a circle with our heads together like we did back in the Silo, though Brohn and I tend to move closer together each night as the cold sets in. More than once, I've awoken with his arm around my waist and a smile on my lips.

Exhausted to the bone, we set ourselves up in our usual tight circle. We tuck ourselves into our black military-style jackets. Brohn settles into a spot next to me, with Rain just over on his other side. As usual, Rain is curled up tight like a potato bug.

Brohn and I both lie on our backs. When his hand touches mine, I look over, and he smiles at me through the gray gloom. I smile back and try to say something, but my lips won't move, and my eyes start to flutter shut from exhaustion. His touch is comforting and gentle, a reminder that he's still a protective force in my life.

He always somehow manages to make me feel small yet strong. But with all that's happened and so much unknown left to come, my mind has been a constant, dizzying whirlwind of fear and doubt. Not just about our past or our future, but about our present. I can't help wondering what we're doing. Does Brohn feel the same way about me as I do about him? If he does, how do we allow ourselves to get close when tomorrow might bring death?

As I feel the warmth of his touch on my skin, the whirlwind goes still. His fingers close around mine, and I suddenly feel like I've got an anchor in a hurricane. His smile and bright blue eyes are the last things I see before I drift off.

I have no idea how much time has passed when the deep sleep I've fallen into is interrupted by a series of earth-shattering screams coming from somewhere outside of the cave.

3

_____

Startled awake, I bolt upright.

"There's someone out there," Rain says, leaping up to one knee, eyes wide and on full alert.

Cardyn shakes his head as the rest of us clamber to our feet. "Sounds like there's an entire army out there. Plus, some escaped zoo animals!"

I glare at him and throw on my jacket as Brohn pulls out one of the pilfered knives. Just for good measure, he also grabs a fist-sized rock from the ground and inches along in a half-squat toward the opening of the cave leading back out into the desert. I start to follow, but he waves me back.

"Let me just have a look first," he whispers. He holds up his hand, palm out with the knife handle wedged against his thumb, and inches forward.

Rain and I follow him anyway, leaving Cardyn and Manthy to keep an eye on Kella, who's awake but looking half-dead. Not surprising that she doesn't react. She doesn't care if she lives or dies, so what does she care if something goes bump in the night?

Slipping from the mouth of the cave with Rain and me just behind either shoulder, Brohn shuffles out into the desert gloom.

The sound of shouting and a serious scuffle rises up from behind a nearby sand dune. There are multiple voices, and my heart does a little tap-dance in my chest at the thought that the Processor goons might have tracked us down. No. It can't be. Why would they be arguing loudly with each other if their mission was to hunt us down and kill us? Based on what we know and what we've seen them do, if their mission was to take our lives, we'd be dead by now. And if they wanted us captured, we'd be chained up and gagged in the back of a transport truck.

I try to tap into Render's mind, but he's in a deep sleep. I could push myself in, startle him awake. But that would be counter-productive. Besides, by the time he got himself oriented enough to scout out the situation, whoever is making all this noise could decide to turn their attention to us.

Brohn takes several more steps in the direction of the commotion. Like the sound of the voices and shuffling bodies, his footsteps are muffled by the sand but magnified by the stillness of the desert night. I follow him as closely as I can with Rain clinging to the back of my jacket as we go. With all the sharp rocks, deep crevasses, and generally unpredictable terrain, she's wise to stay close. I follow as carefully and quickly as I can behind Brohn.

He skids to a stop, peering around the sand dune and over a wall of serrated rocks jutting up from the ground like enormous crocodile teeth. Rain and I bump into each other as we come to an abrupt stop behind him. Together, the three of us peek around the rock formation at what turns out to be a small clearing. It's still the dead of night, but there's enough moonlight to give us a shadowy but otherwise fairly good look at the scene.

Two men and a woman, probably about our parents' age—or rather, the age our parents would have been—are shouting and shoving each other in a three-way free-for-all. Right in front of us and thankfully unaware of our presence, one of the men tackles the other one. The two of them slam to the ground, rolling and punching each other in the shoulders and ribs. Swinging her arms wildly, the woman leaps on top of both of them. Because of the dark and the flurry of motion, I can't tell if she's trying to pull them off of each other or if she's trying to kill them both.

The three of them roll around some more on the rocky ground, screaming, coughing, and kicking up clouds of dark red dust while we look on, baffled.

Before I can stop him, Brohn leaps into the fray and grabs one of the men by the back of his tattered jacket, dragging him out of the pile. Even after all that we've been through—the months in the Processor and the weeks we've spent on the run—Brohn is remarkably strong. For a second, he reminds me of Terk: large and in charge, slinging a full-grown man through the air like I might toss my boots across a room.

Startled by Brohn's sudden appearance and intervention, the other man and the woman leap to their feet, their eyes wide with terror.

"Who are you?" the woman asks. Her voice is broken and hollow, and she's tucked her chin practically into her chest in an act of fear and submission. For a second she reminds me of Kella.

"We're not going to hurt you," Brohn assures her, his chest heaving slightly.

He has more faith in our position and abilities than I do. I'm more worried that we might be the ones who end up getting hurt in this situation. My faith in my apparent skills hasn't yet caught up to all the combat training I've done, and I'm not eager to test myself out on three strange adults who might be crazy enough— or desperate enough—to attack us without provocation and leave us for dead in the middle of nowhere.

Brohn has dropped the rock he was holding as a weapon, but he's got one hand tucked behind his back, so I know he's ready to flash his knife just in case. He exchanges a quick look with me and Rain that says *Don't worry. We're in control here.* Rain and I nod our acknowledgement and follow his lead.

Even in the near total dark, I can see now that Brohn has read the scene correctly. Now that we've taken measure of the situation, I realize the three adults are in no position to hurt us. They're breathing hard and barely able to stand. Whatever we've been through while on the run these past few weeks looks like a summer vacation compared to the mess the strangers seem to be in.

"We were captured by the Patriot Army," the woman sobs. Her shoulders slump down in the resignation of total defeat. "We escaped and joined up with a Resistance Colony." Her eyes are barely focused. Her hands tremble at her sides. "Back in Santa Fe. They tracked us all down to St. Francis Cathedral, where we'd set up headquarters. I don't know how many of us they killed. The three of us might be the only ones who made it out."

Rain steps forward. "The Patriot Army?" she asks.

The taller man lifts his head and gives us a pleading, frightened look. "They're the ones responsible for sealing off the city."

"We've never heard of them," Rain tells him. "We were Recruits."

"Recruits? Recruits for what?"

"For the war," I say, surprised and more than a little confused. "The war that we were fighting against the Order. We're Seventeens. Cohort of 2042." I deliberately don't mention that the Order might be a total fiction. For all I know, these three are on Hiller's side.

"What's a Seventeen?"

This time, Brohn, Rain, and I all exchange a look of shock. Rain leans toward the three strangers. "You do know about the Recruitment, right? And the Seventeens? We get taken away every year. For the war effort."

Now it's the three adults' turn to exchange a look. The two

men turn to the woman for guidance, but she shrugs and pivots back to me, squinting, like I'm suddenly not speaking English.

"You do know about all this, don't you?" I ask. "The way we were supposed to help win the war?"

The woman shakes her head.

"What about the Processor?" Rain asks. "The Agora and the Cubes?"

This time, the woman doesn't even bother to shake her head. Instead, she stares at us through the desert gloom and takes a full step back.

Her two buddies follow suit, stepping away from us. The shorter of the two men asks if we're part of the Patriot Army.

"No," I assure him. "We don't know what that is. We were training, but not for the reason we were told."

"Then you're I.C.A.?"

I shoot a glance from Brohn to Rain and back to the three quivering strangers who might as well be speaking a foreign language themselves. "We don't know what that is either," I assure them. Either they're crazy or else we are, and, right now, I'm not sure which scenario is worse.

"I-I-I don't understand," the taller man stammers. A shudder runs through his shoulders and neck.

"It's just...we don't know what to believe," the woman says as she takes the man's hand in hers. "They buried us. Buried us under so many lies."

Now, the taller man drops his head and starts crying.

"It's okay," Brohn says. "Look—we don't have many supplies, but we've got shelter back in a cave close to here. We're setting out first thing in the morning. You're welcome to come with us."

"To where?" the woman asks. Her eyes dart side to side, but I can't tell if it's out of suspicion, if she thinks there are more of us about to leap out at her, or if she's just looking for something heavy to hit us with.

Brohn points to the faint outline of the mountain range just across the dark desert. His voice is even and soothing. "We're going to head for the foothills. We think there might be a camp and other people there. Maybe people who can help."

The woman still looks skeptical, but she agrees to come with us. She puts her arm around the taller man, who is wiping tears from his face with the sleeve of his shirt.

In a group, we walk back toward the cave with Brohn and Rain in the lead. I follow behind to keep an eye on our three new friends who, for all we know, could be about to turn into our three worst enemies.

4

CARDYN IS WAITING FOR US AT THE MOUTH OF THE CAVE WITH Manthy just behind him, still watching over Kella. Once we're all inside, Card starts to ply us with questions. Brohn quickly explains the situation, but Cardyn doesn't look too convinced. He's staring at the three strangers like they're time-bombs with the timer about to hit zero.

"Hey," he whispers when he's taken a few steps toward me, "I trust Brohn, but I don't think we're really in any position to be inviting a bunch of strays into our little cave."

"They're not strays," I whisper back. "They're people in need. Like us. They're scared. Confused. We couldn't just leave them out there to kill each other."

"No. Much better to bring them back here so they can kill us." Cardyn's voice is barely audible, but the sarcasm in it might as well amount to a scream.

Resigned, he crosses into the deepest part of the cave and pulls our last phosphor-pack from Rain's supply bag. He clicks it on as he walks back, and the small cube struggles to glow warm and yellowish-white in the middle of the cave. We've used these cubes many times over the past weeks for heat and warmth, but

31

this one's charge is clearly on its last legs. We have to get right up to it now to warm our hands, and the feeble light is barely strong enough to cast our shadows on the cave walls.

At least the light from the cube reveals the extent of the trio's suffering. The two men and the woman are clearly defeated, barely hanging on to life. In the weak light, we're now able to see in detail that their clothes are in worse shape than ours, with big holes showing off patches of red skin and thick scars. The taller man is bearded and haggard. His hair is a dreadlocked mess of dirt and tangles. The shorter man is bald on top with long straggles of graying hair on the sides.

The woman looks feral. Her face is dirty and deeply creased. Her piercing green eyes dart around in the gloom of the cave like she's looking for something to eat or fearful that one of us is going to eat her. She jumps and shrieks when she spots Render, still napping on his little ledge. The sound startles him awake, and he barks an irritated *kraa!* before ruffling up his feathers and glaring at her with his jet-black eyes then clawing at the rough surface and trying to fall back to sleep.

"Don't worry about him," Cardyn says with a flick of his thumb. "That's Render. He's one of us."

The three strangers look like they've been fighting hunger, thirst, and the elements for as long as we have. How they managed to summon enough strength to fight with each other is beyond me.

Rain invites them to sit down and starts digging a hand into her shoulder bag. She takes out what's left of our bag of protein chips and empties the contents, one small pile at a time, into the outstretched, cupped hands of the three strangers. They all nod and mumble their thanks then begin scarfing down the brittle white flakes in greedy gulps.

Rain gives me a worried look, glances into her bag and back at me. She motions that it was pretty much the last of our food. None of us has said it out loud, but making it safely to the woods in the morning and finding some help is truly our last and only hope now.

"Where did you say you come from?" Brohn asks the woman as the six of us sit in a semi-circle facing the three strangers around the phosphor-pack in the middle of the cave.

I'm grateful to him for taking the lead on this. The truth is that guiding us along various highways, backroads, and over some pretty rough terrain over the past weeks has been tough, but at least I had Render to help me along. Interrogating three adults in a shadow-filled cave in the middle of the desert isn't exactly my wheelhouse.

"Santa Fe," the woman says after a panting pause. She gestures south and east, deeper into the desert. "That way...I think."

"What's your name?" I ask.

"Asha," she mutters, her head down, chin back to being buried in her chest. She pushes up the sleeves of her army-green jacket and gestures half-heartedly toward the two men. "This is Wes and Theron."

Theron, the taller, bearded man, raises his head, pushes aside a clump of hair dangling over his eyes, and gives us a forced smile. Crumbs from the protein chips speckle his tangled moustache and beard. The smaller man named Wes doesn't look up from the spot on the ground between his crossed legs.

Rain turns to Cardyn and Manthy. "They say they don't know about the Recruitment or the Seventeens."

"How's that possible?" Cardyn asks. "The Recruiters came for us every year. Every November first."

"November first," the woman says, suddenly alert. "2032. That's the day the Freedom Wars started."

"So you know about the war?"

"Of course. The Eastern Order invaded ten years ago, and we've been struggling to survive as a nation ever since."

"Yeah," Cardyn starts to say, "about the Eastern Order—," but I shush him with a look and an elbow to his arm. Now is not the time to push these three distressed strangers into a sensory over-load of too much ugly truth...not that we even *know* the whole truth.

"What can you tell us about them?" I ask. "The Order, I mean."

"What's to tell?" Theron says. "They're the enemy. They invaded. We fought. We lost."

Asha disagrees. "We haven't lost yet."

"The government's turned against us," Theron mumbles from behind his dangling hair. "Our own government. Once we lost our democracy, we lost the war."

"What do you mean 'lost our democracy'?" I ask.

A look of anger washes over his face. He squints hard at me, then at Brohn. "Where are you kids from?"

"The Valta," Brohn snaps. "It's a small town up in the mountains. And we're not kids. Not anymore. Not after what we've been through."

Wes drops his gaze. "Apologies."

"What don't we know?" I ask. "All we see is empty roads and abandoned towns. Where is everyone?"

Asha rubs her arm and then runs her hand through her mop of thick brown hair. "The government decided the small towns were too scattered," she says. "Too hard to control or keep safe. So they centralized everything. Started moving everyone into a few of the big cities. All under the pretense of keeping us safe from the Order. The people who refused were 'convinced.' Ever since the Arcologies—those are the giant skyscrapers they build in the big cities—started going up, choices were limited anyway. If you weren't a Wealthy, you couldn't get a spot. That meant having to figure out how to survive on your own down below. So the shantytown settlements went up in the shadow of the Arcologies, and we just got used to fighting each other and living in fear all the time."

A picture begins to form in my mind's eye. A picture of mass, forced migrations. A type of herding where people have become cattle, expendable commodities to be used, abused, or discarded at the whim of the cattle-herders.

The man named Wes drags his finger along the cave floor in front of him. The light is weak, but I'm pretty sure he's crying. "The government's got everyone fighting each other so there's no one left to stop them from taking total and absolute control."

"Well," Brohn says, his voice in full man-mode, "we plan on doing something about that."

When he talks like this, when he takes over, Brohn has a hypnotic effect on those around him. I feel it right now. I don't think he's right, but I believe him. And that belief is a welcome comfort in a moment of anxiety and uncertainty.

The three strangers don't object when Rain finally insists they get some rest. In fact, they seem grateful for the chance to sleep.

They're out before their heads hit the ground.

Brohn summons the rest of us outside the cave, where we debate whether it's really best to take them along. Kella doesn't want to come outside at first, but Cardyn convinces her that we need to stay together now more than ever.

"I don't trust them," Rain says with a skeptical glance back into the cave where the three strangers are snoring in a discordant chorus.

"They seem harmless enough," Card says. "Not counting the snores. Or the smell."

I give him a punch to the shoulder. "Knock it off. This could be a matter of life or death."

"Yeah," Card says. "But whose? Theirs or ours?"

"There's a lot we don't know about those three," Brohn cautions.

"True," Rain adds. "And there's plenty they don't know about us. Like how can they not know about the Recruitment? It's been going on for ten years. It's all over the viz-screens."

"Maybe we're the only ones who saw the viz-screens," I say slowly, pulling my eyes up into the night sky. "We need to face the possibility that the Eastern Order isn't the only lie we've been fed."

Kella glances up at me from where she's been leaning on Cardyn for support. "What do you mean?" she asks.

"For all we know, the Processor could have been even more top-secret than we thought. I mean, what if there *was* no Recruitment?"

Kella shakes her head. "But we know there was. They came for us every year."

"We've been assuming it was a nation-wide program. A kind of military draft. A way to combat the Order. But what if the Order isn't the only thing that was made up?"

Now it's Cardyn's turn to shake his head, like he doesn't want to hear what he knows I'm about to say. But I have no choice but to say it anyway. "What if it was just us? What if it was just the Valta? Hiller said they were going after kids who showed a certain sign of genetic mutation at our age. What if she didn't mean everyone? What if she just meant those of us who lived in the Valta?"

"Can't be," Brohn says. "What about the thirteen kids we saw outside the Processor? They must have come from somewhere."

"Okay," I concede. "You're right. Maybe it's not just us. But maybe it's *mostly* us."

Cardyn frowns at this. "There's nothing special about the Valta. It's got to be the most boring town in the world."

"So we think. Maybe there was more to it than met the eye."

"Which means maybe there's more to us?" Rain asks. She flicks a thumb at Brohn and me. "We already know about you two and Manthy."

Now a visible tremble rips through Kella's frail frame. "And you think this whole thing…the Recruitment, the Processor, the Eastern Order…you think it was really all about us? You think we're all alone in the world?"

"I don't know if I'd go quite that far," I say, trying to keep my voice low for our guests' sake and calm for Kella's. "But yes, I think there are some pretty important things about this whole situation that we still need to find out."

"So where does that leave us and our three smelly friends?" Card asks. "Do we take them or leave them here to kill each other?"

"No one's killing anyone," I reply in a voice so authoritative that it surprises me. "We'll take them with us. It might not be the safest thing to do, but it is the *right* thing to do. I'm still trying to sort through the images I got from Render, but I think we need to keep going and get to whoever belongs to that fire out there."

Kella puts her head in her hands and whimpers. "You said it could be dangerous."

"Maybe. It's hard to say. For Render, anything unknown is potentially dangerous. But remember, he's looking out for us."

Kella nods, but she doesn't look any less worried.

Brohn looks from one of us to the other, and I'm thankful for the dimness of the desert night. If it were light out, I'm afraid he'd see the terror and uncertainty I'm trying so hard to hide.

"Okay," he says at last. "Let's turn in and get a fresh start in the morning."

With that, the six of us tip-toe back into the cave and settle down into our now-expanded circle.

Kella and Cardyn drift off first, and it's not long before Brohn, Rain, Manthy, and I are out cold as well.

WHATEVER SLEEP we manage doesn't last long. I'm in the middle of a pleasant dream for a change—one about watching through Render's mind as he flies over huge, healthy fields of wheat and corn—when the shrill cries of *kraa!* I hear in the dream morph into the sound of someone screaming in the real world. I leap awake to find Asha and the two men arguing again. Brohn and the others jump to their feet with me, instantly shaking off the trance of sleep.

When he sees what's going on, Brohn thrusts his arms protectively in front of us.

Asha has a small gun clamped in both hands. But she's not looking at us. She doesn't even seem to register that we're still here. She's shaking wildly and looks like she's about to throw up.

The two men are on their knees in front of her, their arms extended with the palms of their hands facing out. They plead with her not to shoot as they inch their way backward toward the cave's exit.

"Wait!" I shout.

But I'm too late. The woman shoots the two men in the head, one after the other. Their bodies pitch forward, sagging to the ground like bags of water.

Over on his ledge, Render shrieks awake and spreads his wings.

Instinctively, Cardyn leaps in front of Kella. Manthy and Rain slip to either side of the cave and assume defensive positions like we were taught to do in a hostile situation in close-quarters. Brohn and I approach Asha and try to talk her down, but she doesn't seem to hear a word we say.

"They're out there!" she shouts.

"It's okay," I say as calmly as I can, despite the fact that every inch of me is shaking. "There's no one out there. There is no enemy."

"There is," she moans. "There has to be." She waves the gun around casually like she's forgotten it's in her hand, and for a second, I think she's going to accidentally shoot us all. With her eyes wide, she gurgles a kind of half-laugh, half sob. "There has to be an enemy. There always has to be an enemy."

Brohn steps forward, his hands out. "Take it easy. There doesn't have to be an enemy."

"Ha! Of course there does. Always has. Call it what you want," she says. Her eyes flutter and dart around like two angry bees. "Eastern Order. Patriot Army. Terrorists. The government. Rebels. Men. Women. Immigrants. Black. White. Human. Modified. It's all the same. It's all just names." She taps the barrel of the gun to her temple. "In the end, they'll get into your head just like they got into ours. They're already in there," she warns in a whisper, pointing her gun at us one at a time. "Don't think just because you escaped that you really got away. You can't get away from your own people. You can't get away from yourself."

Moving out of his defensive position, Cardyn eases up next to Brohn. His voice is surprisingly calm, practically melodic. "We survived. We're going to fight back, expose the lies. We can help you figure things out."

"There's nothing left to figure out," she sobs. Her face is a mess of dirt and tears. "They won. Whatever they are, whether they exist or not, they've already won. We don't even think for ourselves anymore. We're conditioned. We're taught to hate everyone until there's no one left to hate except ourselves."

Brohn starts to say, "Whatever you're thinking about doing —," but he doesn't get to finish.

The woman presses the barrel of the small gun to her temple and pulls the trigger. In a flash of light and an explosion of bright red blood, she pitches sideways and crumbles to the floor of the cave next to the two men.

5

IN A RARE DISPLAY OF RAW EMOTION, MANTHY SLAPS HER HANDS over her mouth, her eyes wide with shock and horror. She points at the cluster of three dead people in the cave. "Why did she do that?"

Brohn tells her to take it easy, but his rapid-fire breathing and the rocky rise and fall of his chest tell me he's barely holding it together himself.

"She sounded crazy," Rain says. "The enemy may not be what she thinks it is, but something spooked her."

"More than just spooked her," Cardyn says. "Sounds like someone put her brain in a blender and pressed 'frappé.'"

As usual he's trying to sound flippant, but the quiver in his voice betrays the distress we're all feeling. The only thing worse than being in a crazy situation is meeting someone who's even crazier than the situation you're in.

Kella drops to her knees and starts to cry, which makes me start to cry. With tears of his own welling up, Cardyn takes a step toward me to try to comfort me, but I wipe my eyes and wave him off.

"Don't worry about me," I tell him. "See to Kella."

Cardyn pauses but seems to realize that Kella definitely needs more emotional support right now than any of us. He kneels down next to her and puts his arm around her shoulders. She leans her head against his and asks, "Why?"

"I think maybe she had some kind of mental illness," Card says. "Maybe she'd just been through too much."

Kella shakes her head. "I don't mean about them. I mean about the world." She swivels her head from Cardyn and then up to the rest of us. She has little streams of tears trickling along her nose and down to the corners of her mouth. She wipes the tears away with the heels of her hands. "Why does the world look like this? It's all come apart. Everything…everyone is dying. Are we going to disappear? Or go insane like them? Are we next?"

I cross over and kneel down by her other side, wondering if it's possible to bring hope back to a person who's lost it. "We're not next," I assure her. "We'll survive this. We'll find others, get help. We'll find out what's going on, and we'll fix it."

I'm aware that I'm making promises I can't possibly hope to keep, based on facts I don't know. But Kella is on the edge of something dangerous, and the murder-suicide we just witnessed is more than enough to push her the rest of the way over. Right now, I just need to talk her down, get her back to a neutral place where she can try to recover from the onslaught of tragedies we've experienced. Cardyn gives her shoulders a comforting squeeze and talks gently to her about how this is as bad as it'll get and about how the only way to a better future is by putting one foot in front of the other. "You always have one more step left in you," he promises. "There's always that one more step."

Kella nods, but I can tell by her face that she's not convinced.

"What happens when I can't even take that one more step?" she asks in a whisper.

"Then I'll take it for you," Cardyn says. He looks over at me, and I give Kella what I hope is my most reassuring smile.

"We'll all take it for you until you can move forward again on your own," I say.

With Kella still crying but at least not hyperventilating anymore, Brohn goes over to the three strangers. Rain joins him as he kneels down and presses his fingertips to each of their necks one by one. He leans in to see if he can feel their breath and checks for any sign of life.

"Dead?" I call to him from across the cave.

"All three."

I step closer to him, knowing that I can't avoid the bodies forever. I need to help. To be strong. Now, more than ever.

"Just as well," Cardyn says as he stands up and walks over to join us. "If she hadn't done it to them, she'd have likely done it to us."

I pick up Asha's gun. "Empty."

"Any more ammo on her?" Cardyn asks.

Rain volunteers to check. She pats Asha down, flips her jacket open, and slides her fingers along Asha's legs and into the pockets of her pants. She slips Asha's boots off and shakes them upside down. Some red sand slides out but nothing else. Cardyn and I go through the men's clothes, but they've got nothing we can use.

"We'll hang onto the gun. Just in case," Brohn says.

"Pretty worthless, though, isn't it?" Cardyn asks. "Without bullets, I mean."

"Not necessarily. We may find compatible ammo somewhere along the way." Brohn brushes red sand from the barrel of the gun. "Besides, if there's anything Hiller and her people taught us, it's that a fake threat can be every bit as powerful as a real one."

He's right. Having a gun, even an empty one, is empowering. As long as no one decides to call our bluff.

Brohn tucks the gun into the waistband of his cargo pants and gets ready to step out of the cave. The rest of us start to follow.

"Should we do something with them?"

It's Kella who asks the question. She's behind us in the cave, standing over the three bodies.

Brohn walks over to her and starts to try to nudge her along, but I stop him. "It's okay," I say. "Let me."

I slide over and stand next to Kella. She's still staring at the three dead people. Her eyes are red, but she's not crying anymore. In fact, her voice sounds oddly calm, all things considered. "We should bury them. Or cremate them. Or something."

"It's too dry here," I say. "Too much sand and dried brush. And we can't risk a fire."

"I'm just so tired," Kella mutters.

"Tired?"

"Of leaving people behind."

I know instantly what she means. Over the years, we witnessed hundreds of people die in the Valta. Friends. Family. We were able to recover and bury some of the bodies in what became a growing graveyard. Those who died in the bombings were gone from our lives, but we still always knew exactly where they were. After losing Terk and Karmine in the Processor, that changed. Now there's a distance between us even greater than death. It's the distance of the unknown, and I can feel it hitting Kella full-force. I put my arm around her, but I can't think of anything to say.

Fortunately, I don't have to. Cardyn steps in front of Kella and lifts her chin a little with his fingertips.

"I have an idea. Let's take something of theirs."

"What do you mean?"

"If we took something it'd be kind of like a souvenir. A way to help them stay connected."

"Connected?"

"With us. With each other."

"We have the woman's gun," Brohn reminds him.

Cardyn shakes his head. "But we took that for ourselves, Brohn. Let's take something as a reminder of them. It doesn't

43

have to be much. A scrap of clothing. A belt. Anything. That way, something that touched them can keep going with us. Kella's right. They deserve that much."

Kella manages the closest thing to a smile I've seen on her face since we escaped from the Processor. I've always been thankful to have Cardyn as my best friend. It feels good to share that feeling with Kella as I watch the way he's able to ease her mind with a soothing hand and just the right words.

Kella points to the woman's jacket, which has a patch on the shoulder. It's an eagle with a snake in its beak and a cactus in its talons. A larger eagle stands behind it with its wings spread. Around the image are the words, "Great Seal of the State of New Mexico" and the number 1912. The words *Crescit Eundo* appear on a faded yellow banner just below the image. Cardyn kneels down, rips off the patch, and hands it to Kella.

"What's it mean?" she asks Rain as she fondles the patch like it's a rare seashell she just found on the beach. *"Crescit Eundo?"*

Rain shakes her head. "I don't know. Brohn?"

"Got me."

"It's Latin." I say. "It means 'It grows as it goes.'"

Rain's eyebrows go up. "How do you know that?"

"I don't know," I shrug. "I guess I just remember it from when we took Latin lessons from those Sixteens a few years back."

Rain gives me a skeptical look. I know she's been keeping track of my collection of weird knowledge and all the trivial bits of memories I suddenly seem to have, but I'm still not ready to tell her my hypothesis that it has something to do with my growing connection to Render.

Kella is absorbed with the patch. She runs her fingertips over it and holds it up to her nose to smell it. "And what's that mean?" she asks. "It grows as it goes?"

"I think it has something to do with a storm gathering force and increasing in strength as it rolls across the sky," I tell her.

"Gathering force...," Kella mumbles. "I like that."

She slips the patch into her pocket, and we head outside. As we step into the waning hours of the desert night, Rain gets an idea. "We can pile rocks up and seal the cave, kind of like a burial," she says to Kella with a half-hearted shrug.

Kella grins and starts helping the rest of us shuffle as many loose rocks as we can find up to the opening of the cave. It's already getting hot out, but we work fast, and we work together. Before long, we've managed to cover the opening as best we can and fill in some of the gaps with dried shrubs and crisp, black vines we scrounge from the desert floor.

When the cave is as sealed off as it's going to get, we wipe the sand and red dust from our hands and begin the hike toward the plume of smoke still fluttering skyward in the distance.

It's near morning, and the first streaks of pink sunlight give the world an eerie glow. I look out toward the East in the direction we came from. I wonder what's happening back in the Processor. Hiller is dead. Terk, Karmine, and Trench. All dead. Is that ominous silver Halo still rotating up there somewhere? Are the guards still coming after us? For a second, I contemplate sending Render back. Maybe he can tell us what's happening or let us know if we're being followed.

In the end, I decide against it. Too much focus on where we've come from will only distract us from what's up ahead. Cardyn's words to Kella echo in my head. *One more step*, he said. *We can always take just one more step.*

As we walk along, Kella fidgets with the New Mexico patch we took off Asha's jacket. She smells it again and holds it to her cheek. My heart breaks for her and for what she's turning into. In the Processor, she was a fierce fighter and an instant expert with any weapon our trainers put in front of her. Now, she's more like one of the Neos, skittish and scared, latching onto anything she thinks will give her a hint of stability in an unstable world. Cardyn sticks by her side, occasionally offering a helping hand when the terrain gets too rough.

After a few hours, we make it across the desert. As we take our first steps up the small embankment and into the scraggly forest that forms the treeline, Kella collapses. Brohn and Cardyn try to help her, but she refuses to move.

It's taken a long time, but she's finally given up.

Rain seems desperate to connect with her. She puts a gentle hand on the small of Kella's back. "What happened to Kar affected all of us."

"It's not just Karmine," Kella says. "It's all of it. Those three back in the cave...? That could have been us. That could still be us. We can't go back to what we used to be." She fights off our attempts to help her before her eyes glaze over and she slips into unconsciousness.

Brohn and Cardyn take turns carrying her limp form slung over their shoulders. She's lost a lot of weight, but Manthy, Rain, and I aren't strong enough to carry her like that. It's an uphill climb into the woods, and we're all hungry, thirsty, and exhausted.

Render leads the way now. Darting among the tree branches and down into the dry gullies along the way, he clicks, chirps, and *kraas* out to guide us toward the best paths. It's easy for him, of course. He gets to fly. The rest of us non-bird types have to trudge over the uneven ground that gets steeper and more hazardous with every step.

Just when even Brohn and Cardyn look like they might not be able to go on, we finally get a whiff of the smoke we've been following. The smell gets stronger as Render leads the way.

"Can you do your Render-surveillance thing again?" Rain asks.

"I can try," I tell her. "It's a good time to take a break, anyway."

We lean against some of the trees that surround us. The events from last night, the physical exertion of crossing the red desert and now hiking up this hill that's practically a wall have taken their toll on me. My leg muscles burn. My brain is mush.

Still, I scan my arm tattoos, and flickers of Render's perspective come into view but then fade out again. I take a deep breath and try to concentrate.

We link up again, but just like before, the link quickly fades.

"I don't know if I can do it right now," I say to Rain. "My mind's not in it."

A soft voice from behind me says, "Don't try so hard." It's Manthy. I turn to see her sitting cross-legged on the forest floor. She's staring down and fiddling with a dried twig in her hands. "Don't reach out," she mumbles. "Open the space between you and Render. He'll meet you halfway."

I'm stunned at first. Partly because Manthy almost never talks unless it's absolutely necessary. And she never offers advice. But she's right. In trying to activate my connection with Render, I've been pushing and pulling and ultimately failing.

"She's got a point," Cardyn says. "It's like the way water avoids you the more you reach for it."

I must be giving Cardyn a confused stare, because he laughs and explains what he means, like I'm some ignorant Neo.

"We're used to being able to grab onto things," he explains, "so when we come across something like fog or water or sand, or even feelings and emotions, we treat them like a solid, something we can hold onto and manipulate instead of treating them like what they are."

"And what's that?"

"A different state of being with their own characteristics and their own rules. I think maybe Manthy's right. Instead of trying harder, you might be better off trying softer."

"Okay," I say. "But it might be easier said than done."

"Everything's easier said than done," Brohn says. He's leaning against a tree, and Kella, barely alert, is leaning against him. He flashes me a knowing smile from across the small clearing. "That's never stopped you from doing some pretty amazing things."

I know he's talking about the time I somehow managed to fly when we were in the Processor. Well, I didn't *actually* fly. But I did leap across a distance I had no business being able to clear.

When Brohn, Manthy and I finally told Rain, Cardyn, and Kella what happened leading up to our escape, we filled them in on Hiller, the Order, and even about how Manthy was able to read the strange code and communicate with the Processor's tech-system. But we didn't talk about my impossible soaring leap. Not even with each other. It's like we made a silent pact to keep it under wraps just in case it didn't really happen.

Or because we know it really did.

With the vote of confidence from my friends and fellow Conspirators, I tap my forearm implants again and clear my mind. I imagine a wide, open lake, the calm blue kind we used to read about but that doesn't seem to exist in the real world anymore. Right now, I'm on one side of my mental lake. Render is on the other. Our reflections form in the water, and the gently rippling waves carry our images toward each other until we overlap. I can no longer tell one of us from the other.

In the hypnotic rhythm that follows, I reach out with my mind and ask Render a question. He flies off, and I can only hope he understood what I was asking.

It's not long before he disappears into the tangle of trees off in the distance.

Render's feelings meld into my mind like rolling waves. He seems to think it's safe.

I don't talk to the others about the depth of my connection to the raven, partly because it fades in and out in ways I can't entirely describe. Sometimes it disappears, leaving me to wonder if I've only just been imagining it, or if it was real for a time, but now it's over. Other times, though, the connection is beyond crystal clear. During those times, I feel like I'm only one step away from *being* Render.

I'm having one of those moments now. Like I'm strolling

through an open door, I tap into Render and enter his mind's eye. He's seen the source of the smoke. He's seen what's there: Kids like us. Tangles of trees. Thick bushes. Anxious breathing. Footprints.

I pull out from our connection and relay what Render is seeing to the others.

"There are more than ten of them," I say. "Maybe as many as twenty. Two are tending the fire. The rest are waiting."

Cardyn chews nervously at his fingernail. "Waiting? Waiting for what?"

"For us."

6

CARDYN AND I HELP KELLA MAKE HER WAY ALONG THE UNEVEN
ground. These woods, like most of the rest of the world we've
encountered since leaving the Processor, are a husk, a dried and
tangled mess of bombed-out wreckage barely hanging onto life.
There is some green, but not nearly as much as there should be.
The earth is soft in places but scabbed and crusted over in many
others. Half of the trees we pass are blackened out and leaning
against each other. Their singed, tired trunks and entangled
branches form dark, enclosed mazes, which we navigate by the
columns of light beaming down from above. The atmosphere is
sad, even a little scary. I keep feeling like something with fangs is
going to leap down at us from the twisted canopy above and
eat us.

Elevating past the lowest foothills, we clamber up a natural
stairway of rocks that juts out from under feeble patches of crisp,
yellow grass. Thankfully, the air grows more breathable and
cooler as we climb. We all inhale deeply as we try to purge our
lungs of the harsh desert dust we've been breathing in for the
past two days. At one point on the steep climb, we come to a
faint trace of a path, but it disappears after a few hundred yards,

and we're left pushing and shouldering our way through more dried vegetation as thorny vines snag at our clothes and skin. I've been wearing my jacket tied around my waist, but now I sling it back on before the skin on my arms winds up shredded beyond repair.

As we trudge along, it occurs to me that my friends and I aren't too different from the world we've been stumbling around in over these past few weeks. Like us, the natural world around us feels like it's struggling to survive a trauma. It feels like it's on the verge of collapse or—less likely—recovery.

There's a creepy tension in not knowing which way either of us will go.

Every once in a while, we pause while I ask Render to scout up ahead to help us get our bearings. Rain still insists on calling it "sending" him up ahead. "Kress," she says, "can you *send* your bird up ahead again to scout the area for us?"

And then I have to remind her that, one, Render isn't "my bird" and two, I don't "send" him anywhere.

"Well, if you don't 'send' him," she asks, flicking her eyelids rapid-fire and making invisible quotes in the air with her fingers, "how does he know where to go?"

"I don't know, Rain," I sigh, unable and unwilling to keep the exasperation out of my voice. "How do your legs know what to do and where to go right now?"

"My brain tells them," she snaps.

"And how does your brain know what to tell them?"

Rain opens and closes her mouth like a fish puckering up for food. She glares at me out of the corner of her eye as we walk along. "That doesn't make any sense," she says at last. "I *am* my brain. And my brain is me."

"But your legs also tell your brain when they're tired, right? They let your brain know when they need to rest."

"So?"

"So they work together. One isn't the slave of the other."

"Look, either you're in charge or the bird is, and I don't like not knowing which one of you we're getting advice from."

Right now, Rain is making me feel like I'm being interrogated under hot lights, and I feel like slapping her. I can tell she's annoyed too. Partly with me, but also with herself, for not being able to grasp my relationship with Render. Rain is a problem-solver. An answer-getter. For her, a bird is either a wild animal or a pet. In her more flexible moments, she might accept Render as a guide and maybe even as a kind of loyal mascot. But there's no room in her imagination for a mental connection based on something she can't see or feel for herself.

"It's not magic," I tell her, more than slightly irked as I push my hands down hard onto my knees to help propel myself up the steep path. "And I don't have a super power. I don't care what Hiller told us. My connection with Render is just micro-tech my father decided to implant to connect the two of us." I utter the words as convincingly as I can, but I know perfectly well that saying them doesn't make them true. On some level I know Hiller was right. My bond with Render goes far beyond microchips. I just wish I understood what was happening to me. To us.

"But you see what he sees?" Rain asks.

"Kind of. But he doesn't see like we do."

Card chugs along next to me. "His vision is better than ours, right?"

"Well, it's definitely different." I'm thankful to Card for talking to me like I'm still me, as opposed to Rain, who latches onto anything she doesn't understand like she's a tiger shark on a minnow. "It's hard to explain. He can see wide and narrow at the same time. It's not like us, where we have to shift our focus from near to far and left to right. He has a much wider field of vision, and nearly everything is in focus all the time. It can be…"

"Overwhelming?" Card finishes as I search for the word.

I nod. "To say the least. And sometimes the connection works.

Sometimes it doesn't. Sometimes it's a blast of blurry images, and I don't really know what I'm seeing."

Brohn's told me before that he doesn't totally understand what I'm seeing either. But he was with me in the Processor when Hiller revealed that there was something unusual about him, Manthy, and me. He knows there are things happening to the three of us that none of us fully grasps, so he's willing to accept some of it at face-value, whether he understands or not.

I think Manthy's in denial about the whole thing. Her only wish in life has been to be invisible, a desire I can relate to. Now it turns out she may be some highly-evolved techno-genius who can control machines with her mind. Yeah, I can see why that would freak her out.

Cardyn, unlike the others, gets it. He has an intuitive understanding of what Manthy and I are learning to do. He even has his own name for it. He calls it *telempathy*.

"It's a different way of connecting, right?" He's huffing and puffing from the hike, and I don't know how he has the breath or energy to keep talking, but on he goes. "See, I think you and Manthy just do what we all do. We feel sorry when we see others in pain. We share happiness and sadness. We even yawn when we see someone else yawn. I think you and Render are sharing like all of us do, just on a level the rest of us aren't used to or don't know how to access."

"That's about as close as I can describe it myself," I say as I duck under a cluster of low-hanging branches arching over us. I'm thankful that Cardyn has taken it upon himself to help me to explain something profoundly unexplainable.

"It's like how sometimes, we can tell instantly what someone else is feeling just by subtle clues," Cardyn adds.

"Subtle clues?" Brohn asks.

"Sure. Like pupil dilation, speed of eye-blinks, skin flush, fidgeting, perspiration patterns, tension lines around the mouth and the eyes. Things like that." Cardyn's continuing his impressive feat of being able to pant and talk at the same time. "I think Kress and Manthy are doing the same thing. Just on a micro-micro level."

Brohn's forehead scrunches up. "Micro-micro?"

"I don't know what to call it. But just because something's so small we can't see it doesn't mean it's not there. And it definitely doesn't mean it doesn't have power or value."

I can tell that Brohn doesn't like hearing all this. Maybe he's scared, not knowing what power he supposedly has—some undeveloped, hidden force inside him that may show itself at any time and overwhelm us all. It's strange knowing something's developing inside you without having a clue what effect it will have on you or on those you care about. I know as well as anyone how frightening it can be.

Brohn says, "I guess" and slips into the lead, guiding us through a small gully, over a cluster of egg-shaped rocks, and through another thicket of thorny vegetation. Valiantly, he stands with his back to the brambles and holds them back as the rest of us pass.

As thanks, I give him a hearty salute, which he returns with a dip of his head and a sweet smile.

"So, does Render actually talk to you? Like with words?" Rain asks me as we continue our ascent.

I tell her that he doesn't use language, which is all but impossible to explain. "Not like we're talking right now," I say with an irritated moan.

"So he's not flying back and saying in your head, 'There are people up there, Kress. It might be dangerous if you keep heading toward the smoke'?"

I laugh at this, but I assure Rain I'm not teasing her. It's just that the thought of Render having a voice like ours and speaking like we do gives me the giggles. I can't help picturing some weird, deep man-voice saying, "Hello, Kress. How are you today? Let us begin our melding of minds."

I think Rain would find it just as funny if I started croaking and *kraa*-ing at her.

"If he saw or sensed danger, he'd let me know," I explain in an effort to set her busy mind at ease.

"What if he doesn't know what counts as dangerous?"

Okay. That's a good question. I don't know the answer, so I pretend I didn't hear Rain ask it, hoping she'll move on to something else.

We've walked a few minutes more when I ask everyone to stop for a second. "I just want to check in on Render." I drag my finger along two of the long black lines on my left forearm and tap three times on one of the dots in the pattern. A curtain of white light and a wave of dizziness sweep over me. Shaking off the momentary disorientation, I point to an outcropping just visible through the spindly limbs of a cluster of trees a few hundred yards away. "We need to get up to there."

Rain scans the terrain and calls our attention to a series of rocks jutting out over a small ravine.

"We can jump to there and then back across up there," she says, pointing to various spots along the rough route.

"After you," I say grandly.

Rain takes the lead and guides us over the rocks, across the ravine, around a forbidding cluster of thorns, and back to a more navigable path up the mountain. Cardyn and Manthy help Kella negotiate some of the more slippery and dangerous parts of our little detour. Brohn leaps nimbly from rock to rock and across the ravine like a gymnast-goat hybrid, and seems to be enjoying the chance to exercise his knotted muscles. His breathing has evened out, and there's a gleam in his eye and a smile on his face. It's like his soul has gotten its second wind.

After we've cleared the most treacherous part of the labyrinth of brambles and boulders, Rain slips back a little, and I wind up in the lead again. Personally, I'd like to stop for a few minutes. Between bouncing back and forth in a feedback loop with

Render, concentrating on surviving the rough terrain, fending off Rain's cross-examinations, and talking with the others about what's happening in my head, I'm getting a bit queasy. But the others keep surging on, pushing me from behind, so I trundle on, and they follow.

After a few minutes, we stop, and I initiate my connection with Render who is circling overhead. He sends me back images of the campfire and of hidden figures lurking behind fallen trees and crouched down in the nearby underbrush. His vision is beyond good sometimes. It can be downright predatory, in fact.

In the Processor, we Seventeens were introduced to high-end laser scopes that could put cross-hairs on a target with incredible accuracy, even from a great distance. Render manages to do all that, plus focus on the big picture at the same time. And I swear he could spot the expression on a flea's face from a half-mile away. It's an insane overload of images, much more than my little human brain was designed to deal with.

I take a long breath and try to absorb as many details as I can: four people are sitting with their backs to the trunk of a fallen tree. Its bark is yellow and dry. Another two people are lying face-down in a shallow ditch with only the tops of their heads and their eyes exposed. One person is sitting nervously in the low branch of a tree. The branch bends and looks ready to break. The person pushes back up against the trunk for better balance. Three more people are stationed in a clumsy flanking formation around the perimeter of a clearing. Their shapes stand out clear as day against the speckled pattern of the leafy bushes and scrubs they're hiding behind. Two others are standing farther off, probably leaders of the group hanging back, ready to assess and instruct.

"That's so creepy," Card says as I shake off the connection and return to my normal limited vision. He's staring at me with a look of shock on his face. But something about him looks weirdly impressed, too.

"What's creepy?" I ask.

"Your eyes."

"What about them?"

"Sometimes they do this weird thing where they go really dark."

"What can I say?" I shrug. "I have dark eyes."

"No, it's not that," Brohn explains on Cardyn's behalf. "Not your normal brown eyes. He means they turn *really* dark. Like black. Even the white parts. Your eyes looked like Snoopy's just now."

"Snoopy? You mean Charlie Brown's dog?" I remember him vividly from an old comic book we found among the Valta's salvaged belongings. A white dog with black ears and eyes, who always slept on top of his dog house with a little yellow bird on his chest.

"Yes."

"That didn't used to happen," Rain says slowly. She sounds worried, but I don't feel any different, so I dismiss it as either their imagination, a trick of the light, or just something I don't have time to worry about right now.

"As much as I appreciate being stared at and compared to a cartoon dog," I say with a scoff and a gesture up toward the area where the smoke is roiling up over the treetops, "we have slightly more important matters to attend to."

"Thoughts?" Rain asks after I pass along the final details of Render's newest round of intel to the group.

"How about a Pincer?" I suggest, recalling a military formation we learned in the Processor.

"With a side of Bait and Bleed?" Rain proposes.

"Three and three?" Brohn adds.

I nod my agreement. "Cardyn and Kella with me, then."

Rain gives me a thumb's up, and Brohn gathers her and Manthy around him while I forge ahead with Cardyn and Kella. With Render fluttering up ahead, the three of us walk along for another few minutes until we hear the sizzle and pop of a camp-fire. I smell the smoke and even feel a slight jump in temperature from the radiant heat.

Clambering over exposed roots, Cardyn, Kella, and I finally break into a clearing. Kella is walking on her own again, which is a good sign. She still looks haggard and pale, but at least she's keeping up.

In the clearing, a good-sized fire is burning. The seven or eight logs of black wood cackle and spit red sparks and twisting plumes of dark smoke into the air. It's an odd thing to see—an untended fire in the middle of the ravaged woods. A clear sign of life in the middle of a lot of lifelessness.

I help Kella sit down on a flat boulder in the wide clearing and then Card and I walk the perimeter and look around for signs of life. Kella may be moving better now, but she's still not anywhere close to strong or alert enough to help us out.

"No footprints," Card says, scanning the ground around the fire.

"No. They've been swept away. They've been using mats and some logs and rocks to sit on."

Card nods. "I can see the marks. They're total amateurs. How long do you figure they've been watching us?"

"Since the desert," I say. "Maybe longer.'"

"How many?"

"Only two trackers. And a bunch of others with weapons," I add as I inspect the cracked wounds on some of the trees. "Homemade, though. Broken branches. Probably some rocks. Things like that." I scan the chaos of vegetation—much of it dead or dying—and the fallen trees surrounding the clearing. I glance from the bushes to the mounds of dirt and dried leaves to a few of the trees at the border of the airy glade, and finally back to Cardyn. In as quiet a voice as I can manage, I draw his attention to the twelve people hidden all around us. "Two there. Two there.

Three there. Three more over there. And two more—the two taller ones—just behind them."

"Think we're in danger?"

"Definitely," I say with a smile.

We walk back to stand next to Kella.

"What's happening?" she asks as if she's just coming out of a trance.

Card puts his finger to his lips. "We're about to get attacked."

7

KELLA'S EYES GO WIDE, AND SHE STARTS TO STAND UP.

"Uh-uh," I tell her with a firm hand on her shoulder. "Let it play out."

The tangles of vines and dried bushes around us rustle suddenly to life as five boys and five girls, all about our age or a little younger, lunge out at us from the woods. Some of them carry brittle tree branches as makeshift spears. Others have fist-sized rocks in their hands. One of the girls has a small laser-blade, its blue light flickering to yellow, which means it's losing its charge and probably wouldn't leave more than a slight skin-burn if she managed to slash any of us with it.

In an instant we're surrounded. We've got a high-walled rock formation behind us, thick clusters of trees and brambles on either side, and a horde of scruffy children advancing on us from across the clearing. Three of the kids, their faces caked with dirt and streaked through with sweat, level their sharpened sticks at us and scowl with what I think is supposed to be menace, but looks more like constipation.

"Great," Cardyn whispers to me out the side of his mouth. "We're about to be poked to death by the Lord of the Flies."

"Knock it off," I whisper back. "Put your hands up and look scared."

"We got 'em!" one of the girls shouts back into the woods.

A boy and a girl, both a little taller and probably older than the rest of the kids, step out of the shadows to stand at the back of the crowd of smaller kids. Like the younger ones, they look like they've had a rough go of it. Their faces are also mud-caked and aged beyond their years. Their clothes are a stitched-together mess of frayed fabrics. Still, there is something almost regal about these two. The boy has a sharp jaw-line and a broad nose. He's thin and lanky, but the ropey muscles in his arms suggest great quickness and strength. The girl is slightly taller than he is and has the confident demeanor of someone used to being in control of herself and others. Both of them exhibit a kind of inner strength even though internally, they must be running on fumes.

They look strong, scared, determined…but also famished.

As the two taller kids stand back and the rest close in around us, Card and I hold our hands up higher. I nudge Kella to follow suit, but she's too far gone to care and barely registers any of this is happening. Still, she puts her hands up in half-hearted surrender as if to say, *Kill me or capture me or whatever. Just do it fast and get it over with.*

One of the smaller boys lowers his meager twig of a spear at us and takes another step forward. He's as frail-looking as Kella, and his voice breaks with the in-betweenness of boy and man.

"Who are you?" he croaks.

"They're the Eastern Order!" one of the other boys barks out from behind him.

I manage to suppress an eye roll. "Do we look like the Order to you?"

The kids look puzzled. Like us, they probably just know the Order from the grainy images on the viz-screens in whatever town they came from. Also like us, they've probably never thought much about what the Order actually looks like in person. They were always an out-of-focus, faceless enemy that had to be destroyed at all costs. A foe without features. That was what we were all taught from the day the war began.

I call out over the heads of the ten smaller boys and girls. "We're not the Order, in case that wasn't clear," I assure the tall boy, who, along with the tall girl, must be the leaders of this little faction. "In fact, we escaped from them. Kind of."

"That's a lie!" one of the smaller girls shouts out.

I shrug my shoulders. Technically, she's right. I *am* lying.

Kind of.

"It's a trick," the tall girl grumbles. "They couldn't find us with their drones, so they sent a scouting party out to track us down."

"Who couldn't find you?" I ask.

"You. If you're not the Order, you're Recruiters, right?" She furrows her brow and glares at me like she's daring me to contradict her.

"You told us Recruiters never come out here," one of the younger kids calls out in a shaky voice. "You said we were safe here. You said they'd never find us!"

"So you know about the Recruiters?" Card asks the tall girl.

"Don't try to trick us."

"We're not tricking you."

"It's almost May first. We know why you're here."

"Wait—what happens on May first?" I ask, even though I know in my gut what she's about to say.

"That's when you take away the new Seventeens," one of the girls chirps.

The boy next to her glowers at us. "Thought you could sneak up on us this time." His bark is more of a yip, and I try not to laugh at how thoroughly unintimidating he is.

"We weren't trying to sneak up on you," I assure him with what I hope is my sweetest smile. "We're not the Order, and we're not Recruiters. We were recruited, too. Only ours was always on November first. We were recruited just like you. Every year."

The kids are clearly agitated and confused. They set their little trap with the fire and their weak attempt at an ambush, but now they can't figure out what it is exactly that they captured. They may have known we were coming and prepared themselves for our arrival, but now that they have us, they don't seem to know what to do with us. Classic case of the dog that caught the car. At least, back when there were cars actually moving along the now abandoned roads.

"We've been on the run for a long time," I tell them. "We saw your fire from a distance and thought we might find some friendly faces who could maybe help us out."

"Sorry. No help here," the tall boy says, his voice laced with suspicion. "If you move along, we'll let you go in peace."

"We're not moving along," I tell him. "So you may as well forget it."

The tall boy looks around, flustered, at his group of friends. After a few seconds, he says, "What are you waiting for?" and the Juvens move toward us, their twig-spears and rocks in hand.

With our training, I suspect that Card and I could probably take down every one of the kids before they knew what hit them.

Thanks to Render and his intel, I won't need to find out.

"Listen," I reply. "I wouldn't try anything if I were you."

Coming from three different directions and making barely a sound, Brohn, Rain, and Manthy slip out from the woods and slide up behind the group of nervous and distracted Neos and Juvens.

Silently easing his way forward, Brohn slips his arm around the tall boy's neck and drags him backwards, away from the stunned crowd of kids. In the same instant, Rain snaps a side blade kick to the back of the tall girl's knee and sends her crumpling to the ground. Even as she falls, Manthy snatches her by the collar of her jacket and drags her aside, dropping to one knee beside her and locking her in an immobilizing chokehold. In the flurry of action, and with their two leaders incapacitated, the rest of the startled kids whip around and lose their focus on me, Kella, and Cardyn.

In a synchronous offensive, Cardyn and I melt into the jostling and disoriented crowd. Even Kella gets in on the action, unleashing a straight punch to the nose of one of the kids, whose eyes tear up as he drops heavily to the ground. Cardyn slings two of the kids into each other and then uses them as bludgeons, knocking down three more of their disheveled crew like pins in a bowling alley. With a roundhouse kick and three sharp elbows to three young jaws, I pick up the spare, and, just like that, every one of the twelve kids is down with the six of us standing over them.

Of course, it's kind of an unsatisfying victory. These are just Neos and Juvens, after all. Even the two leaders, on their knees and at the mercy of Brohn and Manthy, are probably just Fifteens, maybe Sixteens, themselves. Weakened and inexperienced ones at that. Still, as far as counter-assaults go, we've managed to dispatch the twelve kids with a blur of efficiency and with perfect control. Other than a few watery eyes and a bunch of bruises and nose-bleeds, they're all down with no major damage done.

"We don't want to hurt you," Rain says as we stand triumphant over the angry but helpless bunch.

"Why should we believe you?" one of the girls snaps from her seat on the ground.

"You shouldn't," Card says. "But you should at least hear us out. You escaped Recruitment, which means you have excellent instincts and great survival skills. So you're smart. You're resourceful. Heck, you would've even gotten the drop on us if we didn't have our flying set of eyes up there."

Card points to a low tree branch just a few feet away where Render is perched. "Between him and Kress here, we can see everything for miles."

Looking over, the kids jump a little at the sight of the glistening black bird peering at them through his eerily lifeless eyes.

Cardyn snaps his fingers to draw the kids' attention back to him. "We're all just a bunch of kids who've been through too much and don't know what to do or who to trust. This can play out in a big stupid fight that'll probably leave a lot of us hurt or worse. Or it can end with us on the same side, fighting the only enemies we know are out there for sure: fear and uncertainty."

As Card talks to the disheveled dozen, it slowly occurs to me what he's doing. He's humanizing us, calming the kids down, painting a picture of the situation, and giving them a solution, all at once. Giving us all a way out of this impasse.

It's an impressive feat of manipulation, and it seems be working. I can feel the kids let go of the breaths they've been holding in.

"Now, there are more of you than there are of us," Card says with a chuckle and a long look around at the rag-tag gang of orphans. "And frankly, I don't know which one of you to talk to."

"Me," the tall girl says with a frown. "Celia."

"And me," the tall boy adds with a raised hand. "Adric."

They're both still on their knees in front of Brohn and Manthy, who are standing behind them on high alert, ready to put them down again if they try to make a move.

"I'm Cardyn. The big guy there is Brohn. Our quiet friend next to him is Amaranthine. We call her Manthy. This little lady here is Rain. You've already met Kress, Kella, and, of course, Render: the eyes, ears, and wings, of our little band of stragglers."

"Where are the three adults?" Celia asks, her voice laced with suspicion as her eyes dart around to look at the trees surrounding us.

"Adults?" Card asks, turning to shoot me a look.

"Asha and the others," I remind him softly. I turn to Celia. "You saw them."

Celia nods.

"They're not with us," I tell her. "We didn't even know them. Not really. Anyway, they're gone."

She locks her eyes on mine for a few seconds before finally offering me a nod that tells me she believes me.

"Where are you all from?" Rain asks her.

Celia glances over her shoulder at Manthy, who nods approval for her to speak. Celia points up and out past the trees surrounding the small clearing. "We're from Miner. It's over on the other side of the mountain. Like you guessed, we escaped Recruitment."

"Then you're like us. We were recruited—like they were going to do to you. They put us on the truck, took us through the whole training program and everything. But it's not what you think. None of it is. We still don't quite know what it is ourselves."

"What's that supposed to mean?"

"The Seventeens aren't being recruited to fight the Order. The Recruiters are weeding us out, using anyone they can, and killing anyone they can't use so that we don't fight back against them or try to expose the truth about what they're up to."

"What truth?"

"The entire Recruitment process...it's a sham. A lie."

"But why? I mean, if they're not recruiting us to fight the Order, why train us at all?"

The million-dollar question. I glance over at Brohn and swallow hard. Much as I want to avoid the subject, I don't have a choice. "They said they found something special in some of us. Something they wanted to use."

The kids look at each other before Celia asks, "How many are there?"

"How many what?"

"Whatever you called the place where they took you."

"Processors? They said dozens, maybe hundreds, but we don't really know."

"We saw just the one," Rain adds. "But there was something else, too—we saw kids from another—"

I shoot her a glare, and she stops talking. The last thing I want is to totally destroy any shreds of innocence these kids might still have by mentioning the thirteen bodies we saw before our final escape.

"How come people on the outside aren't fighting back?" Celia asks. "Why are the Recruiters still allowed to go to the towns?"

"I don't think most people know." I can't help thinking about the three adults we met in the desert. They seemed utterly oblivious to the whole Recruitment system. But even if they had known, I wasn't sure they could have done anything. "People don't know who to fight back against," I continue. "Think about it. All we really know is what we're told. We thought we were being taken away to fight for our country. We didn't know it was all a lie."

"So the Eastern Order…?"

"From what the woman in charge of the Processor told us, the Eastern Order is a made-up enemy. We don't know how much of what she told us is true, though."

"So they could be our own government," Adric says, a look of dread passing over his face.

"We've been on the run for a long time now," I reply, trying to change the subject away from needless speculation about a truth that's beyond our reach. "We've seen mostly mountains and woods. When we did find highways, we saw a couple of military convoys, but no one else. We hid from them, of course. We passed a few small towns that looked like they'd been nuked. Otherwise, there's not a lot out there at the moment. So there's not much to fight for anymore, to tell you the truth."

I feel a pang of guilt as I see the faces in front of me. Expressions of sadness, disillusionment, lost hope.

I step forward and suggest that we might be more comfortable talking somewhere other than this clearing. "Since it looks like we're not going to kill each other, we might as well go the whole way. Maybe we could have this conversation as friends."

"You have a camp set up, yes?" Rain asks.

Adric gives a small flip of his head. "About a hundred yards that way. Just past the tree-line."

"It's not much," Celia admits. "Really just a collection of makeshift tents and assorted shelters we arranged into a mini-neighborhood back there."

Adric nods and looks up at me as if asking for permission to stand up. I tell him it's okay, and he and Celia rise slowly to their feet, their eyes focused on me with laser intensity. When they realize it's not a trick and that we're not going to summarily execute them all right here in the middle of the clearing, they relax and invite the others to stand up as well.

Still a bit skittish but with their guards mostly down, Adric and Celia instruct the younger kids to follow them across the clearing. Flanked by Brohn and me, Adric and Celia lead us over to a small opening in a cluster of bushes and brambles. They crouch down and walk through, with everyone else following close behind.

We hike a short distance through more clusters of low-hanging vines and half-dead vegetation until we arrive at a small semi-circle of the crude tents and shelters Celia described.

Three of the kids duck into one of the tents and drag sleeping pallets and smoothed-down logs out into the small clearing. They set up the logs as seats for us. We sit down with the ten younger kids gathered in a cluster in front of us, Adric and Celia standing just behind them.

"This isn't a bad set-up you have here," Brohn says, glancing around at the tents, the mesh canopy, and the surprisingly intricate system of wood and stone supports that hold everything together. "Concealed. Cool. Stable. Decent shelters. I'm assuming you have food and other supplies?"

"Not as much as we'd like," Celia says with a sad shake of her head. "Or as much as we need."

"Still," Cardyn says, "you're way better off tucked up in here than we were out there."

"We've been too afraid to stray too far from camp," Adric says. "Too afraid of running into Recruiters if we got too close to the roads. We knew the fire was a risk, but we knew our best hope was to attract someone. We just weren't sure if we'd catch friends or enemies."

"Don't worry," Cardyn announces with a toothy smile, probably for the benefit of the younger kids still staring at us wide-eyed. "We're definitely friends. And, if you have anything around to eat, we can even be *best* friends."

The ten Neos and Juvens in front of us giggle as Manthy rolls her eyes.

"We're not sure what all is out there," Brohn says to Adric, gesturing with a flick of his head up the mountain. "Right now, I'm focusing on what we have left up *there*."

"Where are you from originally? I mean before the Recruitment."

"We're from a small town called the Valta," Rain says.

"We need to get back there," Brohn adds. "To find out if Wisp —I mean, if everyone—is okay." As I listen to his voice, I can hear the emotion in it. He hasn't talked about his sister in a long time, but I know he thinks of her every minute of every day. Wondering if she's still alive, just as I wonder about my dad and Micah. "The Recruiters," he says, "or whatever they're calling themselves, might try to go back there. We'd like to get there first."

"We may know where your home is from here," Adric says, gesturing to two Juvens who are sitting close by. "These two can probably get you there."

The two Juvens each raise a hand. They can't be more than

about eleven or twelve years old. Both are small, but there's a strange alertness and intelligence dancing behind their eyes.

Adric nods toward the girl. "This is Chace," he says. "And her twin brother here is Trax. They led our escape, helped us find this place on the far side of the mountain where the Recruiters couldn't easily get to. If anyone can help you find home, it's them."

"They've got a better instinct for direction and terrain than anyone I've ever seen," Adric boasts. He steps forward, puts a hand on each twin's head, and musses their hair. "They're great artists, too." They push his hands off but don't seem overly irritated by the gesture.

Brohn leans toward me and whispers, "You should tell them more about Render. He can get us home just as easily."

From my other side, Card, who's overheard, shakes his head. "They need to be able to trust us. Let them help."

"Card's right," I say under my breath to Brohn. "They need affirmation right now. Besides, we can protect the twins better than their group can."

Brohn gives me a slow, respectful nod before turning to Adric and Celia. "Okay. We'll take you up on your offer."

"Wait—what about Kella?" I say, turning to him with a sudden twinge of guilt. Instinctively I grab his hand as I tend to do when moments of intense emotion hit. I hate the idea of leaving Kella behind. But we all know that dragging her across miles of mountains to the Valta would be a cruel and unusual punishment.

Brohn squints like he's thinking hard and motions Adric over. "We won't be able to take our friend with us," he tells him with a half-nod in Kella's direction. He's whispering, but he doesn't need to. Kella is so out of it right now—staring off blankly into the woods—he could shout it in her ear, and I don't think it would register.

Adric gives us a nod. "I understand," he says, turning to Celia.

"Can you see to her for now?" he asks. "I think you'd be better company for her than I would."

Celia smiles, pulling her eyes first to Brohn, then to me. "Don't worry. She's in good hands," she says. Her voice is soothing as a snowfall and makes me want to curl up under a warm blanket somewhere and drift off to sleep. "We'll take good care of her while you're gone."

As we thank her, I choke back tears. I feel like we're betraying Kella right now, but leaving her behind is the only thing we can do. Finding home means finding Wisp and the others. It means helping them. It's what Kella would want us to do, with or without her.

Adric digs around under a canvas tarpaulin and pulls out some food and two bottles of cloudy water. "We don't have many weapons or a lot of supplies to spare, but these will keep you going for the couple of days it'll take for you to get home."

"Thank you," I say, gratefully accepting the gifts and stowing them in my bag.

When everyone's ready, we follow Chace and Trax on what they tell us will be a two-day hike uphill toward the Valta. There are no roads and no discernible paths, yet, somehow, the twins easily weave in and out of walls of brambles, vines, and root systems from hundreds of fallen trees.

Brohn stays right on their heels, and I stay right on his. Render soars overhead, letting out the odd cry to let us know he's still with us.

The twins seem to have an endless supply of energy. We're tired, but they urge us to keep going. We stop a couple of times to rest and once to sleep. We continue on for the whole next day, and it's only when I see the murky dark turn wispy pink that I realize we've walked through the entire second night. Every once in a while, I look up through gaps in the trees to see Render gliding along overhead.

I don't even feel tired anymore. Maybe it's because we've

finally found others like us. Or maybe it's because we're finally so close to home. Either way, I feel invigorated. Revitalized.

The others must feel it, too. Except for Manthy, we've all joined Cardyn in prattling away at light speed about how great it's going to be to see the Valta. The past and the future roll into one as we reminisce about what was and about how excited we are to experience what will be.

"We're going to be the first Recruits to see home again," Rain says with a beaming grin.

Those words are enough to deflate me slightly. "Except for Micah," I say quietly.

Immediately, Rain's expression fades to a frown. "I'm so sorry," she says. "I forgot."

"It's okay."

"Who's Micah?" Chace asks.

"Kress's brother," Cardyn explains. "He was recruited before us. He's amazing."

I send him a mental "thanks" for using the present tense. The last time I saw Micah, he was being hunted down and dragged away by Recruiters. Holding onto the hope that he's still alive is hard at the best of times.

These days, though, most of my thoughts and memories of him are the good ones. The kind of recollections that now come back to me in vivid waves, as if he's sitting right next to me, his voice in my ear. I remember every inch of his face. I remember his voice when he was a boy, then the depth and roundness of it as he grew into a man. He was a great brother, and an inspiration to everyone who knew him. "Micah proved the trip home was possible," I remind Rain with a smile. "We're just following in his footsteps."

"True," she replies quietly.

After we've hiked for a while longer, she asks, "Do you think anything will have changed in the Valta while we were gone?"

With a chuckle, Brohn says he's sure of it. "The 2043 Sixteens are a hopeless bunch. Messiest pile of slobs I've ever seen, and not a hunter among them."

Picking up on his old "Remember when…" refrain, Cardyn launches into a long-winded recollection about how we all came together after the last of the adults disappeared or died. "I personally helped patch the roof of the school," he beams with pride at Chace and Trax. "We re-built the walkway down to the beach, cleared the roads, perfected our pulley system for transporting building materials, fixed the water cistern, filled the storage lockers with all the food we'd gathered. Let's face it," he announces, giving me a hard slap on the back, "we were awesome!"

Manthy pushes past Cardyn. "The roof kept leaking anyway," she reminds him.

He's lucky she isn't looking when he sticks his tongue out her.

AFTER ABOUT ANOTHER hour or so, we break out of the woods and climb an embankment up to a steep, narrow road. Pushing along, we march up the road and around its snaking curves for another hour or two until we arrive at an abandoned military checkpoint that leaves me breathless.

It's the same checkpoint that kept us isolated in our mountain town for a decade.

But now there are no soldiers. No trucks. Nothing. A small building, not much bigger than a tool shed, sits alone and empty. A tall fence topped with laser-wire extends from the structure to the left and right and runs out into the woods for as far as the eye can see. Thin spires topped with what look like lifeless motion-detectors jut up from intermittent spots along the fence. The two posts next to the small building must be for an energy-gate, but there's no power here anymore.

Still, when we step through the gate, I expect alarms to go off or troops to leap out at us. But nothing happens.

"Well," Rain says, looking up the last stretch of road before the Valta, "we're nearly home."

As we advance, memories of our last days here come flooding back: Final Feast. Saying our goodbyes. The arrival of the Recruiters on the morning of November 1st. Thinking I was losing Render for good. Wisp being ripped from Brohn's arms before our Cohort of Seventeens was gathered up and loaded onto a transport truck.

Rain leads us in a jog up the pitted and overgrown road to the open plateau at the top, the same big, open space where the Recruiters came for us all those months ago. Embedded tire tracks, old ones and new-looking ones, overlap in the crusted ground in the clearing, reminding us of the trauma of being carted away from home.

It's when we look ahead that we discover that our worst nightmare has come true.

8

———————————————

Most of the Valta's buildings were destroyed in the waves of drone attacks at the beginning of the so-called war. But now, even the few buildings that were still standing when we left our town are devastated beyond recognition.

Not a single structure is left, not even the school. No area is left unscathed. What was once home is now as burned out and blackened as the ruined head of an old match.

Eleven years ago when my family moved here, the Valta was an idyllic, picturesque little town. Ten years ago, the drones wiped much of it out. A few years after that, they reappeared and nearly wiped out the rest. We rebuilt what we could and did our best to make it our town again. We cleared away wreckage, made it as safe as possible, and turned it into a new home for the survivors.

Now, it's nothing but a devastated and smoldering expanse of rubble like the towns we passed after escaping the Processor.

But the demolition of the structures and the remaining fragments of road, it turns out, are just the beginning.

Lying along the roadside, half-buried under debris and

charred beyond recognition, are the scattered and lifeless bodies of all the friends we've ever known.

I want to throw up. To double over at the sudden pain in my gut.

To scream at the top of my lungs.

"Oh no." Card drops to his knees in the dirt, too weak to stand.

I hardly dare look at Brohn. But when I do, I can see that he's shaking his head. He's saying, "No, no, no," over and over again. But it's so quiet, it sounds like a gentle wind blowing across my ears.

My chest is clamped tight. Tears fill my eyes. I feel like I'm breathing hard but can't catch my breath at the same time, like my body is collapsing under the weight of my mind.

High overhead somewhere, Render lets out a cry that tells me he can feel it, too. The residents of the Valta were his extended family. They loved him, and he loved them.

And now they're gone.

Rain's fists are clenched at her sides. She takes a small step forward. Then another. Then she stops, frozen at the horror of the scene before us.

Next to me, Manthy is sobbing so hard I think she's going to choke to death. She's never been an emotional person. Never worn her heart on her sleeve. It always seemed like she didn't care about anything, not even herself. But now, watching her collapse to the ground next to Card, the dam bursts in my own heart, and I'm crying along with her, harder than I ever have in my life.

Chace and Trax hug each other, their faces red and wet. They may never have lived here, but this could just as easily have been their home. From what we know of them, they lived like we did: in a small mountain town in uncertain isolation. Always waiting. Always afraid.

Our pain is theirs. Their tears are ours. They know.

I can't help feeling glad Kella didn't come. When we said goodbye to her, she was barely hanging onto sanity. Seeing this… our town and only home reduced to a field of flattened structures and the burned and twisted bodies of our friends, cracked and broken over piles of blistered wood, concrete, and charred synth-steel…I know it would push her over the edge to a place from which she could never return.

This is Hell, I tell myself. There is no other word for it. This is the end, the fate worse than death. I can't keep going. I don't want to keep going. It's too much. I'm done. I give up.

Brohn and I exchange a look, and, through our overflow of tears, I can tell he's feeling the same thing. *Why go on? What is there left to fight for?* Maybe he's looking to me for strength, but I don't have any to offer him. I have nothing.

Together, we fall to our knees next to Cardyn and Manthy. Rain collapses beside us, and the five of us put our arms around each other. Our sobs combine into one common shudder that rips through each of us, a lightning strike, waves smashing against rock, a tremor tearing through the planet. Chace and Trax stand frozen next to me, their eyes riveted to the carnage in front of us.

Brohn is the first to pull away. He drags a sleeve across his eyes, then smashes a powerful fist to the ground, and I swear I can feel a shudder rumble through the fractured and broken earth beneath us. Seeing his tears, hearing and feeling the deep internal sobs that rattle his body, gives me the answer to my question: there is still something left to fight for. There is still Brohn. And Cardyn. And Rain, Manthy, and Kella. And there are Karmine and Terk to fight for. And all the others who died, and all the rest of us, those who are still alive. This isn't the end.

There are still so many of us, here and out there, worth fighting for.

It's because this is all too much, that's why I will not give up.

My tears burn in my throat until there's nothing left but dry, raspy breathing and the pain of loss that burns its way to the marrow of my bones. The others feel it, too. It's like I'm inside each of their minds, one by one, feeling their loss. Their pain.

When Brohn and I were inside the Halo, we shared a moment where I was inside his head. We spoke to each other wordlessly, just as I do with Render. I've always wondered if I imagined it, or if it really happened.

But now I know. I can feel his emotions, the dark thoughts raging through his mind as clearly as I feel my own.

In a moment of self-preservation, I pull back, shutting myself away. It's more than I can take right now. More than I could ever process.

When we're finally able to gather ourselves, we stand as one and walk slowly through what's left of our town. Heads down, hearts heavy, we follow the path up to the massive expanse of black debris that used to be the school where we all lived. Shoshone High. It's where we all got older without thinking about how much we were growing up. It's the building that saved our lives in the first series of drone attacks. It's where my father taught me about micro-circuitry. It's where I first bonded with Render.

Chace and Trax circle around the huge mass of charred and twisted ruins. The building's walls have collapsed in on themselves to create an array of deformed peaks. Twisted crossbeams and knotted lengths of synth-steel pipe jut out from heaps of smashed window frames and splintered sections of the building's roof.

The twins occasionally bend down to examine the soil and the stray piles of building materials, much of it fused by plasma bombs into smooth mounds of glass, littering the ground. Hunched over, they scurry around, investigating boot-prints and trampled patches of scorched vegetation.

Chace explains that it looks like the remaining kids were rounded up, forced into the school, which was then blown up.

"See," she says, "you can tell from the direction of the smaller prints. The kids were running. This is where the larger prints, the ones with the military-style tread, caught up with them."

"It wasn't a drone strike?" Brohn asks. If it's possible, he looks even more horrified than before. At least a drone strike might have meant a surprise attack. The thought of Wisp and the others dying in a state of terrified confusion is too painful to contemplate.

"No," Chace says. "Men were here."

"They wanted to kill them all in person," Rain hisses. "They wanted to see their faces."

"Your friends…they fought," Trax adds, examining our surroundings. "They tried. Struggled. There was gunfire. A lot of it. Shell casings are all over the place, but all pointing in the same direction." Like Chace, he's holding back his emotions. His restraint makes him sound like he's reciting the alphabet rather than announcing the end of our last loved ones on the planet. I'm about to get angry over his lack of compassion when I realize he and his sister are just doing what they need to do to give us the information we need. "The weapons weren't very high-tech, but there were a lot of them," he says, shaking his head. "There was no return fire."

"We didn't have guns," Rain says. Her voice is even, but her eyes are glassy. Brohn drops to his knees again, and this time he covers his face with his hands. I kneel down next to him, one arm across his shoulders, holding on as hard as I can. He's shaking, trembling like the rest of us against waves of anger and sorrow. I know there's nothing I can say. Nothing for any of us to say. It's like the waves have flooded our lungs and drowned all our words.

After a few minutes we silently rise to our feet and dig through the rubble for a while. We use our hands to excavate what we can. We kick at some of the long beams with our boots and try to team up to lift some of the heavier fragments. It's a mess of concrete, synth-steel supports, and alu-iron rebar.

But there are also bodies.

Some are lying along the edge of what used to be the school parking lot. Others are half buried in the crush of the fallen building. Everyone we knew and thought we were fighting for. All the Juvens, the Neos, and the Sixteens. As carefully as possible, we extract the ones we can. I recognize some of the kids. Others are too badly burned, or else their bodies have suffered too much trauma to enable us to identify them. I know without asking that Brohn is looking for Wisp, but there are too many bodies under too much debris for us to get to them all. I don't tell him that any one of several of the unidentifiable, disfigured or partial remains could be his little sister. I don't need to tell him. It's written all over his face.

After a couple of hours, we manage to pull twenty-six of our friends from the one place they all thought was safe. Most of them are either burned or crushed nearly beyond recognition. As far as we can tell, none of them is Wisp.

The thought that we have already found her but weren't able to identify her remains churns my stomach and brings tears to my eyes all over again.

While we continue to dig, Brohn finds a gap in the wreckage and calls us over to help.

"If we move this slab," he urges, "I can get deeper down in there."

I'm thinking it's hopeless, but I'm not about to stand in his way. If he thinks there's a chance Wisp, or anyone for that matter, might still be alive in there, there's no one in the world dumb enough, strong enough, or suicidal enough to stand in his way.

We get to work prying apart sections of wall and cross-beams as best we can until we've created a small opening. Brohn kneels down in front of it. He slips off his jacket and tosses it off to the side.

"I'm the smallest," Chace says, her small hand on Brohn's muscular shoulder. "I should be the one to go."

Rain says, "No. It's too dangerous. I'm small enough. I'll go in."

She's just stepping forward and bending down to slip into the dark gap when Brohn puts his arm out to stop her. "It's big enough. I'll go."

Without waiting for any of us to object or volunteer ourselves, he drops to his stomach and pulls himself down into the small opening. He crawls forward until his boots disappear, and all we can hear is the heaviness of his breathing and the scratching and clawing of his hands as he pushes and pries his way deeper inside.

"It's tight," he calls back, "but there's space. I can't see much, but I can almost stand up. There are more down here. Neos, I think…"

His voice gets distant and hollow until it fades away completely. There are no more sounds of breathing. No more sounds of digging.

I call out, "Brohn!" into the opening, but he doesn't respond. I shout his name again, and when he doesn't answer, my throat gets so tight I can't even gather enough breath to try again.

Card, Manthy, Rain, and I exchange the same horrified look. Before anyone can stop her, Rain throws off her jacket and dives down into the hole. Manthy, Card, and I rush forward and peer down into the darkness, but we can't see or hear anything. It's as if Brohn and Rain have just vanished into another dimension.

Card cups his hands around his mouth and yells down to them. When he doesn't get a response, he tries again, then starts walking along the top of the rubble. He swings his head from side to side, scanning the debris beneath his feet, still calling out to Brohn and Rain in desperation.

"Be careful!" I shout across to him. "If this stuff shifts…"

Cardyn gets the idea and eases his way back down to where Manthy and I are still standing helplessly with the twins.

I'm just about to give in to panic and despair when we hear Rain's voice call out. Her voice is muffled, but we can hear her.

"I've got him!" she shouts. "We're okay."

Rain's hands appear first. Card and Manthy grab her by the wrists and help to guide her out. Brohn is next. He clambers his way out of the small opening and stands in front of us, his face a mess of dirt and tears.

"Did you find any—?" I start to say.

But Brohn cuts me off and pushes past me toward the road. "I can't free the rest. There's nothing. There's no one left."

"I'll take care of him," I tell the others. "Just give us a minute."

Cardyn looks around at the wreckage and at the bodies of our friends. He drops his head, and his voice quivers. "It's okay. We'll start...looking after all of them."

I thank him quietly and walk over to stand with Brohn on what's left of what was once Center Street. The blacktop and concrete are buckled in places and smooth as glass in others. White plastic pipes from the old sewer system poke out like jagged splinters. It's barely recognizable as a street now. More like a deep, infected scar gouged into the skin of the earth.

Behind us, Rain, Card, Manthy, and the twins go about transporting the bodies as best they can to the small field next to the school where Card says he hopes to give them a proper burial. Render lands on a broken section of rocks on the other side of the burned and brittle field from where Brohn and I are standing. The cracked and blackened blocks form the ruins of what used to be part of an old perimeter wall between the school lot and the road. Render flaps his wings wide and *kraas* at me. I can feel him in my head, wanting to connect with me, to see if I'm okay. I swipe my forearm tattoos, and his consciousness comes into focus. He's calling me over.

"What is it?" I sigh. My heart's too heavy to deal with little things right now. I've got my arm around Brohn's waist. His arm is heavy on my shoulders, but I don't want to move away from him. We're supporting each other, physically and emotionally, and I don't know how either of us would stand up right now without the other. Render *kraas* again, and I turn to him, annoyed. "I don't have any food for you. You're going to have to be on your own for a bit, okay?"

Inside my head, Render's mental voice, urgent and raspy, makes his wordless meaning clear from across the black field:

Come here! Important!

9

"Something's up with Render," I mutter to Brohn.

"Go ahead. See what he wants." Brohn is still teary-eyed as he slips his arm from my shoulders. "I'll be okay."

It kills me to disrupt this moment. We're all grieving, and Brohn needs me right now in a way no one's ever needed me before. Losing Terk and Karmine was devastating. The loss of Wisp, though, is something beyond even that. Brohn lived for his little sister. He was more protective of her than I've seen anybody be over another person. In return, she made his life worth living. She could switch him on and light him up with a smile. Now, there's an emptiness in his eyes and a flatness in his voice that fills me with dread. For the first time since I've known him, which is basically my entire life, he seems deflated. Defeated.

Render *kraas* again, and I tell him I'm coming. As annoyed as I am right now, I've also learned to trust him over the years. He's been known to launch into loud, dramatic outbursts to draw my attention to an animal carcass, to drag me out to a field to watch him tumble and dive, and sometimes for no apparent reason at all. He has a mischievous and playful side. Right now, though, he's all business.

As I approach the broken wall where he's perched, Render flaps his wings again but doesn't take off. I cough at the dust he kicks up, and I walk over to stand in front of him. He gives me a series of croaking groans, another *kraa!* and another flapping of his wings. This time he does take off, his five-foot wingspan unfurling his shadowy black feathers cape-like around him as he hurtles airborne. I look up as he soars and circles overhead.

"What was that all about?" I ask the air. But I get no answer.

Although my connection with Render has proven to be quite strong at times, there are plenty of other times—right now, for example—when I have no idea what he's thinking, feeling, or trying to convey. At the moment, he reminds me of a Sixteen named Peter from the Valta. I was just a Neo when I knew him, but not surprisingly, I remember a lot about him. He rarely spoke, but when he did, nearly nothing he said made any sense. He rambled off a jumble of philosophy, science, and religion— usually to himself. He squirreled himself away in a corner of a small room, a broom closet actually, on the top floor of Shoshone High School.

That little room became his sanctuary, his bedroom, and, more often than I care to remember, his bathroom. No matter how much the other Sixteens tried to intervene, Peter lived his life on his own terms. He came out and went back in when he wanted. In between, he muddled around on the fringes of his Cohort, spouting off random phrases from books he'd read or spewing out long speeches about alien space probes, genetic experiments, or how we were all really just digital simulations living out our lives in a virtual-reality game being played by a cabal of secret government operatives. In the month after my father died, Peter started following me around. He'd track me down in the school or by the beach and would lecture me about taking care of my implants and about how I would one day help to "save the fallen from themselves." I tried to be nice and listen, but eventually, those encounters became overwhelming, and I found ways to be where Peter wasn't. Eventually, he lost interest in me and latched on to a Juven named Werner who wasn't the most patient person in the world and was constantly pushing Peter away and telling him to get lost. The Recruiters would normally leave someone like Peter behind, but instead, they took a special interest in him. On November 1st of that year, when the Recruiters loaded the new Seventeens into their transport truck, they gave Peter the royal treatment. They fussed over him, threw a blanket around his shoulders, wiped the sticky saliva from the corners of his mouth, and then let him ride up front in the escort vehicle.

I never did manage to understand Peter, and I wonder if he was as frustrated with my inability to communicate as I was with his. And now I'm wondering if Render ever feels the same. After all, he's probably clear as day in his own head. He knows what he's thinking and what he wants. Surely, I must seem pretty ignorant to him when I get as confused about his intentions as I am now.

Overhead, Render banks hard and vanishes behind a grove of tall trees. I wait for a second and watch, but he doesn't come back.

"Thanks for nothing," I say, still irritated about being lured away from Brohn for no reason.

But before I turn to head back over to Brohn, I glance down at the broken wall Render was perched on. There seem to be markings of some kind etched into the surface of one of the gray-brown stones. At first, it just looks like random chips and cracks, and I'm about to turn away when I realize it's actual words. I push aside a bundle of prickly green vines and brush away a layer of dirt with my hand. It *is* words, jagged and slanted, like they were carved into the stone by someone in a hurry.

It says, *Follow Render to San Francisco for your answer. It's been an honor.*

"Hey!" I call out to Brohn, a flicker of hope springing to life inside me. "Come here a sec."

Brohn looks half-upset and half-relieved at having to move. Head down, hands plunged deep into his pockets, he walks over to where I'm standing and looks at the cryptic message. He kneels down and feels the imprint of the markings in the stone. He scratches his head and looks up at me. "San Francisco?"

"Yes. But look at the last part. The part about honor."

"So what?"

"So, that's the last thing Granden said to me before he helped us get away. I think he must have been here. I think he left this message for me."

Brohn stands up and wipes his hands on his pants. "You think Granden was here?"

"It makes sense. He helped us escape from the Processor. He knows about Render. He was still an insider as far as I know when we got away. There's no reason to think Hiller's people suspected him of anything."

Brohn clenches his jaw and looks back to where Rain and the others are sorting out the bodies of our dead friends. "Then he was here when they…"

"I don't think he would have been part of this."

"How can you know that?" Brohn snaps.

"I don't know how. I just…feel it."

"So you *feel* that he just stood here carving mysterious messages in stone while his buddies wiped out our town?"

"I-I-I'm not, I mean I don't think he could have…Maybe he came here later?" I stammer. "After they…"

"Killed everyone we know?"

I nod, tears welling up in my eyes.

"And the 'answer'? What's that about?"

"I'm not sure," I say, wiping my eyes. "But Granden used to look at my tattoos all the time. I don't think he knows I noticed. Once he asked me about them."

Brohn says, "Okay" and reaches over to wipe a tear from my cheek with his thumb. He tucks some of my stray hair behind my ear and offers me a weak but warm smile. "I remember that. We were in the Agora. Walking back to the Silo after one of our war-games exercises."

"I told him I had all kinds of questions about my dad and Micah and about the war. I wanted to know what my connection to Render really was and what I was supposed to do with it. I told him I felt that knowing about my tattoos was the one thing I needed in order to make all the other answers fall into place."

Brohn seems to think about this for a second. He looks down at the stone and then back up at me. "Hey guys!" he calls out to the others. "Come here. Kress found something."

Cardyn, Rain, Manthy, and the twins turn away from where they've been carefully lining up the recovered bodies of our friends to prepare them for burial. With Cardyn walking slowly in the lead, they come over to where Brohn and I are standing at the low, broken wall.

I show them the writing etched into the stone.

"What's it mean?" Trax asks.

I explain to him and Chace about how Granden helped us Seventeens escape from the Processor. "He grabbed my arm right before I got ready to run into the woods with the others. There was gunfire and shouting behind us. He could have killed us himself if he wanted. By then, it was probably his job. Instead, he told me to follow Render and that 'It's been an honor.' Then he led the Processor guards in the wrong direction so we could make our escape."

"She also had a conversation with him about getting an answer," Brohn adds.

Chace looks up at me. "An answer to what?"

I push my jacket sleeves up and hold out my arms. "To these. To Render. To everything."

"And you think this Granden person wrote this here?" Chace asks.

I tell her that I think so. "It's possible, anyway. Probable, in fact. I can't imagine who else it could have been."

We all look over at Render, who has just flown back over and is now busily preening himself on the trunk of a burned and fallen tree just down the way from where we're standing.

Rain kneels down and looks closely at the writing. "So, I guess this means we follow Render to San Francisco?"

"Yes," I say with more certainty than I'm feeling. "That's exactly what we need to do."

Cardyn raises his hand and clears his throat like he's a little kid in a classroom. "Not to throw water on this happy little bonfire, but there may be a couple of potential problems here, Kress."

"Like?"

"Like for starters, we don't know where San Francisco is from here or how to get there. We don't know who or what might be standing in our way. We don't know if this is just another trick of some kind. And we don't know for sure who left this message here or if it was even meant for us."

"I agree," I say. "There's a lot we don't know. But the only way we're going to find out anything is by having a little faith."

"In a bird? Or do you mean in a man who helped kidnap and manipulate us?"

I suddenly feel very defensive, but I'm not sure if it's more about Render or about Granden. "Even if Granden didn't leave this message, we know we can trust Render. We've already put our lives in his hands more times than I can count."

"Wings," Cardyn says. "Technically, we've put our lives in his wings more times than you can count."

I'm about to punch Cardyn in the face when he smiles, and I realize that I'm smiling, too. Even here, in the middle of our ruined town with all of our murdered friends and my eyes red and raw from crying, Cardyn has a way of balancing me out. He doesn't augment or reduce my rage. He just keeps it from totally taking over my common sense and sanity.

"Thanks for the clarification," I say with a sneer. "Now, tell me what you really think. What do all of you think?"

Rain stands up from where she's been having a closer look at the message. "Granden may or may not be on our side. But Render's never steered us wrong. I say we see where he takes us."

Manthy shrugs and walks over to where Render is perched and starts running her hand along his feathered head. He leans toward her and ruffles the feathers on his neck. I think he'd smile if he could.

"I'm up for anything that will get us as far away from this place as possible," Brohn says evenly. I can tell he's struggling to keep his voice measured, and I can only imagine how hard it is for him. "San Francisco can't be any worse than being on the run in the woods. How long to get there from here?" he asks Chace.

She closes her eyes like she's visualizing a map. "Not sure. Four weeks on foot. Maybe more."

"Then we'll need supplies," Brohn says, taking charge like he used to back when we lived in the Valta, before I somehow became the leader of our Conspiracy. "First, we need to finish giving our friends a proper burial. Then we need to get back to your camp. From there, we can head out."

I swipe my fingers along my tattoos and re-connect with Render, who is practically purring over on the log where Manthy continues to stroke his head while she gazes absently into the distance.

When the connection is made, he looks up at me and lets out a contented *kraa!*

"Thank you," I whisper.

What he sends back to me aren't words, of course, but I get the idea.

He's saying something along the lines of *What are friends for?*

1 0

WITH THE DECISION MADE TO FOLLOW THE CRYPTIC MESSAGE carved into the stone, we talk for a bit about the logistics of the next leg of our journey. Having something to focus on seems to be giving Brohn some respite from his grief. A reason to keep breathing for now.

Chace and Trax assure us they can point us in the right direction. Their knowledge of everything from the terrain to the now-obsolete highway system is impressive.

"We've always been interested in geography," Trax tells us. He's a funny combination of child-like and knowledgeable. His voice is high and chirpy, but on occasion he sounds like a professor. At least, how I imagine a professor would sound.

His sister nods her agreement as she looks over to where Manthy is still petting Render. "Maps. Guidebooks. Atlases," she says. "Topographical diagrams. You name it."

"We didn't have a lot of paper books in Miner," Trax explains. "Just the ones that survived in an old archive section of the library. And it wasn't much of a library."

"But it was enough for us," Chace says. "No power meant no digi-texts. So all we had were the maps."

Trax blushes. "So we maybe got a little obsessed with them."

"Your obsession might just be the saving grace we need," Rain says. "In all our time in the Valta and then the Processor, it was hard for us to really know where we were in the world. We studied some geography, but because we never traveled to any of the places we learned about, we didn't have any context."

Chace looks at Rain then drops her gaze to the ground at her feet. "Not knowing where you are in the world sounds sad to me."

"Well, with your help," Rain says, "we can change that." She gives Chace's shoulder a friendly shake and then gives her a full-on hug. "Thank you for helping to give us direction," she adds softly, and I understand exactly what she means. We need it. We need purpose now, more than we ever have. Without it, we'll break. Shatter into a million pieces, never to be put back together again.

Chace smiles and walks over to stand next to her brother, who takes her hand in his own.

"I hate to be the one to bring us back down to reality," Cardyn says. "But we still need to take care of..."

We follow his gaze back to the crushed school and to the waiting bodies of our departed friends.

"You're right," Brohn says, his voice low, beaten down by the weight of the world. "We need to give them the respect they deserve."

It takes us the rest of the day, but we're finally able to transport what's left of our friends to the makeshift graveyard we started so long ago. In those early days after the first wave of drone-strikes, our all-too-frequent burial ceremonies were a constant reminder of the horrors of war, the temporary nature of life, and the need to keep the reins on our emotions in a time of crisis.

While I knew I'd be facing the horrors of war once again after

Recruitment, I somehow thought the days of burying my friends were behind me.

I thought wrong.

As we did in the past, we've managed to fashion some primitive shovels out of lengths of synth struts and alu-iron. It's slow going, but we silently bury the remains in graves dug as deep as we can get them with the limited tools and supplies we have. The ground is rocky and dry. The only remotely soft earth in the Valta is down by the riverbed, but we decided long ago not to bury our dead there. Partly because it was the safest spot for us to congregate and have fires, but also because we always hoped the water would return someday, and we didn't want the bodies of our dearly departed to get swept away by the river.

So we're left up on the plateau with semi-sunken tombs, half-graves that are nothing more than shallow ditches with stones and unsalvageable building materials piled on top. It's a strange and creepy mess of rocks and clutter laid out in neat rows like heaps of well cared-for garbage covering our dear friends.

It's the middle of the night by the time we're done digging and burying.

"Does someone want to say the final farewells?" Cardyn asks quietly.

I look at Rain, Brohn and Manthy. It seems too cruel to ask Brohn to muster the strength to speak. Manthy is still a mess. And I suspect Rain is, too, though she hides it well.

"Why don't you go ahead, Card?" I ask.

"Okay," he replies. He shoots a glance at Chace and Trax, who are standing by, watching curiously. "I...I wanted to tell all of you I'm sorry," he begins, looking around at the rest of us for a second before continuing. "I'm sorry we weren't here for you. We all are. We're sorry we didn't get here faster, so we could warn you what was happening out in the world. We're sorry to the Sixteens who never got to see their next November first. We hope you're in a nicer place now. But most of all…" Card presses a hand to his chest, "we want to say goodbye."

Twenty-six times he says goodbye, each time naming one person we left behind.

As he speaks, the rest of us let our emotions go. With the grim awareness that we're now the last of our town, every choke, sob, and tremble is allowed to come out. I move over to stand close to Brohn, knowing that even if he's not asking for support, he needs it. We hold hands and hug each other, hoping this will be the final time we bury someone we know and love, but knowing deep down that it won't be.

Our own personal war has only just begun.

When I've managed to gather myself enough to speak, I rub my eyes and promise out loud to set things right for our fellow Valtans, to honor the memories of our time together, and to help us get our revenge.

"Revenge won't make any of us feel better, you know," Manthy says.

"I know," I tell her with a glance toward twenty-six new piles of rocks and scraps laid out in orderly rows among the black weeds and dry grass. "But I'm not out to feel better. I'm going to feel bad for a very long time. I'm okay with that. Because I'm not out for revenge for my sake. I'm doing this for our friends."

Manthy sighs and offers me an almost imperceptible nod. She's not exactly a pacifist. She'll bicker, argue, and even engage in combat when necessary. She can be brutally efficient in a fight when it's called for. But she has a strange relationship with violence. It's like she thinks every act of aggression, no matter how minor or how justified, might lead to full-scale war. So she keeps her feelings in check and refuses to see anyone as an enemy until they don't give her any choice but to take a stand. I don't think she agrees with me about getting revenge, but, in the grimness of the moment, she seems willing to let it slide.

"It's too late to head back to the camp now," Rain says as she drags a dirty sleeve across her sweaty forehead. "We need to get a fire going. See if we can keep warm. Maybe find something to eat."

Brohn looks around at all the scrub-brush and crisp vegetation. "Better not do it here," he says. "We'll head down to the beach. It'll be safer there."

When Chace and Trax hesitate, Rain tells them it's okay. "We used to eat down there all the time."

With Rain in the lead, we turn toward the decimated woods and to the path leading down to the beach. Brohn lags behind, so I tell the others to go on without us. "We'll catch up," I promise.

As they continue on their way, I hear Manthy as she starts crying again. Cardyn puts his arm around her shoulders. I watch them for a minute as they disappear into the gloom of the black woods. I'm glad Manthy has someone to watch out for her when I'm not there, and I'm especially glad it's Cardyn.

I turn back to Brohn, who's still standing in the dark, looking out through the dim moonlight at the field of graves.

"She might not have been one of them," I say with a nod toward our homemade cemetery. "Maybe she got away somehow."

"I'd love to think so," Brohn says. "But I need to go back into the school. Or, what's left of it. I can't leave here without her, without knowing."

"I'll support you in whatever you do. I know she meant the world to you. All I ask is that you also take into account what you mean to the rest of us." Pointing back to what used to be our home, I remind Brohn how dangerous it is in there. "If that rubble collapses, if it even shifts, you'll join Wisp in a way you don't want to—a way she wouldn't want you to. And Brohn, just like you can't imagine going on without her, I don't see us getting very far without you." I'm trying to be strong for him, like he's been so many times for the rest of us. Trying to be rational, reasonable, even though pain and sadness are eating away at me from the inside out.

Brohn shakes his head and tips his chin toward the woods where Rain, Cardyn, Manthy, Chace, and Trax have now passed through the tree-line, down the path, and out of sight. "They have you, Kress. They don't need me."

"They need you," I assure him. "More important, *I* need you."

Brohn finally looks me in the eye. "I need you, too," he says. He lays his hand on the side of my face and tilts my head up so my eyes are on his. Even in this dim light, I can tell how hard he's fighting to hold things together. "I need you."

A moment later he leans down and kisses me. It's a warm, soft kiss. Part apology, part gratitude, and all love. I can taste the salt from his tears. I want to savor the moment, but knowing how broken his heart is only makes me start crying again. It's a kiss I've wanted for days, even weeks. But not like this. Not with all the sorrow in the universe pulling us both down like gravity.

Eventually the realization that we're simultaneously weeping and kissing seems to strike us both at once, and we pull back from each other just a little, only to start laughing.

Brohn gazes into my eyes, clasping his hands on top of each other against my lower back. He's smiling through his tears, probably relieved to have allowed himself a moment of levity. "We've been through a lot, haven't we?"

"I've got a feeling we have a lot more to get through," I say. "And it probably won't be fun."

"Or easy."

"True. But it's what we need to do. Not just for everyone we've lost, but for everyone still suffering under this great big lie. We need to find out the truth and expose it."

I drape my hands over his shoulders and play with his hair for a minute, then press my head against his chest. We hold each other for a long time. But it still doesn't feel like long enough.

After a brief silence, Brohn kisses the top of my head and steps back.

"We should catch up with the others," he says. "We need to figure out what we're doing next."

I agree reluctantly, and we head through the woods and down to the beach. Render is flying somewhere overhead, no doubt craving sleep.

The path is dark and overgrown, but it's a trail we know well. Brohn and I have walked it a thousand times, but never like this. Never together. Never holding hands amid the cyclone of fear, grief, and purpose our lives have become.

When we arrive at the beach, I remind myself that it's the same place where we celebrated Final Feast just a few months ago. That night seems like a dozen years ago and a million miles away. It's a ghostly feeling, seeing how little has changed out here, but knowing how much all of us have changed inside.

Rain is working with Chace and Trax to start a fire in the same pit we used to roast the deer Brohn caught on our last day before Recruitment. The river bed is, as always, dark and dry, with creepy shadows from the thin strips of moonlight slipping past the charcoal-colored clouds overhead. The old log where Brohn and I planted the first seeds of our relationship is still sitting undisturbed, exactly how we left it. Off in the distance, a series of mountain tops, every one of them as familiar as a best friend, rises up under a field of winking white stars. Every inch of it—the sand, the rocks, the dead leaves, and the broken branches that litter the beach—is something I hoped I'd see again.

But not like this. If I knew then that I'd be sitting here with the last of the Valta burned beyond recognition, I would never have let those men put us in their truck. I would have fought with every last ounce of strength I had to keep myself at home. To keep myself and the others safe.

On the beach, the mood is somber. We sit in a circle around the fire that Chace and Trax made. Some of us sit cross-legged.

Manthy has her knees pulled tight to her chest, her arms around her shins like she's trying to make herself as small and as invisible as possible. Card puts his arm around her shoulders, but she shakes her head and says, "Don't. I'm okay. Really."

Card pulls away, but he gives her arm a squeeze as he does. Without looking up, Manthy smiles a little and thanks him.

"We lost a lot of people, too," Chace says, her young voice breaking the stillness. "At home, I mean. We're sorry for what you're going through."

"We never had to come back to find them gone like this," Trax adds. "The pain must be beyond...anything."

"I don't recommend it," Rain says bitterly. She's sitting across the fire from me, her face a flickering palette of emotion. I've seen her sad, determined, focused, and furious to the core. Right now, she looks like she's somehow all of those rolled into one. "We need to find out who did this," she says at last through gritted teeth.

Cardyn smirks. "What do you mean 'who?' We know perfectly well who. It's that psycho Hiller's gang of fake military."

"We don't know how fake those men were, or how deep this thing really goes," Brohn interjects.

Chace sits up straight and sweeps her long hair back behind her ears. "Wait—I don't understand. Back at our camp, you told Adric and Celia that the Eastern Order isn't real. I thought you said it's just our own government."

"That's true," Brohn says. "That's what Hiller told us. And at that point she didn't have any reason to lie to us. But she killed herself before we could get the whole story out of her. According to her, the government fabricated the entire thing."

"That's not exactly what she said," I correct him. "She said, and I quote, 'the Eastern Order was an invention created nearly fifteen years ago as a way to keep us at war, so everyone stayed scared and no one asked too many questions.'"

Rain turns to Chace and Trax and brags to them about how

amazing my memory is. "You may know your way around a map, but Kress here has apparently memorized everything in the world anyone has ever written or said since the beginning of time. The girl's a walking bio-mainframe."

"I'm nothing of the sort," I scoff. "I've just been oddly clear-headed about certain things lately. Like about what Hiller said. She said the Order was created. She didn't necessarily say it was created by our government. For all we know, it could've been made up by some splinter faction or a gang of rogue geneticists. Who knows, really?"

"It could have even been real," Card says. "At the start anyway."

"Either way," I say, gesturing back up the path to the town, "we need to avenge our friends, and we can't do that unless we know exactly who we're going after."

Brohn scratches his head and sighs. "And how are we going to figure that out?"

"We're going to follow Render to San Francisco and get some answers."

Trax looks over at me out of the corner of his eye, like he wants to ask me something but is too scared to do it. When he catches me looking at him, he turns away.

"It's okay," I say. "You can ask me anything."

"I was just wondering about Render."

"What about him?"

"Well, birds have an excellent sense of direction. They have a mineral called 'magnetite' in their upper beaks that helps them navigate using the Earth's magnetic fields. It's called 'magnetoreception.' The ability, I mean."

I chuckle to myself at Trax's funny, kind of robotic way of talking. It's like someone combined an eleven-year-old boy with a digital encyclopedia.

"Plus," he continues, "birds have a type of protein called cryptochromes in their eyes that enables them to see the Earth's magnetic fields just like we might see waves in the air above the ground on a hot day."

"Is that so?"

"Oh, yes. They use two systems—a compass system and a map system—to orient themselves and to get from one place to another. They can migrate for thousands of miles and find their way to the exact nesting spot where they were born even though they've never been back there in their lives."

"And they do it all without studying maps like we do," Chace jokes, giving her brother a light slap on his knee.

Trax flinches but otherwise ignores his sister. "And you have a connection with him, right?" he asks me.

"I do."

"So can you tell him to lead you to San Francisco, and he'll do it?"

"She doesn't 'tell' Render anything," Rain interjects, turning to me. "Do you?" She gives me a playful push, and I put my hand down into the sand to stop myself from falling over.

"Ouch," I say before turning back to Trax and Chace. "Rain's right. I'm not Render's boss. I'm his friend and partner, and we're all part of his Conspiracy."

Chace's eyebrow goes up. "Conspiracy?"

"It's what you call a group of ravens," Brohn says.

"To answer your question, I can't ask Render to help us get to a place I've never been," I add. "It doesn't seem to work like that. Sometimes he can sense what's in my head, but since there's nothing in my head about San Francisco, he'd just wind up as lost as I'd be."

Trax grins. "Then you really do need us?"

"Yeah, we really do."

That seems to make him and Chace doubly happy, and I'm grateful. Their smiles in the flickering halo of the campfire inspire me to think fondly of our lost friends, instead of angrily about our enigmatic enemy...or fearfully about our upcoming journey.

Brohn stretches his arms above his head and yawns before turning to Trax and Chace. "We should try to get some sleep. We have a long hike back to your camp."

"At least this time it'll be downhill," Card points out.

It's a simple observation, but it's one that makes me feel slightly more hopeful about the future.

I fall asleep telling myself that at least tomorrow, we don't have to face another uphill climb.

WE ALL WAKE as the first glow of morning begins to push back against the grim murkiness of night. After ensuring the last embers of our fire have been safely snuffed out, we follow Chace and Trax along the beach, through the woods, and down the mountain.

It takes us another two days, but we manage to get to Adric and Celia's camp without any real problems. Rain has to help Cardyn at one point along the way, after he slips and gets his boot stuck under a protruding tree root.

Brohn asks Chace and Trax a couple of times if they're sure this is the right way back. They assure him each time that it is. I have no idea how they know their way around so well, maps or no maps. The twins seem to have an uncanny sense of direction beyond anything I could ever imagine.

Maybe it's their gift. Their super power, much as I hate the thought of using that word. Apparently, Brohn shares my theory, because he expresses amazement at their gifts on the second day of our march.

"Maybe they're like you and Manthy," he tells me with a nudge.

"Or you," I reply. We may not yet know his supposed special ability, but according to Hiller he definitely has one.

"Whatever it is the twins have," Rain says, "they can probably rival Render when it comes to having a great sense of direction."

"Who knows?" Cardyn jokes from behind me. "Maybe they have some magnetite of their own in their upper beaks."

I laugh and agree. "Maybe they do, Card. Maybe they do."

Actually, I think, *maybe they really do.*

11

When we arrive back at the camp in the middle of the night, we're greeted by Adric and Celia.

"The others are asleep in their tents," Celia tells us quietly.

As if sensing we'd like to be alone with their leaders, Trax and Chace announce they're tired, too. I watch as they slip off to their tent, where they pull back the tattered pink and yellow polka-dotted sheet that serves as a door and disappear from view.

Adric invites us over to crouch down and file in to his tent. Exhausted physically from the trip and emotionally from its outcome, we plop down heavily on the mats of cloth and leaves that line the floor.

Adric sits down cross-legged on the edge of the palette of folded canvas sheets and cloth that serves as his bed. "Did you find...?" he starts to ask, before stopping himself. No doubt he's read our faces by now.

"Nothing," Brohn answers, his voice numb. "We didn't find anything." He bows his head to convey he has nothing more to add.

Adric looks over to me, and I somehow summon the courage to describe the devastation and death that greeted us. "It was pointless and cruel," I say, fighting off a lump in my throat. "Just kids. It was all just kids. They were barely surviving day to day as it was. We'd already lost so much. Our parents. Our town. To die like that. Afraid. Helpless. The government was supposed to protect them. Why couldn't they just leave us alone? Why couldn't...?" I shake my head, unable to go on. When I look down at the ground, Brohn slings his arm across my shoulders. The tremble wracking my body slows as he gives me a gentle squeeze.

I can all but feel his voice inside my head. *It's okay. It'll be okay.*

When we can manage to, we talk for a while more about what we found in the Valta and, more sorrowfully, about what we lost. Adric and Celia nod their heads sympathetically, a look of understanding in their young eyes. I hate the thought that they've been through similar pain, but somehow it helps to know our pain is shared.

"Sun'll be up soon," Celia says after a few hours. "Adric, are you okay gathering more wood for the fire?"

"Sure. I can get started, anyway. The Neos can help out when they wake up."

Rain raises her hand and offers to help. "I feel like I need to contribute something, even if it's just to keep my mind off the Valta."

"I can give you a hand, too," Cardyn volunteers.

"That'd be great."

"I'll go, too," Manthy says.

Cardyn beams at her. "Really?"

"I'm not tired," she says. "If I don't do something useful, I'll just lie here and think too much."

After the four of them have pushed themselves up and ducked out of the tent, Celia asks if Brohn and I want to check in on Kella.

"I've been taking care of her as best I can," she tells us. "Though I can't say she's doing all that well."

I shoot Brohn a look. "We should check in," I say.

All I can think is *This is going to be brutal.*

We accompany Celia toward another improvised tent at the end of the semi-circle of shelters where she tells us she's been tending to Kella during the four days we've been gone.

"We use it as our emergency room," Celia explains. "We've patched up our share of bumps and bruises. The Neos are really good at tripping and landing on sharp rocks."

As we walk, Brohn asks, "How is she really, Celia?"

Celia stops in her tracks and shakes her head. "She's eating a little. But she's so frail. Not just her body. Part of her soul's been broken, and I don't know how to help her."

The words come from a person who knows all too well what it is to see someone who's been crushed. I tell myself angrily, silently, that no seventeen-year-old should know that feeling.

Celia walks us the rest of the way to the canopy fashioned out of pieced-together green canvas panels, an impressive network of branches forming the framework of the whole thing. Long, dark shadows cast by a small, struggling phosphor-pack inside flicker and dance.

"I'll leave you to catch up," Celia says. "I'm going to go help the others gather wood. If we wait too long, it gets too hot out to do much of anything."

With the first hints of a pink morning peeking over the horizon, she heads back toward the tree-line while Brohn and I duck into the small shelter where Kella is lying on a blanket of leaves and moss. Her blond hair is splayed out around her head. She has one arm slung across her eyes, and her breathing is raspy and shallow.

Brohn leans over her and asks how she's doing.

She drops her arm from over her eyes and looks up at him and then over to me. "You're back."

"We're back," Brohn confirms.

"Did you...what did you find?"

Brohn sits down and shakes his head, and Kella's lip starts to tremble. "It's what we were all afraid of, isn't it?" she sobs. "There's no one?"

Brohn shakes his head again, his eyes welling up with tears. Kella shifts her gaze over to me as if hoping I can offer her a better answer, but, of course, I can't. She must recognize the pain etched on my face because she rolls over on to her side like she can see the Valta in my eyes.

"I've caused everyone quite a headache, haven't I?" she whispers. I get the feeling she's steering the subject away from the overwhelming trauma of home on purpose.

"You haven't caused anyone anything of the kind," Brohn says.

"We're just concerned for you," I tell her. "We may have a lead on where to go next, and we need you with us."

Kella tries to push herself up onto her elbow, but she's clearly too weak right now, and Brohn urges her to lie back down.

"I'm fine," she says in a voice I practically have to strain to hear. "No need to fuss over me."

I kneel down next to Brohn and run my hand along Kella's hot forehead. We sit in silence for several minutes before I ask her, "Do you remember that time in the Processor when we had the shooting competition?"

I know it's a risk bringing up our time in the Processor. It's where Kella bonded so closely with Karmine and where we all saw him die. But it's also, strangely enough, where Kella was at her happiest.

Fortunately, she seems grateful to reminisce and turns her head to look up at me.

"Which one?" she asks, rolling onto her back. "Bow, pistol, or rifle?"

"As I recall, you beat everyone at all three."

"Even Trench," Brohn adds.

Kella's eyes sparkle. "He was pretty cocky for a guy who couldn't hit the ground if he fell out of a tree."

The three of us have a good laugh. Kella coughs a bit, and I move to help her tilt her head, but she waves me off.

"Twelve arrows into a forty-centimeter target from twenty meters in sixty-two seconds, wasn't it?" Brohn asks.

Kella gives him a dirty look. "Sixty-*one* seconds."

"I stand corrected! And you aced clay pigeon-shooting."

Kella coughs again. She turns her head to wipe her mouth against her shoulder before turning back to us. "Thirty pigeons in twenty-five seconds."

"Trench only hit twenty-two."

"What'd you use for that? The Beretta twelve-gauge?"

"Yeah. The one with the recoil reducer. I would've won the distance competition, too, but Karmine..."

When she mentions Karmine, her eyes get glossy with tears, and she looks away from us for a second.

"He got lucky," Brohn assures her.

Kella shakes her head. "No. He beat me. Fair and square. He handled that Inferno stock twenty-two like it was part of his body. Hit a seven-centimeter target at three-hundred meters. I don't think he even needed the telescopic sight."

"None of us even came close," I say with a laugh. "I thought the kickback alone was going to blow my arm off. You, though... you were like a surgeon out there."

"I was good, wasn't I?"

"The best," Brohn says.

Kella nods, and her eyelids flutter.

"Better let you get some sleep," I offer.

She answers with a quiet moan and closes her eyes. I stroke her hair one last time before Brohn helps me to my feet, and we duck back out of the shelter.

With the sun now rising along with the rest of Adric and Celia's band of orphans, Cardyn and Rain get the rest of the crew caught up on what we found in the Valta. The kids are beyond sympathetic, embracing each of us and telling us how sad they feel.

Brohn asks Adric if he knows anything about San Francisco. When he says, "Not really" and apologizes, Brohn informs him, "It's where we need to go next. You should come with us."

"How long do you figure it would take to get there?"

"Chace and Trax tell us maybe four weeks' hike."

Without a second's hesitation, Adric shakes his head. "We can't. There's no way."

"Why not?"

He pulls Brohn and me aside. "Listen. The younger ones wouldn't survive even half of a trip that long. Not yet, anyway. We don't have the provisions or resources to be of any use to you. These kids are mostly Neos. The truth is, we'd drag you down. Just promise me..."

"What?"

"If you make it out there, out to San Francisco, don't forget about us. Come back for us. Save us...if there are any of us left to save."

When I promise Adric we will, he looks genuinely happy. We also agree to stay a few more days. Just long enough to help get them on their feet, refresh their supplies, and give them a fighting chance at some semblance of life.

Rain and Brohn team up a few more times to try to convince them to come with us, but Adric and Celia, protective of the Neos and Juvens, remain adamant.

"We really should stick together," Brohn urges Celia as the five of us sit in a small circle on a sunny ridge near their camp later that evening. He uses his knife to strip the knots and bark from a thin stick and tosses it onto the growing pile of finished arrow shafts at his feet.

Celia says it's too risky as she continues to carve small notches into the end of each new shaft with another one of the knives that Brohn pilfered from the Processor before our escape.

I'm just sharpening up some small stones to use as arrowheads when Adric returns with a canvas sack full of bird feathers he's collected from the forest floor.

He plops down heavily next to Celia, pulls a spool of twine from a small satchel draped over his shoulder, and starts tying feathers to the ends of some of the arrows. His fingers are long and slender, flying and flitting in a mesmerizing bit of dexterous choreography. "She's right," he says with a deep sigh. "The two of us can make it, but we've got ten others we're responsible for. When the Recruiters came last year, there were only four new Seventeens. This time, there's just us two." He makes a sweeping gesture with his hand toward the younger kids scurrying around over by the fire. "They're just too inexperienced, too young, and frankly, too small to make that kind of trip."

"Not to mention the drain on supplies," Celia adds. "No. You need to travel light. You've been together a long time. You've got your own…what did you call it?"

"Conspiracy," Brohn says with a wink in my direction. "Kress says that's what you call a family of ravens. Or, in this case, a family with a raven and a raven-whisperer."

Celia laughs at that, and the gloomy mood that comes with being immersed in a struggle for survival lifts a little. "You're doing the right thing for you," she says. "You're doing what you need to do. We've got a different path."

"What will you do?" I ask. "You can't stay here forever."

"That's true," Adric says through a deeply contemplative squint. "But thanks to your help, we can get through the next few weeks. Maybe even months. We'll store up supplies. We'll take some smaller excursions first. Maybe see if we can find a transport or something in one of the towns you say you passed on your way here. Once we feel everyone's strong enough for the trip, we'll set out and see what we find."

"Don't get your hopes up of finding anything in those towns," I say. "There really isn't much of anything left."

K. A. RILEY

Adric plucks chunks of crusty mud from some of the arrow feathers. "A chance we'll have to take. Besides, based on the path you say you took, you might have missed a few towns. Trax and Chace say they've found a bunch of places on their maps, and who knows—maybe there'll even be people out there."

I shake my head, but I don't dispute his suggestion. As sure as I am that they'll find nothing out there at best—and enemies at worst—Adric seems just as sure that hope, no matter how slim, is worth holding onto. I can't blame him, really. Although we're older than these kids and have been trained for combat and problem-solving, even our upcoming journey could benefit from a healthy dose of Adric's optimism.

"We're thinking about heading east," Celia says. "Nearly all of us have family back there. Me and Adric and most of the others. Most of our families came here to escape the violence when the war first broke out. I'm sure if we can get back there, we can track down relatives, find safe places to stay."

I'm doubtful about that, too, but again, I decide not to say anything. If the government is set on recruiting people our age, leaving the safety of the woods and the mountains to head back east where the so-called war started seems to me like sticking your own head in the hangman's noose and helping him to tighten the knot.

Still, despite the overwhelming odds against them, Celia's right. Their path and circumstances are different from ours. It's not my place to offer advice. After all, I don't know if where we're headed is any better. In a few days, we're going to follow a mysterious black bird toward a city none of us has ever been to, in a world we don't begin to know.

All on the advice of a cryptic phrase carved into a rock.

A phrase that might lead us into a whole new trap.

"Okay," Brohn says to Celia and Adric as he stands and stretches. "We'd like to have you with us. We can relate to what you've been through, but we respect what you need to do." He squints into the setting sun and points. "If you change your mind, San Francisco is in that direction, I think."

I know they're tempted.

"Who knows?" I say. "Maybe you can do some good back East while we see what kind of answers we can find out West, and maybe someday we'll meet up again somewhere in the middle of the country, and things will be good again."

"I'd like that," Celia says. "Not sure if I'd bet on it. But I definitely like the idea."

Brohn sits back down and the five of us continue making arrows, stitching together some basic carrying sacks from extra clothes Adric and Celia have lying around. Steering clear of sadness and negativity, we talk about all the great things the future might hold. They tell us more about growing up in their small town, which, miraculously, was even smaller than ours.

When we swap stories about the Recruitment the mood turns sour again.

Adric turns to Brohn. "Do you think they'll still try to come for us?"

"I don't think so," Brohn replies. "It's past May first. Past your Recruitment Day. I think they'll be more interested in tracking us down than figuring out where you all got off to."

"Then...Recruitment's over?"

"I'd say so. For you, anyway. I don't know how many other towns like ours are out there."

Adric's flighty fingers pause for a moment. "Do you really think there's something special about us? Kids in these mountain towns, I mean."

"I'm not sure what to think," Brohn says. "There's so much we still don't know, and guessing isn't a strategy. But I've seen Kress and Manthy do things they shouldn't be able to do. Things no one should be able to do. And yet..."

"And yet, they've done them," Adric finishes. "They're...special."

Brohn laughs at this. "Well, they were special long before they started to develop their abilities. These new things they can do just makes them…very handy in certain situations."

"Just what I've always strived to be," I say with a playful sneer and an exaggerated eye-roll. "Handy." I deliberately avoid mentioning that Brohn is supposed to be gifted just as we are. I can't help wondering sometimes if it bothers him to know he has some mysterious, hidden skill that may or may not prove incredible.

"We could use a little 'handy' around here, ourselves," Adric says. "I have a feeling we're in for a rough time ahead. Maybe a dangerous time."

"You'll be okay," Brohn assures him. "You're survivors."

"So were the rest of the people from our town." Celia hangs her head. "Right up until they died."

12

OVER ON THE OTHER SIDE OF THE CAMP, CARDYN AND MANTHY have teamed up to continue taking care of Kella. They take turns bringing her water from a nearby trickle of a creek. The water doesn't look too healthy, but Card and Manthy, with some help from a few of the Neos, have been able to filter it and boil it without losing too much.

For the rest of the night and into the next day, Brohn and Rain shift gears and help Adric, Celia, and the other members of their camp gather more firewood and show them which trees provide the best building material and which are best for fuel. They teach them how to assemble and use the bows and arrows we made for hunting. They even help them bring down a mule deer, which is a cause of massive celebration in the form of fists to the sky and howls of triumph from the Neos and Juvens.

I'm reminded with a smile of Final Feast back in the Valta on the night before Recruitment. Brohn fed us then, too.

He's taller than everyone here, and he prowls the camp like a panther, helping out, offering advice, and inspiring a type of reverential awe with every determined stride and authoritative command. The Neos and Juvens hang on his every word. Although he doesn't seem to notice, some of the boys have even started trying to walk and talk like him. It's really something to see.

I can't help but feel a surge of pride and affection at the thought that I share a connection with the broad-shouldered titan.

In the afternoon, Rain and I team up to lead the ten Neos and Juvens into another part of the woods. We give them a whole series of lessons about which berries and plants are edible, which are medicinal, which are borderline, and which are just plain deadly. Using a dozen or so of the sacks we sewed together the day before, Rain and I help the kids gather enough food to last for several weeks at least.

"It will keep better if you have a nice, cool place to store it," Rain tells the kids. "We'll help you build an underground storage space when we get back to your camp."

The Neos and Juvens absorb every word and spend the walk back to camp quizzing each other on everything we've taught them.

When we get back, I check on Cardyn and Manthy, who are still taking care of Kella.

Kella offers me a weak smile as I sit down with them under the canopy.

"Feeling any better?" I ask her.

"I'm not feeling much of anything these days."

I slip onto my knees next to her and squeeze her to me. She lets out a gentle purr and nuzzles her cheek against mine.

"You're going to be great," I assure her. "We're all going to be great."

"I'd settle for just 'okay,'" she says.

After that, I don't have a lot to do, so I mosey out to the clearing and sit on a flat rock by the fire. It's nice to have a break from the constant worry and busyness that comes with the struggle to survive. I cross my legs and focus, like I learned back in the Processor. It's funny. For all their lies and evil intent, the things Hiller and her crew taught us have actually been helpful during our adventures. Ironic that they're the reason we've survived this long.

I'm just settling into a pleasant meditative state when a few of the Neos and Juvens spot me and start gathering around.

The younger kids are feeling more comfortable and courageous around me than they were a few days back, and start asking me about my tattoos. A little girl with a frizzy mane of orange-brown hair asks if she can touch them.

"Sure. Go ahead."

I ask her name, and she says, "Livvy."

"Okay, Livvy. It's just micro-circuitry under my skin. You'll find you can barely feel anything."

She reaches out with two fingers and traces the pattern of black dots and dashes leading into the long, swooping curves running from the backs of my hands up to my elbows.

"How'd you get them?" she asks. Her voice is hushed in what feels like an act of reverence.

"They're a gift," I say. "A gift from my dad."

"Are you a Modified?" a little boy asks.

"I don't think so. From what my dad told me, Modifieds were about prolonging life, enhancing physical abilities, things like that. These are supposed to enhance my empathy."

"What's empathy?" Livvy asks. She pronounces it "empafy."

"Well, in this case, it means my ability to connect with a certain special someone." I point over to where Render is skulking around in the branches of a nearby tree. As if he knows he's being watched, he lifts his head, puffs up his hackles, and struts along a branch like a runway model.

Livvy's mouth hangs open. "Wow!"

Now the other Neos and Juvens come rushing over. Render's

been keeping himself scarce since our arrival, so this is the first time they're getting a good look at him.

"Is he your bird?" one of them asks.

"Well, he's *a* bird. But he's not 'mine.' Let's just say he's my friend."

"Does he bite?"

"No. He doesn't even have teeth. He's more of a gnasher and a gulper."

"Does he do any tricks?"

"Actually, he can do tons. He's slightly on the brilliant side." I put my finger to my lips. "But, shhh…don't call them 'tricks.' He thinks it's demeaning. He likes to think of what he does as 'talents.'"

A tallish boy with freckles like Cardyn's but dark hair like Brohn's introduces himself as Ven. He asks if I can show them all some of Render's "talents."

"I can't make him do anything he doesn't want to do," I tell him. "But I'll ask him." I swipe my fingers in a special pattern along the tattoos on my left forearm. "This helps me to connect with him," I tell the kids. "I'm sure he'll be happy to help out. He's a born show-off." The sequence I employ is an old one that my father taught me. I don't want to connect too deeply with Render just now. If my eyes go black, I can only imagine the screams and nightmares the smaller Neos might have.

With a few flicks of my fingers and a couple of verbal requests, Render jumps into an elaborate performance for the wide-eyed, open-mouthed crowd. He leaps from his perch, his wings extending out and beating in powerful strokes. He ascends to near invisibility, barely a speck in the sky high above the camp. At the height of his flight, he stalls out in mid-air, then dive-bombs like a glistening black missile.

With gleeful shrieks, the kids leap back as Render skims the ground at our feet, kicking up a vortex of dirt and debris from the forest floor before ripping his way up into the sky again. He completes a series of barrel rolls, skirts along the tree-tops, appearing and disappearing from view. He streaks upward again in a steep climb and drops into a dizzying corkscrew descent. He spreads his wings out like a billowing black cape, narrowly avoiding the ground below. He seems to defy gravity as he hovers a few feet above the earth and then, with a whoosh, he's off again, rising back into the expansive sky he calls home.

I call Livvy over to my side and hand her a buckle I've detached from one of the pockets on my military jacket. "Try holding this up," I tell her. "He's got a soft spot for shiny objects."

With a slight tremble in her hand and a matching one in her voice, she asks if it's safe.

"Don't worry. He's not only smart and precise, he's also super nice and would feel terrible at the thought of hurting you."

She holds her slightly shaking hand up with the glittering silver buckle pinched between her thumb and forefinger.

The kids crane their necks and look up until one of the girls points to a small black dot out in the distance. "There he is!" she squeals.

The black dot gets bigger, banks hard to one side, and disappears behind a golden cluster of Narrowleaf Cottonwood trees. The kids hold their breath, waiting for Render to emerge from the other side of the dense woods. Instead, there's an explosion of feathers and brittle brown leaves from the woods right in front of us. A blur of black blasts past our eyes and vanishes on the far side of the clearing like a ghost.

We all turn to look at Livvy. Her eyes are wide with shock. Her hand is still held high in the air, her thumb and finger pinched together. But the buckle has vanished. In total and absolute awe, the kids burst into applause even as they run in a screaming group toward the dark patch of forest where Render disappeared. They shout out to him, begging him to come back and show off some more of his "talents." When they don't get a response at the tree-line, they seem crestfallen at first, until they turn back toward me and see Render perched smugly on my shoulder, my silver belt buckle clamped firmly in his black beak.

Laughing, the kids swarm back toward us, and I have to stand up and take a big step back to avoid being trampled to death.

"How does he do that?" Ven asks.

"I didn't even feel him take the buckle," Livvy squeals.

"Ravens are talented and complicated animals," I tell her. I sit back down cross-legged, and the kids all plop down in a semi-circle in front of me. I put my hand out under Render's beak, and he drops my buckle into my open palm. "Ravens have great memories. They can imitate a wide range of sounds. This guy here does a great wolf. He can also make a sound like a processor microbit-drill. He's even been trying a bit of human speech from time to time." I put my hand to the side of my mouth and whisper, "Although he's not very good at it just yet."

The kids laugh and continue to stare wide-eyed as Render twists his head around and ruffles the hackles on his throat again. "Cultures all over the world have complex relationships with ravens. In some cases, they're considered evil demons because they eat carrion. In a few places, they're considered gods. They're often thought of as tricksters, but they're also known as creators. In some legends," I tell the kids, "ravens are actually responsible for the creation of the world."

I'm greeted with a chorus of *Wows*, and a bunch of the kids ask me to tell them more. "I don't know how much more I can tell you," I say with a shake of my head. "Just that these guys have a world-wide reputation...at least they used to, in the days before the war began. The raven is a guardian god in the nation of Bhutan in Asia. They're an honored bird in the Yukon and the Northwest Territories in Canada. There even used to be a sports team called the Baltimore Ravens, right here in the United States. The coat of arms for a city called Lisbon in a country called Portugal features two ravens and the quote, 'most noble and always loyal city of Portugal.' In Norse mythology, the god Odin is accompanied by two ravens, Huginn and Muninn." As I recount all the snippets of random raven trivia, I'm astounded once again at my ability to recall this wealth of information I didn't know I had.

"Huginn and Muninn? Those are funny names," a little boy with patchy blond hair says.

"They mean 'Thought' and 'Memory,'" I tell him. "Two things Render here is very good at."

"What else?"

"Well, the Tower of London is said to keep ravens around at all times. If they don't, a legend says that the entire kingdom will fall."

"Is that true?"

"That's one of the nice things about legends," I tell him after a brief pause. "They're as true as you believe them to be. Shakespeare makes a lot of references to ravens in his plays: *Titus Andronicus*, *Othello*, and *Macbeth*. A poet named William Wordsworth once wrote, 'We saw a raven very high above us. It called out, and the dome of the sky seemed to echo the sound. It called again and again as it flew onwards, and the mountains gave back the sound, seeming as if from their center; a musical bell-like answering to the bird's hoarse voice.'"

Although I'm not sure the kids understand the quote, they seem super impressed with the fact that I remembered it.

"But the most famous quote is from another poet, one named Edgar Allen Poe. He wrote a poem about a raven who keeps reminding a terrified and heart-broken man that he'll never again see his lost love, Lenore. No matter how angry the man gets, how much he pleads, or how many times he asks the bird to tell him if he'll ever see his love, the raven just sits there above his bedroom door and tells him 'Nevermore' over and over again."

The kids shiver like I've just told them a ghost story. I laugh and tell them not to worry. "Render here is more of a happy raven than a scary one. And he's very protective. My friends and I are part of his Conspiracy. And now that you and I are friends, you're part of ours. That means he'll always help you and take care of you. He'll let you know if there are dangers coming, and he'll remember your faces forever."

The kids all beam at this, and one of the girls asks if she can pet him. I say, "Sure. I think he'd like that. But one at a time."

The kids approach one by one and reach out to touch the very happy bird. Some kids give him a small, gentle stroke. Others barely make contact with him. Some of the braver kids give his head and body good, firm pats, which Render leans into, rumbling deep in his throat like a jungle cat.

After the kids have all filed through and had their turn with Render, he gives a few little chirps and then a jubilant *kraa!* and launches himself from my shoulder, soaring over the clearing and then zipping like a missile into the woods.

When the kids turn their attention to Brohn and the others coming back with canvas sacks of rabbit, roots, and berries, I decide I could use some alone time, so I decide to make a quiet exit and have a quick hike through the woods.

I give Brohn a wave and mouth, "Going for a walk." He gives me a thumb's up, and I slip out of the clearing to head into the dense, dry forest.

After a zig-zagging clamber up a steep embankment, I come to a clearing on a wide plateau. I call Render, and he glides his way down to my shoulder and outstretched arm. His heart is still racing from his impromptu performance for the kids, but I can feel he wants more. "Such a show-off," I say. "And a total adrenaline junkie." Render responds with a happy *kraa!*

Finally, we slip solidly into each other's minds. I let him know how much he means to me and how proud I am of him. He may have just given those kids a much-needed break from this castaway life, not to mention a reason to go on trying to live a better one.

Render's thoughts are simple at the moment, and crystal-clear: *More play.*

"Okay," I sigh. "Hide and seek?"

Kraa!

I hand him my Special Ops pin—the symbol of a black bird with its wings spread wide—which I've had tucked away in my pocket. He snags it with the tip of his beak. He flies out over the canopy of trees while I sit cross-legged on a bare patch of ground with my back to him and my eyes closed. When he returns a few minutes later, I know he's dropped the pin somewhere out in the woods. It's my job to figure out where, find the token, and bring it back to him. Normally, I'd just connect to him, tap into his ocular implants, and infiltrate my way into his neurological memory pathways where I'd see what he's seen and remember what he's remembered. But I know that would mean breaking the rules of this particular game. So instead, I have to try to tap into him without *really* tapping into him. I have to think like he does, to find my way to where he's gone.

This form of treasure hunting is a game we used to play in secret in the Valta. The first few times we played it, I *did* tap into him, and he made it crystal clear, across any inter-species barrier that might exist, that what I was trying was a total cheat.

Keep your mind to yourself.

For someone who doesn't talk in human language, Render sure knows how to make himself understood.

So now we have new rules: I must find the object on my own. It's a perfect diversion. Thinking like him without connecting with him is exactly the distraction my overburdened mind needs. Forget yoga, warrior poses, meditation, and Buddhist chants. Those aren't enough to make me forget about the possible treachery of President Krug and my government, the loss of two of my closest friends, or my destroyed town. Even if it's just temporary, Render's game calms my mind, soothes my breathing, and evens out my soul.

A thunderous flutter of wings and a vortex of kicked-up dust let me know Render's returned. Just in case I'm not paying attention, he hops up next to me and lets out three shrill *kraas!* and a guttural grunt in my ear.

That's my cue.

I spring up and sprint toward the tree-line. Bounding into the woods, I skip over shallow ditches in the ground and vault over a series of downed trees. Following nothing but instinct and intuition, I plunge deeper into the scarred forest and over the perilous terrain. It's a dizzying array of vegetation and towering White Fir trees, Blue Spruce, and Quaking Aspens. Many of the trees are leaning over, brittle from bombings or perhaps from infected, irradiated soil. Tendrils of some kind of vine whose name I don't know and whose small leaves I don't recognize twist their way up many of the trees. I wonder if the sinister-looking parasitic vines are feeding off of whatever nutrients remain in the trees that have managed to survive the chaos of the last ten years.

I can't think about it too much, though, and I can't do anything about it anyway. I've got a game to win.

Looking skyward, I see openings in the forest canopy where light streams through. I imagine myself soaring overhead. Which opening is the most inviting? Which offers the best point of entry? Once I narrow it down, I begin scouring the area of fallen leaves and scrub-brush dotting the forest floor. I kick at some of the leaves and roll a broken tree branch over to expose the soft patch of earth underneath. *Nothing.* I keep looking. I've got a good feeling I'm close.

Out of the corner of my eye, I catch a series of small marks in the soil. I scurry over, and sure enough, it's the tell-tale marks of Render's four-toed feet, three toes facing forward and one facing back, pressed into the ground. Most tree-dwelling birds leave side-by-side tracks. But Render, like other birds who mostly hang out on the ground, leaves footprints in a nearly straight line.

There are probably other birds—crows, jays, warblers, and owls —in these woods. But I can tell these tracks belong to Render. He leaves a distinctive drag mark with his backward-facing claw. Also, most ravens have an inward-tilted middle toe on each foot, but Render's middle toe sits relatively straight.

I spot a rock sitting at an odd angle at the foot of a small tree. Render is strong. He can fly for hours, and he can move branches and stones and even carry fist-sized rocks in his powerful beak.

Gotcha.

I kick the rock over with the toe of my boot, fully expecting to see my Special Ops broach underneath. But no. Render's tricked me. Led me to the wrong place on purpose. But he was here, which means I can figure out where he probably went next.

I backtrack and am able to pinpoint the direction he was facing when he took off from this spot. A black feather clings to the bark of a tree at the edge of the clearing. Another feather sits at the base of the tree after that one.

"Fool me once," I say out loud. Dismissing the two feathers as another red herring, I turn in the exact opposite direction. Render knows I can't fly, which means he knows I can't get up to the top of most of the trees around here. He also knows that much of these woods have suffered from the drone strikes and radiation fall-out from the war. He wouldn't risk my safety by hiding the badge anywhere too high or in any tree that might crumble to ash if I try to climb it.

The dark tree that's leaning on a 45-degree angle over a narrow ravine and against an outcropping of smooth white boulders, however, is a perfect hiding place. It's strong enough to hold my weight, slanted enough so I won't drop to my death if I slip and fall, and challenging enough to push me to my physical limits but not too far beyond.

"Stinker," I say as I leap up onto the large tree trunk. The bark is brittle under my boots, but it holds. I swing myself under one of the protruding branches and clamber over another. Shuffling sideways, I work my way through a tangle of thin branches toward the top of the tree as the trunk thins down to the size of my wrist. From here, I cling to a spindly cluster of twigs and brace my feet against the tall tree's final feeble branch.

There's about ten feet between me and the nearest flat-headed boulder. I take a deep breath and leap out over the chasm beneath me and land with both feet firmly on the other side. I'm greeted by a small pyramid of white and gray stones, which I topple to reveal my Special Ops badge.

Panting from the effort, I give a wheezy little laugh and say, "Clever bird" out loud. My voice echoes back at me from against the side of the mountain.

Now, I just have to get back down from here. Jumping from a weak branch onto a strong rock is pretty easy. Reversing it might be more than I can handle. I look down into the narrow ravine. There was probably a gurgling little creek running down there at one point. Now it's just an uneven, empty trench. It's bone dry, fairly wide, and about thirty feet to the bottom.

It's something I'm suddenly certain I can do.

Before I have a chance to think about it, strategize, or weigh all the pros and cons, I leap from the rocky outcropping and down into the scraggly void. The ground rushes toward me, but it slows as I get closer until one of us—me or the ground, I'm not sure which—seems to be moving in slow-motion.

Out of instinct, I brace myself and prepare for the shock of landing, but I barely feel it when my feet hit the ground.

It's the first time I've "flown" since the day we escaped the Processor, and a sudden surge of euphoria pushes its way through my delighted mind and body.

Laughing like a crazy person and waving the Special Ops badge above my head, I bolt from the woods and back to the plateau where Render is waiting patiently for me.

His emotions flood my mind like they were my own. He's surprised and a little annoyed that I found the badge and won the game. He also senses my delight at surviving a thirty-foot jump I had no business attempting.

But another feeling is swirling around in that little black-feathered head of his as he launches himself into the air and glides off to find something to eat.

He's proud of me.

13

AFTER THREE MORE DAYS AND NIGHTS OF HELPING, BONDING, AND trading stories about small-town life and about the pain and guilt of surviving when others haven't, Brohn and I tell Adric and Celia it's time for us to say goodbye.

It's been good to have a little time to grieve, to think about everything that's happened, to hold each other in silence when the pain grew too strong.

But we both know the longer we stay here, the farther we'll be from the answers we need.

"We've done what we can in the time we've had," Brohn tells Adric.

"Don't worry," I add. "You have enough supplies to keep you going for weeks. Maybe months. At least until you feel the Neos are prepared to move on to the next camp."

I know Brohn's been anxious about hitting the road ever since we returned from the Valta. "There's nothing here for us anymore," he confided in me one evening when he and I went for a walk in the nearby woods. "And if San Francisco has even a single answer, we need to get there, find it, and figure out who's responsible for everything that's happened.

Not having answers is almost as bad as not having our freedom."

There's more to it, of course, even though he's reluctant to talk about it. He wants closure. He wants to know what happened to Wisp, and if Granden's the one who left us that message. If he's the one summoning us to San Francisco, there's a chance we can get the answers we need.

I understand Brohn's desperation. For years now I've tried to accept the possibility that my brother and father are dead. But as long as I have the faintest hope, I find myself aching to believe they could still be out there somewhere. I'd give anything in the world to see them even just once to say goodbye. I know Brohn feels the same hole inside that's torn me up all these years, only his wound is fresh and raw.

Card and Manthy have just returned from tending to Kella when the rest of us get started on loading up supplies.

"How is she?" I ask softly.

Cardyn shakes his head and pulls his gaze to the ground. "She's not good. Not even close. It's like...like she's not even in there anymore."

"Karmine's death hit her so hard," I remind him. "She never really recovered."

"It hit all of us hard, Kress."

"Come on, Card. You know they had a special bond. I think she loved him more than any of us ever knew."

He shoots me a look that tells me he gets it. Much as we've all denied tacitly that love in a world like ours is possible, there's no doubt in anyone's mind that Kella and Karmine were a perfect match. I've never met two more compatible people in my life. When Karmine died, part of Kella went with him, and it's a part she'll never get back.

I ask Adric and Celia to give us a minute while we duck into Kella's tent to check on her. As always, she's lying on her makeshift mattress, a glazed-over look in her eyes.

Brohn kneels down next to her, his brow furrowed. "We're leaving tomorrow."

Kella stares out of her tent at the Neos who are shuffling around, poking at the fire, and dragging heavy sacks of food and other supplies over to the underground bunker we helped them build.

Brohn tries again. "We need to stick together, Kella."

"He's right," I add. "We're a Conspiracy, remember?"

Kella looks from me to Cardyn to Rain, and finally back to Brohn. "I'm going to turn into that woman, you know."

"What woman?" I ask.

"The woman from the cave."

"Asha?" Brohn says. "That crazy woman?"

"She wasn't crazy, Brohn. She was hurt." Kella taps her temple with her finger. "Here. Like me. She couldn't take any more."

"We're not leaving you behind."

"You're not leaving me at all. I'm leaving you." Kella turns her head to look away. "I'm sorry..." Her voice trails off, and her eyes close.

I give her a shoulder a gentle shake and check her breathing. "I think she's fainted," I tell the others.

"We can't leave her here," Rain says.

"We can't take her with us," Brohn replies. "You heard her. She can't take it physically. And emotionally, well, if the trip doesn't kill her, her own head will. I'm not about to force her to come on a hike that will take weeks."

With that, Adric, who's apparently been listening, steps inside the tent and sidles up to our little huddle. "Don't worry. We'll take care of her."

I'm thinking, *How? You can barely take care of yourselves*. But I don't say it.

Brohn stands up and puts a hand on Adric's shoulder. "Thank you," he says.

It's the only realistic solution, and we all know it. But Rain is crying now, and I'm on the verge. "She's been through so much. We all have. But Kella has really...just, please do everything you can to keep her safe."

"We will. She's one of us now. You have your Conspiracy. We have ours. We'll protect her like our own."

With a grim series of quiet thanks, we walk out of the tent and into the clearing, where the Neos and Juvens all gather around and squeeze in tight. Some of them are crying, sorry to see us go.

Chace and Trax are the first to give us each a tight hug.

"I did these for you," Chace says, handing me a small stack of white paper. When I riffle through the pages I discover that it's a series of pencil drawings.

"You drew these?" I ask, astonished.

Chace blushes and pulls her chin down as Trax leans over her shoulder. "My sister loves to draw," he brags. "We weren't able to take much with us from Miner. Mostly food, blankets, and a few other things. But she insisted on bringing along her sketch books and a backpack full of pencils and markers. She even uses charcoal sometimes."

Brohn, Cardyn, and Rain huddle around me as I flip one at a time through the drawings. Manthy pretends not to be interested, but I catch her casting quick glances in my direction, no doubt curious to see if Chace has drawn her.

"They're of us?" I ask.

Chace blushes again and nods. "I draw what I like."

"They're so good," Rain says.

Cardyn shakes his head. "Good? They're amazing!"

Brohn agrees and tells Chace how impressed he is. "You have a gift," he says, his voice deep and mature. "You should develop it."

She's managed to capture all of us on paper. The drawings are sketchy but wonderful. There's one of Brohn leading us through the woods.

A bunch of us gathered around the campfire.

Me with Render.

My tattoos.

Some are drawings of Render in flight, some of Adric and Celia, and one of the Neos and Juvens gathered around me from yesterday, when I told them about ravens.

My eyes tear up at when I come to a sketch of the Valta's ruins.

One image is of Brohn going through the rubble, looking for any signs of life. Somehow Chace managed to capture the tightness of his body. The hesitation in his movements. The fear of what he might find…all with a few pencil strokes.

When we get to a bunch of drawings of me and Brohn together, my mood lightens a little. It's like Chace is reminding us of what's important, of what we still have in this world.

The first sketch is of us sitting on the ground, talking. The second is hard to make out at first. But as I stare, I realize that I can see our hands firmly clasped together, like we're holding onto one another for dear life.

There are other drawings. Some of Cardyn and Manthy, others of Rain. It's a strange sensation, seeing all of us represented like this. It makes me feel like we're really a part of the world, rather than just a bunch of orphans passing through.

After I've stared at them for a long time, I go to hand the drawings back to Chace, but she shakes her head. "I want you to have them."

I start to object, but she cuts me off. "Don't worry. I have lots more back in my tent."

A tug from a small hand on the sleeve of my jacket draws my attention away from Chace and Trax who have slipped away behind Adric and Celia. I look down to see Livvy—the owner of the little hand—beaming up at me with her saucer-sized eyes and a giant smile.

When I kneel down, Livvy and Ven run up and throw their arms around my neck.

I drop my Special Ops pin into Livvy's small hand and close her fingers around it.

"I can't accept a gift like this," she says. "It's yours and Render's."

"Oh, it's not a gift, it's a loan," I say. "Don't worry. We'll be back for it."

14

WHEN WE SET OUT ON OUR LONG JOURNEY, WE FIND THE HIGHWAYS abandoned once again. Endless open fields stretch out on either side of the road, leading us through a landscape devoid of any evidence of human life.

"These used to be crops," Brohn guesses. "Probably corn or beans or something."

I nod my agreement, but I have no way of knowing if he's right. It's hard to imagine anything ever growing in what are now huge red expanses of rocks and dust. Outside of the mountain, it's hard to imagine anything green out here, period.

"It really is like the world's given up on itself, isn't it?" I ask with a shudder.

"Unfortunately, yes. But that doesn't mean we have to give up on it. Or on each other." Brohn takes my hand and pulls it to his lips. I breathe a long sigh, grateful as always for his touch.

We march for two days. At night we do our best to light fires in concealed locations. I spend the hours of darkness curled up with Brohn's arm around me. By now there's probably no doubt in the others' minds what's happening with us, but no one comments on it. Even if they wanted to, they're probably too exhausted to bring themselves to care much.

The other three stay close together for warmth. Even Manthy, who usually keeps as much distance as she can from other people, lets herself press in close to Cardyn with Rain curled upon the other side.

During one long hike, Cardyn complains non-stop that we should have just stayed back in the camp with Adric and Celia. "We had food. Not much, but some. And shelter. Not the best, but it kept the heat out in the middle of the day. This is brutal."

"We may have had food, but we didn't have answers," I say. "Or revenge for what happened in the Valta or the Processor. And there's no way I'm hiding out in the woods with a bunch of Neos until I get both. Don't forget why we're going to San Francisco, Card."

He goes quiet for a few more minutes before he announces, "I think maybe Celia had a thing for me."

Brohn and Rain burst into a peal of simultaneous laughter. Rain is still wiping tears from her eyes when she asks the deeply-blushing Cardyn whatever gave him that idea.

"Just a look here and there," he says meekly. "This one time, she touched my arm...right here, near my elbow. And she talked about how good I was with the Neos. Besides, is it so strange to think a girl might find me interesting? Maybe even...attractive?"

I give Brohn a little wink before turning to Cardyn and promising him that he's the most interesting and most handsome person I know.

Card blushes another shade deeper, hangs his head, and kicks at a small stone on the ground in an "aw shucks" moment of guilty pride.

"Hey," Manthy calls out, pointing to what appears to be some kind of fence in the distance, over the next ridge. It seems she's not interested in talk of Card's hypothetical love life.

"Looks like an army base," Brohn says.

He's right. Even from here, the fence looks tall and imposing, ringed at the top with menacing-looking coils of laser-wire, glittering faintly purple in the darkening night.

It takes us another twenty minutes to get close enough to be sure, but Brohn was definitely right. This place is some kind of military outpost.

I can't speak for the others, but my mind has just filled to bursting with images of Recruiters in transport trucks swarming out to take us away. A wave of nausea sweeps through me to recall the horrors the Recruiters brought with them to the Valta.

It's full-on dark by now, which is good because it gives us cover. The only problem is that we won't be able to see much, let alone get our bearings if we need to make a quick getaway. The halo-like purple light from the laser wire and the bluish glow from a single ionic xenon bulb at the top of a tall wooden post inside the base cast strange shadows that make the night seem even darker, somehow.

Taking care to stay in the dark shadows, we slip from the road and make our way through the edge of the desert up to the synth-steel barriers and along the high metal fence surrounding two buildings, a green shed, and a small parking pad. A monstrous-looking tank-like truck with six huge wheels, a machine-gun turret up top, and a set of shuttered windows on its front sits idly on the parking pad like a napping rhino. Even from here, we can tell that the clunky gray-brown vehicle is covered in red dust, but at least it's intact. Other than the transport truck that originally took us to the Processor, we haven't seen a single vehicle that wasn't a twisted, barely-recognizable wreck listing over on the side of the road.

Brohn points to the boxy truck and whispers that maybe we can get our hands on it, find a way to commandeer it and get out before anyone knows we were here.

"If it's even working," I whisper. "And if we can even get into this place. And if we don't get killed trying…"

Brohn smiles and puts a finger to my lips. "That's way too many 'ifs.' Let's get in first and take it from there."

Rain leans forward and peers through the holes in the wire fence.

"Don't touch the fence," I whisper, pointing up to the laser-wire along the top. "Electrified."

Rain nods. "I don't see anyone in there. Maybe the base has been abandoned."

Cardyn shakes his head. "Or there could be fifty soldiers inside those barracks just waiting to blast away at anyone dumb enough to try to get in."

I point through the dark to the two buildings—one a single-story cabin of some kind, the other a taller structure with a ring of windows up high near its roof—in the middle of the yard. "Looks like temporary barracks. Let's go around. See if there's a way in. We can investigate the buildings first. Then we can see about the truck."

Brohn, Cardyn, and Manthy agree. "But Rain's right," Brohn adds. "If the buildings are clear, our next top priority has got to be checking out that rig. All this walking is for the birds." He looks for Render and apologizes. "Figure of speech," he says.

"Even if he hears you, he can't understand you, you big dope," I laugh. "But I'm sure he appreciates the sentiment, wherever he is."

Even in the hazy moonlight, I can see Brohn's glowing grin.

"Ready?" I ask.

"There are too many of us to move in close and check it out," he replies.

I agree, and we decide that Cardyn and Rain should stay hidden with Manthy while Brohn and I run a quick reconnaissance mission.

"Maybe you should send Render in first," Rain suggests.

"He doesn't like to fly at night," I reply.

Rain pauses but doesn't take her eyes off my face. I can tell she's being protective of us, trying to give us every chance to survive the next few minutes.

"Okay," I say at last. "But only if he wants to."

Rain smiles. "Fair enough."

I slide my fingers along my tattoos and initiate contact. Render is out in the desert somewhere in the distance. As I thought, he's sleeping. But when he senses my presence and my need for his help, he ruffles himself awake and pushes off from his perch near the top of a rocky butte a few miles up the road. I get the sense he's pleased but trying to hide it, like he's been itching to make himself useful and has grown slightly annoyed that I haven't called on him more these past couple of days on the road.

He arrives after a few minutes and flutters to a thumping hover just above us before dropping down to land on the upper part of my outstretched arm.

Cardyn gives a pretend shudder. "I still say that's about the creepiest-looking thing ever."

"Funny," I say. "Render says the same thing about you."

Brohn and Rain struggle to muffle their laughter, and even Manthy cracks a smile, which she tries to disguise with a pretend cough.

With Render in a quiet, stealth-mode glide just up ahead, Brohn and I start to make our way around the perimeter of the fence that encircles the base.

It's dark but there's just enough light to make our presence here risky. Who knows? We might have already set off any number of heat-sensors or motion detectors.

"Render would probably set off any sensors that would detect our presence," Brohn says, reading my mind as the raven glides up ahead. "If there are any, they don't seem to be turned on."

There are no signs of life from inside the compound on the other side of the fence, but the active lights at the top of the post seem to indicate that someone's around.

"Maybe the lights are on a timer," I whisper, more to myself than to Brohn.

Either way, this is the first time we've seen electricity since we escaped from the Processor. At first, I feel elated to think of it, but then I grimace at how low my standards have gotten.

It doesn't take us long to circle around the back of the base, where we get a better view of the two buildings. They're pre-fab units, the kind they use for military rescue operations and temporary housing after natural disasters. The green synth-steel looks almost black in the night. A quick and stressful image flashes through my mind of the big Cubes in the Processor where we lost our innocence and two of our friends. Not to mention that it's the place where the rest of us nearly lost our lives.

Brohn and I continue to follow Render's barely-visible outline as he slides ahead on silent wings. Once we're around to the far side of the fence, away from the abandoned highway and deeper into the dark desert, Render slips an image into my head of a thin tree, scraggly and twisted, lying nearly on its side. We keep walking along until, sure enough, the tree appears just up ahead. It's dry and in the throes of death, its spindly root system half exposed above the rocky red soil. Brohn asks me to help him, and the two of us are able to push the tree upright and then over a little more until it's leaning against the chain-link fence. The purple lights of the laser-wire emit a dangerous-sounding buzz. I give the crispy, twisted tree a little shake and start to say, "Let's just hope it holds us," but Brohn is already scrambling up the thin trunk and swinging his legs over the top of the fence. "Hey!" I call out in an annoyed whisper. "Wait for me!"

Brohn laughs and reaches a hand down to help me up to the top of the fence. With remarkable dexterity, he hurtles over the laser-wire and drops down to the other side, his boots kicking up a cloud of soft red dust that dances in the straggles of moonlight. As I attempt to duplicate his feat of nimbleness, I stumble and get the cuff of my pants caught on the sharp end of one of the broken branches. Wrenching myself free, I manage to perform the world's most awkward head-first tumble over the top of the fence. Brohn catches me on the other side and helps me keep my balance as I plant myself on the ground in front of him.

"Thanks," I say with a nervous chuckle. "You may have noticed I'm not quite as coordinated as you."

"Don't mention it. But here's a tip: next time you're barreling toward the ground, try it *feet* first."

"I'll keep that in mind," I tell him with a mock scowl.

There are still no signs of life, and I'm starting to wonder if maybe this place really has been abandoned. I'm imagining rooms full of left-behind provisions and weapons. Brohn points to a shorter building about a hundred yards ahead and on the left. "Let's check that one out first. Follow me. Stay low." While we run in a half-crouch, Render soars up and lands on the top edge of the building's roof as Brohn and I scuttle across the desert surface, coming to a stop under one of the windows of the building. Pulling himself up with his fingers braced on the outer window sill, Brohn is able to get up high enough to peek inside.

After a few seconds, he drops back down.

"Well?" I ask.

"It's nothing. I think maybe it was an old rail car. See, it's up on blocks. Lots of red sand inside on the floor. Must be a door or window somewhere, though. Want to circle around front? See if maybe we can get inside?"

"Let's try the other building first," I suggest. "I'd rather check them both out from behind before we try a full-on frontal assault."

Brohn grins and agrees. Ducking low, we scuttle over to the second building.

This time, the window is far too high up for us to see in. Even if I got on his shoulders, there's no way I could get high enough to reach the small square windows. Brohn suggests we sneak around to the front and see if there's a door, but I recommend having a look inside first.

"And how are we going to manage that?" he whispers, looking up.

"We have a pretty clever drone," I remind him.

Render senses my need practically before I sense it myself. He flutters down and alights on the windowsill high above us to peer through the glass. Brohn and I stand with our backs to the building's ice-cold metal wall, where I skim my fingers along the tattoos on my left arm. What Render sees comes back to me in waves of color, which I need a few seconds to sort out. He's looking down into what appears to be an office. I see empty shelves. Empty weapons racks on two walls. A panel of viz-screens, lifeless and broken.

I see a desk down below, with a man seated at it. Green jacket with brown trim. Brown cargo pants. Brown ankle boots laced to the top. An empty holster slung on the back of his chair. He's got to be a soldier. Blond hair, thinning at the top. Pale hands with long, bony fingers. He's wide-eyed and slumped over with a white coffee mug by his head on one side. On the other side, a pool of dark red blood soaks the desktop before meandering off in a trickle down one of the desk legs and to the floor by the man's boots. Two other men, also soldiers, lie hunched against the far wall, their clothes soaked with blood. I blink my eyes, trying hard to sort out what I'm seeing as the images bounce in and out of focus.

Half-tucked under the edge of the desk, I notice another figure. A girl around my age.

I didn't see her at first. She's not moving. Hiding? No. Dead. Her eyes are open but blank.

She died afraid.

I drop down into a squat, my arms wrapped around my stomach. The impact of the scene, magnified in intensity by Render's perceptions, hits me like a sledgehammer to the gut.

Brohn drops to a knee next to me. "What is it?"

"There are people in there," I gasp, blinking and seeing through my own eyes again.

"Who?"

"I don't know."

"Dead…Alive? What?"

"Dead. Or else sleeping very heavily with their eyes open and a good chunk of their heads missing." It's a morbid joke, but dark humor is the only way I can deal with yet another awful scene. "Four people. Soldiers. And, Brohn…there's a girl in there."

"Dead, too?"

I nod, and Brohn takes a deep breath and grits his teeth. I know what he's thinking, so I add, "I've never seen her before."

I can see the relief in his eyes as he asks, "Weapons?"

"What?"

"Did you see any weapons? Anything we can use?"

"None that Render could see. Other than the bodies, it looks like the place has been cleaned out."

"What now?"

"I think we should circle around," I reply, struggling to get my breathing back to normal. "Maybe try getting inside."

"Kress, you can barely even stand right now. We need to…"

"What?" He's staring at me in a weird way, like he's both frightened and fascinated.

"Your eyes."

"What about them?"

"They're still black. You're still connected to Render. You need to disconnect. We have the info we need."

I hold my hand up and ask Brohn to give me a second. I start to disconnect from Render, but he won't let go. My mind starts swirling, and our thoughts spill over into each other like two rivers at a confluence. He circles high in the air, his black form invisible in the night sky. He issues a sharp series of *kraas!* and what sounds like his gurgling version of a running motor.

"He's warning us," I whisper to Brohn. "This way. There's someone over in the lot by that truck."

"Then shouldn't we be going the other way?" he asks, his voice layered with tension and total disbelief. Brohn's brave, not crazy. With three dead men and a dead girl inside the barracks and the possibility that their murderer is over on the parking pad just across the way, Brohn's instinct is to get back to the others, re-group, and come up with a strategy to account for these new circumstances.

I don't totally disagree. "But Render thinks we'll be safe," I tell him. "Trust us." I use the word us without even thinking about it. We've become one, the raven and I. One mind. One entity. At least for the moment.

"Okay. Lead the way. But slowly, please." I can hear how hard it is for Brohn to follow my lead, not because he's reluctant to let me take charge, but because his protective instinct is strong. Giving up control is hard for him if he knows my life is on the line, and I have to admit that I love him for it.

15

WITH BROHN CLOSE BEHIND, I LEAD THE WAY AROUND THE SECOND building, across about a hundred yards of rutted desert sand, and over to the edge of the parking pad. Other than the big truck we saw from the other side of the fence, the pad looks deserted. I'm just starting to wonder if Render sounded a false alarm when I hear a woman's voice followed by the clang of metal over by the truck. With Brohn's knife as the only weapon between us, we inch around behind the huge transport and peer around its hulking rear fender.

A man and a woman are busy cranking a thick bolt near the bottom of the truck with a large red wrench.

Silently, Brohn darts his eyes between me and the two figures in the distance. It's his signal that he's going to confront them. I open my eyes wide and shake my head violently, my not-so-subtle signal that it's a terrible idea, and we're likely to end up dead. I'm about to whisper to him that we should maybe follow his original instincts and gather up Card, Rain, and Manthy before we leap into a confrontation with two potentially very dangerous strangers in the middle of the night. It's possible that Brohn's forgotten our similar encounter with Asha and the two men in the desert, but every second of that memory is burned into my brain.

Brohn moves too fast for me to stop him. Before I can say a word, he steps out into the dim light cast by the flickering fixture at the top of the nearby wooden post and calls out to the two people.

"Hey!" he barks. "What are you doing?" His deep voice rumbles with authority from deep in his chest. If I didn't know him and he snuck up on me like this, that voice alone would make me want to put up my hands and do whatever he says.

The man and woman whip around, clearly startled and unsure whether to confront us or turn tail and run. For the first time I can see their threadbare clothes and dust-crusted jackets. They're definitely not military.

They must have come to the same conclusion about us, because they seem to relax as Brohn and I step fully into the light.

"Who are you?" the woman asks, looking around the shadowy parking pad. "Where'd you come from?"

"You first," Brohn orders. He's got his knife out, but he's wisely got it hidden behind his hip. No sense escalating the situation unnecessarily or giving away a strategic advantage. "Are you with the Eastern Order?" he asks.

The woman holds up her hands. "What? Definitely not! I mean, I used to work for…"

The man shoots her a look that seems to say, *Shut your mouth right now.*

"What are you doing on a military base?" I ask.

"We could ask you the same thing."

I decide to take a chance and lead with the truth.

"We escaped from a government military facility. Like this. Only a lot bigger."

"Escaped?"

"We were being recruited."

"Recruited?"

"For the war against the so-called Order," Brohn says.

"So you *are* soldiers."

"No. We were being trained to be soldiers. But it turns out we were fighting for the wrong side."

"If you're not government and not the Order…"

"Let's just say that we're in favor of fighting for ourselves instead of dying for someone else."

"Seems we have something in common," the woman says. The man next to her looks tense as his eyes skim over me and Brohn. The woman whispers something to the man, and he leans his big red wrench against the side of the truck. "We're part of an underground resistance ourselves," she says.

"Resistance to what, exactly?" Brohn asks.

The woman laughs. "Resistance to the end of our democracy as we know it. Ever since the Eastern Order supposedly invaded, we've stood by while our rights slowly got sucked away. There's a movement. An underground. We're dedicated to ending the war by revealing it for the sham that it is." She taps the side of the big truck with the palm of her hand. "Just going to 'borrow' this transport here for the cause."

"Unless you plan on trying to stop us," the man says with a defiant sneer, though behind his eyes I can see fear.

The woman tells him to back off, and he does.

"We're not the enemy," she says. "In fact, we're the good guys. I promise."

"Then we really are on the same team," I say as I drop my shoulders and take what I think must be my first real breath since we stumbled into this place. "We're trying to get to San Francisco."

The woman laughs and slaps her hand on the side of the truck, harder this time. The sound of her palm echoes in the quiet of the desert night. "Then you're in luck. Just so happens that we can get you halfway there, at least."

"We're on our way to Salt Lake City," the man says. "There's an underground there."

The woman gives us a long once-over in the pale light. She steps forward, and Brohn and I brace ourselves for an attack, but she just extends her open hand. "Vail," she says. "And this is my husband, Roland."

Brohn and I exchange handshakes with the couple. Any thoughts I had about a repeat of our horrifying experience in the cave are quickly washed away. Vail and Roland are about as normal and friendly as anyone we could have hoped to meet, all things considered. Vail's shoals of soft brown hair are pulled back in a loose ponytail tied off with a red leather band. The laugh lines around her eyes and at the corners of her mouth suggest someone who's managed to find joy wherever she can in the world. Roland, thin-lipped and balding, seems a bit more somber, but his eyes twinkle with undisguised affection and unqualified love when he glances over at his slightly taller wife.

"How'd you get here?" Brohn asks. He looks out over the fence. "There's nothing around for days."

"We stowed away with a military caravan until it stopped in Denver. Then we 'borrowed' a skimmer, but it broke down maybe twenty miles from here. We had intel about this little temporary military pit-stop, so we hiked the distance, and here we are."

"What about them?" Brohn says with a flick of his thumb back toward the army barracks where I saw the dead bodies.

"Who?"

"The soldiers," I say. "The dead soldiers and the girl in there."

"Dead soldiers? What girl?"

"You must've checked out the barracks before coming over here," Brohn says, his voice flickering with suspicion.

"Of course. We went into both of them. Searched for weapons. Supplies. Anything we could get our hands on. Didn't find anything, though."

"Wait," I say, stepping in front of Brohn. "You're saying that you didn't see the dead man slumped onto his desk in there? Or the other two up against the wall? Or the girl?"

"Girl?"

"Yes!" I nearly shout. "The soldiers. The dead girl under the edge of the desk."

Vail gives me a curious look and steps toward the truck. She reaches down into a long silver tool box. At first, I tense up, thinking she's reaching for a weapon, but she stands up and shows us a handful of small metal micro-drills. "All we found were these. Going to see if we can get this transport started up. Should be enough to restart the solar cell. Not sure how we're going to de-activate the grav-pads, but we've got to try. As far as we know, this truck's the only dead thing here."

"So you really don't know anything about the soldiers and the girl? You didn't see anything?"

Vail shakes her head, and Roland says it sounds like we've got a mystery on our hands. "Are you sure *you* saw something?"

"We'll show you," Brohn says. "Follow me."

Without waiting for an answer, he jogs back over to the barracks, and we follow him right up the front door, which is slightly ajar.

"This is how we left it," the man says.

Brohn ignores him, flings the door open, gestures inside, and says, "See?"

I step inside with Vail and Roland right on my heels.

The desk is there. The chair. The shelves. The empty gun racks on the walls. And the broken panel of viz-screens. But there's no coffee mug. No blood. And there are definitely no dead bodies.

Brohn's face goes into a knot as he whips around to face me. "What the hell—?"

"He was right here," I say as I walk around the desk and put my hands on the back of the chair. I kneel down, looking for pools of blood that just aren't there before skipping around the rest of the room. "And two more here. And the girl over here."

I take in a sharp breath, wondering if I've lost my mind.

"And you saw these people?" Vail asks.

I'm about to say yes when I realize that it's not entirely true. Technically, Render saw them. But I see what Render sees, so it's the same thing.

Isn't it?

I stammer something about thinking we saw someone, but it was dark, so maybe it was just our minds playing tricks on us in the dim light.

"Pretty detailed tricks," Roland mutters, but Vail shushes him.

"Sorry," I say, shooting Brohn a look. "I guess I must have imagined it."

We head back to the transport with Vail and Roland, clearly not satisfied with my weak explanation, leading the way.

"What happened?" Brohn whispers to me as we pad along behind them. "Did you see bodies or not?"

"Render saw the bodies," I whisper back with a certainty I don't really feel.

"What's the difference?"

When he asks that, it occurs to me for the first time that something's happening with Render and me. Something I can't explain, as though together we're an evolving entity, growing, morphing, and potentially turning into something no one has seen or even imagined before. I don't really understand what it is that we saw. But I do know it was real.

Brohn's question is simultaneously empowering and terrifying, and I'm glad he doesn't insist on an answer.

Instead, we arrive back at the truck where Vail tells us she's "kind of sure" she can get it started and asks if we'd like a lift. "If we can get to Salt Lake City, we can get you some supplies. Help you on your way. The truck holds eight. Two up front. Six in the back. So there's plenty of room for the four of us."

"So, is it just the two of you?" Roland asks. "Or are there others?"

"There are three others," I say, pointing to the section of fence off in the distance where Cardyn, Rain, and Manthy are waiting for our all-clear signal. "Plus Render. But you don't have to count him. He'll fly."

16

"I'll get the others," Brohn says. In a brisk jog, he trots off into the dark, leaving me alone with Vail and Roland.

Normally, the thought of being left alone with two strangers in an isolated, dimly-lit place like this might make me nervous, especially considering I might be in the process of losing my mind. But Vail and Roland are giving off vibes of honesty and authenticity. I sense I can trust them. If anything, they might be wondering to what degree they can trust *me*. After all, I'm the one seeing ghostly visions of bloody soldiers and non-existent dead girls in abandoned military barracks.

I'm puzzling over those visions, and Vail is just reassuring me and telling me not to worry about it when we hear Brohn's voice in the distance, calling out to the others through the fence that it's all clear.

"He's going to guide them around to where the tree is," I explain. "It's how we managed to get over the fence. Speaking of which, how did the two of you get in?" I intend it as an honest question, but I pump the brakes when I realize it might sound like an accusation.

Roland and Vail don't seem offended. In fact, they exchange a pleasant laugh.

"Actually," Roland boasts, "we were locked in."

I must look confused, because Vail laughs again and points to a spot in the fence about a hundred yards away. "The main gate is over there. The only gate, actually. We slipped in when a Transport Truck was shipping out."

"So there were soldiers here when you arrived?"

"About a dozen that we saw. Most of them were pulling crates and trunks along on grav-pads and loading everything into a supply truck. They were cleaning the place out. No guards on patrol. Wide open fence. No scan-cams or detectors or anything."

"Everyone's been relocated to the slums and cities and into those beastly Arcologies," Roland sighs. "Forced migrations and all. No need for little desert outposts like this anymore when there's no one left to watch over."

"I guess."

"Anyway," Vail continues, "we knew we were on all kinds of watch lists from our supposed 'Eastern Order associations' and insurgent activities down south, but we were desperate for shelter and supplies, so we slipped in through the open gate and hid in that green tool shed over there. There was a bunch of shooting and shouting, and we thought we were busted, but nothing happened. So we hunkered down, and when it sounded like it was all clear we came out. Sure enough, the place was abandoned, locked up tight from the outside with the laser-wire activated. Nothing else left except for us and this truck, which, unfortunately, doesn't seem to be in working order."

"Although we're going to see about that," Roland says, flipping a silver hammer-sized tool in his hand.

"It's nothing we can't fix," Vail boasts. "Their loss is our gain. With the micro-drills from the barracks and what we dug up from the supply shed, we hope to be able to scrounge enough good parts to get this monster working again. Otherwise, it's back to walking the highway until we find civilization or else..."

"Or else what?" I ask.

Vail drops her smile. "Well, I guess there is no 'or else.'"

"Did you say 'shooting' before?"

"What?"

"You said you heard shouting and shooting."

"Oh that. Yes. When we were in the shed. Definitely. We've heard enough of them to know what a military-issue Sig Sauer 2040 sounds like. We've seen too many folks like us gunned down over the years. Thought we were caught for sure."

"You were so scared," Roland teases.

"That's because I'm not dumb enough to think I'm bullet proof," she replies with a gentle push to his shoulder.

I scrunch up my face as a dozen tumbling thoughts caper around in my head. "Wait a second. What if the dead bodies I saw, the three men and the girl, what if the soldiers you heard were the ones who shot the people I saw? That would explain the gunfire, wouldn't it?"

Roland digs his pinky into his ear like he's trying to clear water out after a long swim. "I guess it's possible that we heard those people getting shot. But if that's the case, they were taken away in one of the Transport Trucks before you arrived, which means you couldn't have possibly seen them. I mean, they're not there anymore, right? And I don't imagine they got shot, were left for dead, and then decided to spring back to life, climb the fence, and make their grand escape."

Now I've got a major migraine clomping its way through my temples, and I'm hoping Brohn and the others get here quick, because something strange is going on, and I'm terrified it might all be in my head. It's not helping that Vail and Roland are now staring at me like they're having second thoughts about helping out a girl who's not only apparently seeing ghostly visions of dead people but who might also believe in fence-climbing zombies.

I'm saved from having to offer up an explanation by Brohn, who trots out of the dark with Rain, Cardyn, and Manthy in tow. They step from the rough desert floor up onto the silver parking pad. After a quick round of introductions, I explain to Brohn and the others about how Vail and Roland are planning to repair the military vehicle and that they're willing to take us with them.

"More than willing," Vail insists. "We owe it to you. On behalf of our own kids and all the others who are getting swept up in this pointless fear-mongering."

Just as she's saying this, Render swoops down and lands on the top of the big gray truck. Vail and Roland are startled by the sudden flurry of movement.

"Don't worry," I say. "That's just Render."

"A lot of people think of ravens as a bad omen, but not us," Vail boasts as her shoulders relax. "We have a raven of our own back home."

"You do?"

"Jeff," Roland says.

"Jeff the raven?" Rain asks with a chuckle.

Roland shrugs. "He's named after my grandfather. Jeff's one of the family. My folks are taking care of him now."

I can only assume that they're talking about some sort of semi-domesticated family pet and choose not to ask any more questions. I'd rather not explain that Render and I have a semi-psychic connection that turns my eyes black and apparently makes me go slightly mad.

Turning to Roland, Vail rubs her hands together like a greedy diner on her way to an all-you-can-eat buffet. "If you're willing to keep our new friends company, I've got a truck to resuscitate."

Vail drops to the ground and crawls under the big truck while Roland rearranges wires in an open access panel by the side door. As he pulls and untangles the colorful filaments, he tells us about his life back home with Vail. It turns out they have kids about our age. "A girl and a boy. Heather and Liam." His voice gets quiet as he tells us how they enlisted in the fight against the Order.

"We're pacifists. We raised the kids to be opposed to violence in all its forms. But as the Freedom Wars went on, our kids became more and more convinced that some invading horde was going to come breaking down our door at any minute and kill us all in our sleep. They were afraid. Terrified, actually. Despite all our assurances, all our lectures, all the locks we put on the doors and those stupid bars we put up on the windows, they couldn't sleep anymore. All they knew was fear. That's the power of propaganda."

After a few more minutes of hearing from Roland about the kids, parents and the pets they left behind, Vail slides out from under the truck, pops to her feet, and announces that she's fixed the solar cell but that she hasn't had any luck with the grav-pads. "It's a lock-down system," she tells us. "The network pathways need certain lines of code to run, but the processor is loaded with all kinds of encryption I can't come close to figuring out. Which means the truck'll start, but we can't move it off the parking pad."

Roland hangs his head. "No luck here, either. Got the ignition network running just fine, but the navigation system is off-line, and I can't get it back on. But if we can't move the truck, it doesn't matter anyway."

Vail stops and looks at us, startled that we've all gone quiet. "What?" she stammers. "What is it?"

We hear her, of course. But we're all staring at Manthy.

Manthy takes a big step back, shakes her head, and puts her hands up in defiance. "No," she says. "No way."

Brohn says, "Manthy..."

"I don't know how."

Then it's Rain's turn. "Manthy...please..."

"I can't do it. Plus, it hurts."

156

I step forward. "We need your help. You're the only one who can…"

But Manthy isn't swayed. It seems she left her powers back in the Processor and doesn't want to revisit them for anything.

Vail and Roland are looking at us like we're speaking in Chinese. "What's happening?" Vail asks, her face contorted in a puzzled frown. "What are you asking her to do?"

"Manthy here has certain…abilities," Brohn explains.

"Abilities?"

"I don't have anything of the kind," Manthy objects. She looks even more skittish than usual, and I half expect her to turn around and bolt off into the desert night. But Cardyn steps forward, his hands out like he's calming down a rabid dog.

"Think of it like this," he says. "You just happen to speak a second language, and the rest of us can't. There's nothing freakish about it, and it's not an unusual thing to be able to do. Not when you really think about it. All kinds of people have skills and can do all kinds of things. This is *your* thing. I don't know if it's a gift or a curse or just a fluke of nature. But whatever it is, it's yours and what matters is how you use it. It might also be our only chance to get out of here and reach some kind of civilization."

Vail and Roland continue to stare at us while we stare at Manthy, who has her fists balled up tight and her legs tense like she's debating whether to run or tuck herself into an armadillo-style ball.

Vail finally breaks the silent stalemate. "I have an idea. How about if someone tells us what on earth the five of you are talking about?"

"Manthy might be able to help us out," Brohn explains rather cryptically and without taking his eyes off of our quietly-snarling friend. "But she has to want to."

Vail looks from Manthy to Brohn and back to Manthy, who finally looks up, still sporting a furious frown.

"Fine. I can do it," Manthy grumbles as she shoulders past Cardyn and then pushes her way through the rest of us on her way to the front of the truck. "I can fix the problem with the solar cell and grav-pad release."

Clearly stunned, Vail jogs after her, and the two of them disappear around the front end of the massive vehicle. I feel kind of bad about it, but I can't help laughing a little as we explain it all in more detail to Roland.

"Manthy has a way with technology," I tell him.

"An *amazing* way," Card jumps in. "She's not the one you want if you need someone to give a big speech or socialize at a cocktail party. But when it comes to stuff like this, well...there's honestly no one better. I can't explain it, but trust me."

Roland asks a few questions about Manthy's abilities, and we do our best to answer, although we're quick to confess that, like us, even she might not know the extent of what she's capable of.

"And I recommend *not* asking her," Cardyn warns. "She has a temper and a wicked right-cross. Not the kind of combination I recommend exploring."

Roland promises he won't raise the subject again. Instead, he tells us some more about his family and life down south. "We lived in Santa Fe," he says. When we hear that name we all go dead quiet and stare at one another. Finally, Rain steps forward to tell the story of the three people from the cave.

"I don't think we know them," Roland says. "But they definitely sound like some of the folks we ran with down there. In the end, the place was a mess. No one trusted anyone anymore. Everyone had become the enemy. Reason flew out the window. Sanity was optional. Honestly, I'm not totally surprised the folks you met were a little...off the rails."

The sound of the truck bellowing to life startles us, and we all jump in unison.

Vail and Manthy return from inside the truck with Vail

beaming in triumph and Manthy looking miserable and pale, like she's just expended the last of her energy.

"Your friend here is an absolute wizard," Vail gushes. "She said more to the truck than she said to me. And I don't know what they talked about, but she was apparently pretty convincing! Anyway, it works, and it's free of the grav-lock."

Roland claps his hands together. "Let's step inside and have a look around." He pulls open the heavy sliding door, and we step onto the small metal ladder leading into the vehicle. Roland sounds like a proud father as he launches into an explanation of the truck's specs.

"This ugly, boxy baby," he gushes, "is the Tatrapan MPAV. That's a Multi-Purpose Armored Vehicle. They stopped making this particular model in 2022 when the amphibious version came out, so this one is probably more suited to a museum than to being on the road." Ducking down, Roland points to various parts of the truck's interior. "As you can see, it has an eight-seat configuration with two forward-facing captain's chairs up front in the cab and two bench seats seating three-a-piece back here in the cabin. Nav-comm system would normally be here, but, as you can see, it's been ripped out. Pretty carelessly, I must say. This MPAV is strictly a personnel-carrier, but they can be outfitted for ambulance, communication, or combat duty depending on what's needed. This one has a gun mount up top, but, again, as you can see, no ammo and the scope and trigger systems have been removed. In the old days, these ran just on diesel. This one's still an oil-sucker and gas-guzzler, but it's been partially retro-fitted with a magnetic starter and a solar-cell recharger with a rear-mounted back-up tank. Oh, and it's armored top to bottom and back to front."

"Don't mind him," Vail apologizes when Roland finally takes a breath. "He was a purchaser in President Krug's army for about two minutes, and now he thinks he's Mr. Know-it-all."

Roland blushes and drops his hands to his sides. "Not my fault if I picked up a few things."

In the dark, cramped space of the truck's interior, we gaze around at the various storage compartments, gauges, and empty munitions racks. Panels are missing from parts of the inside walls with clumps of wires and copper-colored valves exposed. The seats are barely bolted to the floor anymore, and dark stains of oil and dirt cover nearly every surface. I can see why the soldiers Vail and Roland were hiding from left it behind. Even with the engine in perfect working order, it doesn't look like it'd be much good for anything other than possibly getting from point A to point B, and maybe not even that.

"Stripped clean," Roland says sadly. "Too bad. Would've been nice to have some provisions or weapons or something."

"We don't do weapons," Vail says. "Besides, thanks to Manthy, we'll be in Salt Lake City in four hours instead of a couple of weeks."

Vail crawls through the tight opening between the cabin and the cab and slips into the driver's seat.

"Are you going to join me?" she asks Manthy.

Roland nods his approval to Manthy, and, with her head down and her tangle of dark brown hair bunched into a scruffy ponytail, she follows Vail into the cab and slides into the passenger seat.

Fine clouds of red dust puff up as the rest of us drop down onto the two hard steel benches on either side of the cabin. Brohn eases down next to me, for which I'm grateful. With Vail at the helm and Manthy as her co-pilot, the truck lurches forward, sputtering and grinding in painful spasms. In the cabin, we jostle against each other, and Vail calls back for us to hang on. The rumbling rig covers the length of the base in a bouncy chug until we reach the fence, and Vail pilots the truck straight through without hesitation or resistance. Slamming around hard to the left, the truck plows onto the very road we spent so many days and weeks walking after our escape from the Processor and after we said our sad but necessary goodbyes to Adric and Celia and their crew.

After about twenty minutes of slamming into each other, we all settle in and relax into the liberating feeling of being on the open road. And it really does feel amazing!

The truck's cabin is wide and windowless with low ceilings, and only Rain is able to stand up in it without cracking her head. But it offers a tangible sense of safety and security, something I haven't felt in…well, ever.

In the Valta, there weren't many mag-cars, even before the war began. Everyone made their way around on foot. Some of the kids had mag-bikes, the hovering kind my dad said people used to race back East. The closest I ever came to an experience like this was the seemingly endless time we Seventeens spent in the military transport truck that took us from the Valta to the Processor. But that was a stress-filled, terrifying, and violently rocky ride in a windowless rig with two armed guards ready to blast our heads off if we even thought about stepping out of line.

Compared to that, this is a luxury cruise.

Although the highway is deeply cratered in most places, Vail turns out to be an expert navigator. She skims around the larger blast holes and depressions and manages to glide right over some of the smaller ones. The huge truck bounces and dips like a galloping horse, but it does it all with a certain strength and confidence, like it's a living creature that knows its limits but hasn't yet reached them.

"We've got three wheels on each side with one forward axle and two in the back," Roland tells us. "The absorbers and stabilizers prevent excessive jostling." He goes on to get into all the technical specs about the transport—everything from wheel size to engine torque—but I'm too absorbed in trying to lean close enough to the front windows to watch the scenery fly by to pay much attention. Rain, on the other hand, is hanging on his every word and seems to understand what he's talking about. For all her snarkiness and sarcasm, Rain is a dedicated learner whose brain has gotten us a lot further than anyone else's brawn ever could.

It takes a few hours on the road before I really get used to the feeling of seeing the world outside skimming past the truck's small front windows. The pits, craters, rocks and debris littering the nearly-destroyed and totally deserted highway make the ride perilous and stomach-churning at times. After a while, I grow more used to it and manage to enjoy the experience.

At one point, Rain says this must be what it feels like to fly. I don't reply, even though I don't agree. This is different from the feeling I get when I'm connected to Render. When I'm inside his mind, I don't feel my weight, the relentless force of friction, or the concussive impact of the road like I do in the Transport Truck. With Render, even the turbulence in the air turns smooth as he skims over thermal waves and rides like a surfer in zero-gravity on rolling pockets of wind.

Now *that's* what it feels like to fly.

17

After several hours, Vail announces our arrival in Salt Lake City.

It's been a long but great ride, one I kind of wish didn't have to end. Along the way, I decided I trusted Vail and Roland enough to tell them about my dad and Render, and about how he connected us through the microcircuitry in my forearm tattoos. Vail seemed to find this last part especially interesting and asked me a few more questions about my connection. In the meantime, I could sense Render soaring above the truck, high in the sky, feeling free for the first time in a long while, just like us. I spent most of the rest of the drive with my shoulder pressed against Brohn, who occasionally offered me one of his million-dollar smiles. I could tell he was still concerned about what I thought I saw back at the base. I tried to smile back to reassure him, hoping it was enough to tell him I was fine.

At the city's outer limits, Vail spots a military check-point in the distance.

"How are we going to get past them?" Cardyn asks across the cabin to Roland.

Roland tells us not to worry and to just sit back in the transport and not say anything.

"Vail used to work for an arm of the government," he informs us. "She quit when Krug announced the formation of his Patriot Army, but she's still got a few connections up her sleeve. And the credentials she has will make any guard think twice about snooping too much or asking too many questions."

Vail sends Manthy to the back with us and closes the small but heavy door separating the cab from the cabin. The overhead cabin light goes off, and Roland and the rest of us sit quietly in the dark.

Through a small vent just behind my head, I hear the guard say, "You're cleared," before sending us on our way.

After that, Vail re-opens the dividing door and navigates the troop transport through the city. We take turns leaning into the cab to have a look out of the small panel of windows running along the front of the truck.

For the first time since I was a small child, I set my eyes on people walking the streets. It's like I remember—pedestrians on sidewalks, going about their business. Humans living ordinary human lives, as if the rest of the world hasn't been destroyed.

Some of them are men dressed in tidy suits, accompanying women in light veils and pretty dresses. Each pair seems to have an armed guard alongside them, dressed in something like military fatigues.

When we begin to weave through a shanty town, I spot children and adults in ratty, torn clothing, running around in the shadows of two monstrous buildings.

"Arcologies," I say softly as the others lean forward to look. Two massive structures, the size of entire cities, stretch high toward the clouds. For a little while I contemplate connecting with Render to take a closer look, but after our last experience at the base, I decide to hold back.

"They're so huge," Card says. "I never knew they'd be so big."

"Big enough to hold all the richest, most important people," Vail says, her voice tinged with bitterness. "Listen, there's a safe house not too far from here. Just keep your heads down, and we should be there before you know it."

As promised, she gets us through the city and to an underground parking garage within a matter of minutes. When she's pulled inside, we hear the door sliding closed behind us. I press my arm tattoo to make sure Render's with us and am relieved to find he's swept off into the city to forage for something to eat.

After a few seconds, the truck comes to a stop. Vail climbs out and lets us out the side, a huge smile on her face.

"Good news!" she sings. "We have showers!"

I look around at the others, and suddenly I want to break into song myself. Other than using dirty spring water to clean ourselves up, none of us has taken a shower or bath in weeks.

Vail leads us through a door into a space that reminds me of the locker rooms at Shoshone High School. A ladies' change room on one side, men's on the other, a long series of metal lockers lining the space between.

"Go ahead," says Vail. "You've earned it. There are towels in the change rooms."

Rain, Manthy and I dash into the shower room so quickly that we almost get stuck in the doorway, laughing as we try our best to out-maneuver one another. I'm pleased when I see that there are multiple private shower stalls, each stocked with shampoo, conditioner and body wash.

"Toothbrushes!" Rain squeals, opening a nearby cupboard. "Brand new ones! And toothpaste!"

I've never felt so fortunate in all my life as I do in this moment. I rush over to one of the sinks and turn on the water. The sound is music to my ears, but it's the feeling of warm liquid caressing my hands that makes me all but swoon. I splash some on my face before glancing into the mirror.

What I see freaks me out.

My large brown-green eyes have turned bright and alert, standing out like beacons above my now-prominent cheekbones. I've clearly lost weight, though that's not the most surprising part of it. Somehow, I've turned into an adult. The last time I saw my reflection, I looked like a round-faced teenage girl. But now I've grown into something else. It's like I've spent the last several weeks tucked inside a cocoon, only to emerge as a different person.

I see now what the others see when they look at me. What Brohn sees when he takes my hand. A girl who's transformed, who looks wiser, more experienced, and more confident than she did back in our days in the Valta.

I see Render in me, too, though the thought of it makes me shudder slightly. I can't help thinking that he's the one who's given me this odd energy, this air of alertness…as though I now see the world through new eyes.

Pulling away from my reflection, I stride toward the shower stalls, determined to wash away the last remnants of my past.

WHEN WE'VE all finished our luxuriously long showers and wrapped ourselves in fluffy white towels, Vail leads us over to a large supply closet at the back of the central locker room. She slides the door open to reveal a line of clothes of various styles and sizes.

Blissful sighs emerge from every open mouth. Clean clothes haven't existed in our world in so long that we've all but forgotten what they feel like. I can see joy in my friends' faces for the first time in ages, and my joy mingles with theirs in a sort of collective moment of pure bliss before it fades again to vague worry about our future.

After we've all slipped on our brand-new outfits and swiped as many toothbrushes and toothpaste tubes as we can realistically carry, Vail leads us back out to the truck and hands me a small pouch, which holds dozens of thin silver disks.

"Tap-coins," she explains as Roland climbs out of the truck to join us. "Not sure how much good they'll do. They ran on the old I.D.S. We were still using them in Santa Fe, but I hear most of the New Towns like Reno, where you'll head next, are back to the barter system. So money won't necessarily do you much good."

"What's a 'Reno'?" asks Card.

Vail laughs. "It's a city."

"Like this one?"

"Not exactly. Things are safer in Salt Lake. Everything's about modesty. A woman just needs to be covered. In Reno, they need to be careful."

"We can take care of ourselves," I tell her.

"I don't doubt that. Just watch out." She points to me, Rain, and Manthy. "You three, especially."

"What do you mean?"

"It's just that…well, let's just say that town belongs to whoever has the biggest gun."

I don't get what she means at first, but when Brohn clears his throat and looks down at his crotch, I catch her drift.

"Once there, you'll need to track down a thermonic sensor cartridge."

"A what?" I ask.

"Thermonic sensor cartridge," Roland explains. "This truck won't run much longer without one. It's a fuel supplement and enhancer, and you'll need it to get the rest of the way to San Francisco."

"Wait," Rain says. "You're going to drive us to San Francisco? I thought you had to stay here. You said you had family…"

"We do. And we are. But this truck won't do us any good here. So, we're giving it to you."

"You mean you want us to…?"

"Drive yourselves to Reno, yes," Vail laughs. "Pick up the thermonic sensor cartridge, get to San Francisco, join the resistance, and save the world. Yes, please. All of it."

I'm about to object when Brohn steps forward. "We can do that," he says, extending his hand, which Vail pushes away, leaning in for a tight hug instead.

"I know you can," she says. "I have a feeling about you. About all of you. I wish we could keep you here, have you help out our cause. But something tells me you're destined for bigger things."

"We'll do what we can in San Francisco," I promise as Vail releases Brohn and pulls me in close for a hug of my own.

"Uh, about the sensor thing?" Rain asks. "How exactly do we...?"

Vail wipes her eyes. "We've got someone on the inside in Reno. A friend of the family. Used to be an inventory clerk at a military supply depot back in Santa Fe. She owns a bar now. She keeps her finger on the government's pulse while she hides in plain sight."

"Who is she?"

"Her name is Nora. But she goes by Saucy. She'll help you, and she won't require much in return."

"Much?" Cardyn asks with a raised eyebrow.

"She has a thing for bio-tech in non-human organisms."

"Which means?"

Vail swings around to face me. "She'll want to have a look at your bird."

"Render? What'll she want with Render?"

Vail tips her head back and laughs. "Don't look so shocked, Kress. She'll just want a feather or two. Maybe a little blood."

"From Render?"

"For her DNA collection."

Cardyn leaps in front of me. "Wait. What kind of nut are you hooking us up with?"

"The best kind of nut. The kind that doesn't give you an

allergic reaction or contain cyanide. The kind of nut you don't have to work too hard to crack."

"Sorry," Brohn apologizes on Cardyn's behalf. "We're just a little wary about being blind-sided."

"Not everything in life has to be a struggle. Still, you'll need to watch out for checkpoints. We don't have any surveillance drones, or I'd lend you one to figure out alternate routes. You shouldn't encounter too much resistance on the highway, anyway. As you saw, the roads and the smaller towns have all been abandoned or destroyed."

"That's all right," I say, "We have our own drone."

"That you do. So you know, you'll be on the road a good seven or eight hours to Reno. You'll need to get the cartridge and find a way to install it. Otherwise, the truck won't be much more than a twenty-ton paperweight. After that, you'll head to San Francisco. That'll be another three hours, at which point this beast probably won't have a lot of life left in her, even with the cartridge installed. You may have to walk part of the way, or if you're lucky, you can cruise in on fumes."

"I wish we could stay together," Rain says.

"Me too," Vail replies. "But as you said, we have our family to take care of. And you need to get those answers you say you're looking for. But hey—who knows? Maybe we'll meet up again someday when the world is right."

18

IT'S GOING ON NIGHTTIME WHEN WE'RE FINALLY READY TO LEAVE. After the rest of us have said goodbye to him, Vail kisses Roland on the cheek and climbs into the truck with the five of us piling into the cabin behind her. She drives us across town to the Western Gate, which she explains is the city limit and the dividing line between Salt Lake City and the desert. Using the same credentials she used to get us past the first checkpoint and into the city, Vail drives us out into the desert, where she stops the truck at the side of the road after about five minutes, cutting the engine.

"This is it," she says. She stoops down, climbs back into the cabin, and leads us out the sliding side door. We hop out of the truck and down to the road. The air outside is dusty and hot. The broken road extends in a straight line right into the horizon. On either side, the desert stretches out, red and rocky for as far as we can see.

With a loud *kraa!* Render lands on the truck's roof to let us know he's still with us.

"I'll head back to the city on foot." Vail tells us, tapping the side of the massive truck. "She's all yours now. Should be smooth sailing to Reno."

When she notices us all standing in place and quietly staring at her, she furrows her brow and asks us what's wrong.

Cardyn half-raises his hand. "Um…none of us knows how to drive."

Vail's laugh echoes through the desert. "Okay, I guess I'll give you a quick lesson, then. And don't worry. These things are designed for the military. They're totally idiot-proof."

"I think we've got an idiot or two who can prove you wrong," I inform her.

Cardyn says, "Hey!"

"I didn't say you were one of them," I laugh. "But you've just incriminated yourself. Nice work."

"Come on, then." Patient, supportive, and endlessly smiling, Vail crowds Brohn and me into the cab with her while Cardyn, Manthy, and Rain poke their heads through the portal as best they can to follow along with the instructions. Vail points to an array of lights and gauges on the front panel. "These, you don't have to worry about. Since your communication and GPS systems are off-line, the only thing you have to pay attention to is the read-out here. This tells you your solar-cell charge and monitors the hydraulics. That's what you need the thermonic sensor cartridge for. Without that, the fuel link doesn't work, which means the truck won't run. Other than that, it's about as basic as you can get. Steering wheel. Accelerator. Brake. She's a big machine, and she's older than all of you, so go easy on her. Start turning before you need to. Brake before you think you have to."

Brohn and I take turns driving the truck up the road, turning around and coming back. When we think we have the hang of it, Cardyn takes a turn.

Manthy refuses. When Cardyn tries to convince her to give it a shot, explaining that we'll never know when we might need her to step up and drive, Manthy tells him, "If we're desperate enough for me to drive, it means we're all dead, so what difference does it make?"

Brohn whispers to Cardyn not to push his luck so he drops it. After a while, we get to the point where we all start to feel like we can drive this thing in a straight line without killing ourselves or anyone else along the way.

Brohn, Cardyn, and I take a second turn just to be sure we have the hang of it. Rain, it turns out, has to be disqualified. It's a big vehicle, and her legs aren't quite long enough to reach the foot pedals from the high perch of the Captain's Chair. On top of that, her arms aren't long enough for her to work the hand controls at the same time, even when she pulls the seat up to its closest setting. Vail tries folding up some of the floor mats in the back and tying them to the foot pedals, but they keep slipping off.

We all have a good laugh over it, including Rain. "My poor little legs," she moans in mock complaint.

"I know," Card says, nodding his head in vigorous agreement. "They're barely long enough to reach the ground!"

Rain grumbles at him. "And your brain's barely big enough to fill your head."

Vail interrupts their squabbling. "The truck is equipped with an auto-driver and mobile navigation system, so, technically, you should have just been able to insert a destination or map coordinates into the nav-comm entry panel, and the vehicle would have taken you to Reno on its own. But the system has been disabled or broken."

We try pleading with Manthy to fix it but once again, she refuses.

"But it would make things so much easier," Cardyn whines over the grind of the engine as Brohn takes one last practice run down the road.

Sitting stiffly in the belly of the Truck, Manthy frowns and asks, "Easier for *who*?"

When Cardyn leans forward and tries to explain that her noble sacrifice would be for the benefit of the group, she very unkindly suggests that what might benefit the group even more would be for her to knock out all of his teeth and throw him out the side of the hurtling truck. "That would definitely make things easier for *me*," she snarls as the rest of us quickly and wisely back down.

Feeling comfortable enough at last, we say our goodbyes to Vail and ask her to pass along our thanks to Roland as well. As we exchange handshakes, hugs, and sad farewells, it occurs to me that just once I'd like to say goodbye to someone I know I'll see again.

With that, we pile back into the truck with Brohn in the driver's seat and me next to him in the springy passenger seat. Cardyn, Rain, and Manthy start out in the back. We trundle along the road for several uneventful hours, thankful to be closing in our first destination without any problems.

"This is the life," I sigh from my seat up front, locking my hands behind my head. "No more scratching and clawing our way through the wilderness. It's so much more fun to cruise along in style. Not to mention how amazing it is to smell like a normal human being instead of death warmed over."

"I do like the not smelling like death part, but I'd hardly call this 'style,'" Brohn laughs, practically shouting above the clang and grinding of metal on metal coming from somewhere under the truck. "I'll just be glad if this thing doesn't crumble into a heap of busted parts before we get to Reno."

As if on cue, one of the truck's wheels hits a massive crater in the road, and the vehicle jolts hard to one side, sending all of us flying. By some miracle, Brohn maintains his vice-like grip on the steering wheel and keeps the big rig from soaring off the rutted highway.

Unfortunately, the jostling and jolting seem to have knocked out the bank of lights on the front of the truck, so now we're flying blind. Brohn has no choice but to pull over and ease us to a stop at the side of the road.

This time, it's Rain who comes to the rescue.

"I saw a couple of flashlights when we were rummaging around before. Maybe we can use those."

Despite the darkness surrounding us, Rain manages to scoot into the back of the cabin and flip open a silver panel to reveal one of the vehicle's storage compartments.

"See?" she says. I can just barely make out her silhouette holding something up to show us.

"No," I reply with a chuckle. "I can't see."

With a grunt, Manthy rises to her feet and flicks on an overhead light that faintly illuminates the cabin.

Rain waggles the little light at us. "We can totally use this."

"You think that'll be powerful enough to replace the lights we lost?" Brohn asks. "The thing looks more like a pen-light for night reading."

He's right to be skeptical. The bank of lights on the front of the truck were massive, powerful and bright enough to enable us to see for a good mile down the road. Thanks to that kind of visibility, we've been able to avoid every potential deadly obstacle in our path. That includes overturned passenger vehicles, deep cracks in the pavement, endless strips of melted asphalt, and dozens of boulders that had tumbled onto the road from the steep and spikey cliffs along the way.

Standing under the dim overhead light, Rain fiddles around with the small device, turning it over in her hand as she looks for a switch or some mechanism for turning the little flashlight on. When she can't find anything, she squints at the tiny writing embossed into the side of the delicate-looking device. "It says, 20K-L, MT 900m, and 156K-C. I wonder what that means?"

Before I can stop myself, I launch into what I'm sure must sound like an annoyingly pompous explanation. "Artificially-produced light is measured in Lumens, Throw, and Candelas.

Lumens measure the light's output. Throw is the distance the light travels before it reaches point-two-five lux, which is the approximate brightness of the moon on a clear night. Candelas is the measure of the light at its brightest point. So it's 20,000 Lumens, a Maximum Throw of 900 meters, and 156,000 Candelas."

"First of all," Rain says with a hand on her hip, "you need to stop doing that."

"Doing what?"

"You know. That thing you do where you suddenly have all the knowledge of the entire universe at your fingertips."

"It's hardly all the knowledge of the universe," I whine, irritated with Rain for being so unnecessarily dramatic. "It's just a tiny bit of information I remember from something my dad taught me in the Valta."

"When you were six."

"So?"

"So remembering something like that from when you were six isn't normal."

I don't know whether to blush, scream, or cry, but as it turns out, I don't have to decide. Brohn comes to my rescue and whips around to face Rain. He growls, "Normal is just another word for boring, and Kress is the least boring person in the world!"

Scowling, Rain looks like she might either strongly object or possibly lunge at Brohn, but she thinks better of it and exhales instead. "Fine," she says. "I just think her whole memory thing is…"

"What?" Brohn challenges.

"Well, definitely not boring," Rain admits, chastened.

"And?"

"And it's an amazing gift," Rain concedes, "and I'm glad she's not dull. Now can we drop it?"

Brohn seems satisfied with Rain's pseudo-apology.

And suddenly, I don't feel so bad.

Because it occurs to me for the first time that Rain is jealous.

Jealous of *me*.

How did that happen? How can the girl I was terrified of when we were growing up possibly be intimidated by me in any way? This is Rain we're talking about. Girl genius. Confidence personified. The girl who never met a puzzle she couldn't solve, a person she couldn't control, or an argument she couldn't win. She's pretty, charming, overwhelming in every possible way other than stature.

This strange reversal should probably overwhelm me, but it doesn't. Instead, it gives me a sense of comfort and strength, like I matter because, for the first time ever, I'm good enough to be some kind of threat to the great and powerful Rain.

Brohn, his head scrunched down in the low-ceilinged cab, puts his hand on my shoulder, pulling my attention back to the matter at hand. He smiles and says, "Now Kress, about that light…"

"Based on those specs, it's going to be pretty bright," I offer without hesitation. "Military-grade bright."

"Ha!" Cardyn chuckles. "'Military-bright.' Now there's an oxymoron if I ever heard one."

Rain plops down onto the metal bench seat, the flashlight in her fist. "Okay, Miss Miracle-Memory. How do we turn it on?"

"Let me see," I say, extending my hand.

Rain slaps the little device into my open palm. "Good luck," she mutters.

Brohn scowls at her and tells her to stop being a baby. She throws him a rude *harrumph* and crosses her arms in defiance.

Ignoring them both, I skim my fingertips along the surface of the flashlight. "Since it's bound to be powerful, it likely has a safety feature built in. Yes. Here it is." I hold the black cylinder up to the overhead cabin light to show the others the nearly-invisible finger pads. "See, you have to put your fingers here to acti-

RENDER

vate it. It's so you don't accidentally set it off in someone's eyes, including your own. Dad called it 'poka yoke.'"

Cardyn laughs. "'Poka' what, now?"

"'Poka yoke.' It's a Japanese term for a kind of error-proofing. It's like a safe-guard in anticipation of a potential risk. See?" I press the fingertips of my left hand onto the markings and tap the end of the device with the heel of my right hand, and it suddenly feels like we just drove into the sun.

"Whoa," Cardyn gasps, draping an arm across his eyes. "That's beyond bright! More like blinding."

Shielding my eyes and pointing the light down, I slip into the front of the truck. It turns out that shining the powerful beam through the front windshield causes a painful glare that reflects back at us, and the side windows don't roll down, so I can't even hold it while Brohn drives.

"Great. The most powerful light in the world, and we still can't see anything," Cardyn complains.

Rain reaches into the cab and asks for the light, her mood improving. She's always happiest when she has a problem to solve, and this is a good one. "I have an idea."

Brohn nods his assent in my direction, and I hand the little light back to Rain, who aims it at the floor as she fumbles around in one of the storage compartments and yells, "Perfect!" After a second, she holds up a long white rope for us to see.

She slides the truck's side door open and hops down to the ground. She tosses the braided rope underneath, just behind the front wheels, and loops it back around the top of the hood, where she ties it into a solid knot.

"See?" she beams as she clambers up onto the bumper, "I can hang onto this rope with one hand and keep the light pointing forward with the other. That way, we can still see the road and maybe just get to where we're going without driving off a cliff or into a crater."

Back in the cab of the truck, Brohn and I exchange a look that

177

I'm pretty sure is a perfect blend of *impressed with Rain's ingenuity* and *doubtful about her sanity*. Manthy quickly covers her smile with her hand and turns her head to stare at the truck's cabin wall.

"Great idea!" Card shouts at the window to Rain, who I'm sure can't hear him through the thick and grimy glass. Turning back to us, he shakes his head and cuts loose with a twittering chuckle. "I always figured Rain had a special ability of her own. Who would've thought it would be as a hood ornament?"

"I just hope she tied that rope tightly," I say under my breath. She and I may fight on occasion, but the last thing I want is to lose another friend.

With the transport truck grumbling and pitching, Rain holds on as best she can while Brohn navigates us off the highway until we reach the pitted side road Vail told us about. Just as Rain predicted, the little but mighty flashlight of hers does the trick and proves to be a life-saver. We're able to drive along in relative calm, avoiding nearly all the big gaps and cracks in the long-neglected road as she angles it perfectly.

Until we reach what looks like a dead end, that is.

Just when we think the road is going to disappear completely, we spot a shadowy structure up ahead.

"That must be it!" Brohn says as Rain points to what appears to be a large square shed of some kind. "The garage Vail mentioned." Sure enough, as he limps the truck closer, we're able to make out the edges of a building made of corrugated metal nestled within a semi-circle of large red boulders.

"Not exactly a five-star hotel, is it?" Cardyn jokes.

"We don't need flashy," Brohn says. "Just safe."

When we've pulled to a stop, Manthy and I hop out to find a long double chain rising up from the ground and disappearing into a large housing at the top of the banged-up garage door, which has been painted in splotchy patches of red, orange and brown to camouflage it within the splotchy desert surroundings.

Together, Manthy and I grab the chain and pull, hand over hand, until the big metal door rises high enough for us to get the truck through.

Manthy steps to the side to inspect her red and blistered hands while I wave Brohn forward.

He inches the truck into the garage, bringing it to a final grinding halt. The engine sputters and coughs like it's decided we've arrived at our destination, so it's okay to finally die.

Brohn, Manthy and Cardyn hop down from inside the truck, and Render, who's either ridden on top of the cabin or flown above us for the entire trip, comes fluttering in to land on a nearby table. Rain releases her grip on the rope and slides off the truck's hood, landing with the perfect precision of a champion gymnast on the smooth concrete floor.

"Not bad for a baby, huh?" she says to Brohn.

"No," he concedes with a laugh. "That was pretty impressive for a baby."

Rain gives him a playful, two-handed push to the chest, and Brohn fake-stumbles backward.

I spot a sensor-pad on the wall by the door and wave my hand in front of it, and a bank of overhead lights flickers to life.

The garage is a dingy mess, but the temperature is good, and it seems like it'll make a good home base while we collect ourselves, get our bearings, and, hopefully, fix the truck up enough to get us to San Francisco in one piece.

"First things first. We need to track down this thermonic sensor cartridge," Brohn says, getting right to business.

"And you really think this Saucy person will have what we need?" Rain asks.

"Vail said she was good for it, and I trust her judgment."

"So what are we supposed to do? Just waltz into town and go door to door asking if anyone knows someone named Saucy who happens to have a thermonic sensor cartridge we can borrow?"

"Vail gave us enough information to get started. Riverwalk

District, just north of Wingfield Park. That should help narrow it down enough so we can do a bit of investigating and see what we can come up with."

"The five of us walking around together might look suspicious," Rain says, and I nod my agreement. She's right. We can't keep lunging blindly into unknown situations. We've been lucky up until now, maybe even a little skillful on our better days. But all the luck in the world will only get us so far, and it's bound to run out sooner or later. "We need to take care of whatever's broken on the truck, anyway," I suggest. "How about if we split up? Brohn, you and Rain can help me track down the cartridge. Manthy, you've kind of become our resident mechanic. I hate to ask, but do you think you could have a look at the truck?"

Manthy turns to rummage and clang through a tangled pile of tools on the long wooden work table against the garage wall. "If the problem is what I think it is, maybe I can fix it," she mutters.

"Really?" Cardyn asks.

"I think so."

Cardyn taps his finger against his temple. "Using your...uh, thing?"

"No," Manthy snaps, holding up a lethal-looking silver sonic-wrench and brandishing it menacingly at Cardyn. "Using this."

Cardyn takes a step back, apparently unsure if Manthy is bluffing or if she really plans to club him to death. He puts up a hand in a desperate attempt to calm her down. "I was going to say, 'using your...uh, sonic-wrench.' That's all, I swear."

"No you weren't," Manthy growls.

Probably in an attempt to get as far away from her as possible, Cardyn walks the length of the truck and drops to one knee to peer underneath it. "Probably the drive shaft," he says with a macho false bravado I can tell he doesn't really feel. "I'll stay with you, Manthy. Help you get this thing fixed up."

She scowls at him and crosses her arms. "I don't need help."

"That's fine," he replies, leaping to his feet. "I don't know what

I'm talking about anyway. How about if I just watch, and you can enjoy my charming company while these three are off on their mission?"

"Your company is a lot of things," Manthy sneers. "Charming isn't one of them."

"It's better if he stays with you," I tell her. "We don't want to attract too much attention out there. We'll need to move fast, and Mr. Charming here will just get in our way."

Cardyn plunges his freckled hands deep into his pockets and stares at the ground. "I'm feeling pretty unloved at the moment."

"Don't worry, Card," I tell him, striding over and dropping a hand on his shoulder. "We still love you just as much as we always have."

"Thanks...I think?"

With a grin, I mime a tip of the hat and give him my best rolling-hand royal salute before turning back to Brohn and Rain.

"We should probably set out now, before the sun comes up and it gets too hot to function," Brohn says.

"Any idea how to get where we need to go?" Rain asks.

"I'm going to see if I can stay in contact with Render while we're on the move," I tell them. "Vail and Roland gave us enough information that I think I can pass it along to him. It won't be perfect, but it does include specific geographic locations in the city, so I think he can get us close. Besides, if what Vail said is true about this place being dangerous, we're going to need as many eyes on our backs as possible."

"Can you stay in contact with him for that long?" Rain asks. "Like, in his head?"

"Not sure. I've never tried to do it for more than a few minutes at a time. I could wind up getting pretty dizzy. It might even be painful. If I start to go wonky, you guys..."

"Don't worry," Brohn says. "I'll stick close and keep an eye on you."

"Thanks," I tell him as my cheeks heat up. Brohn's promise to look out for me is music to my ears. If I do pass out, there's no one whose arms I'd rather fall into.

I look around the garage until I locate a pair of sunglasses and pull them on. "In case my eyes go dark," I tell the others. "We don't want people asking questions about the weird raven-lady."

"Good point," says Rain.

As the other two are getting ready to leave, I pull Cardyn aside. "Please try not to annoy Manthy too much, okay?"

"Wouldn't think of it," he says with a sly smile. "I'll just be here if she needs help with anything. You know, if she needs me to fetch any tools or hold anything for her or, you know, tell her some totally hilarious jokes."

"Oh, God," I say with a massive eye-roll and a slap with my hand on the side of the truck. "Please just let her do what she needs to do to fix this thing, and don't bug her. We need this truck in working order, and I don't want to come back and find that the two of you have killed each other."

Cardyn crosses his heart with his finger. "I'll be every bit as sweet as an apple pie."

"And hopefully every bit as quiet as one, too," I say.

He sticks his tongue out at me.

"Yes," I say as I turn away. "Definitely Mr. Charming."

Leaving Cardyn and Manthy to get to work on the truck, Brohn, Rain and I head out of the dingy garage.

It's a short hike the rest of the way down the road toward the Reno city limits. In less than an hour, we find ourselves stepping into what feels like the middle of an old Western movie.

I SCAN MY TATTOOS AND CONNECT WITH RENDER. FROM HIS location high in the sky, he helps us navigate the dirt roads and plank-covered sidewalks of Reno, sending me signals—sometimes images, other times feelings—that let us know which roads to take and which ones to avoid. Some parts of the town are deserted. In others, people walk along, most with their heads down. Although we do get a few odd stares, for the most part, our hike is pretty uneventful.

Until we round a corner and Rain stops, points down the road, and says, "Look!"

A few thousand people are shuffling between endless rows of long tables at what looks like a massive farmer's market.

"No wonder the town's mostly deserted," Rain observes. "Seems like everyone's here."

"And the place we need to go is on the other side of that chaos," I say.

There are more people in this one place than we've ever seen in our lives. It's like every person from every bombed-out ghost town we passed during our months on the road has found their way here, to this square in this otherwise quiet town. I suggest this to Brohn, and he says that's probably exactly what happened.

"From what we've heard from people like Asha and Vail, it sounds like the only way to survive these days is in these bigger communities. The Recruiters made sure the little tucked-away towns like the Valta weren't the safe havens our parents thought they'd be." I can feel his bitterness on the air, and quietly reach over to grab his hand for a second. No, indeed. The Valta was no safe haven.

Rain stares out at the throng of busy and bustling people who flood the market in the square. "Do you think they cleared them all out and brought them all here because of people like us?"

"You mean to try to find more people with...abilities?" I ask.

"Yes."

I'm not sure if Brohn if shaking his head at Rain's extreme suggestion or at the insane possibility she might be right. "It's funny," he says with a cynical chuckle. "These people could've started out like us. All that time, we thought we were being kept safe when really we were all just being imprisoned. The government was keeping us caged until they could figure out which of us was worth saving while they killed off the rest."

"Great," I mutter. "Just what I've always wanted to be: a chicken in the big poultry farm of life."

Brohn gives me a sad half-laugh and starts walking toward the crowded market.

"I wonder if there will ever be quiet mountain towns again," Rain says sadly.

"Probably not," I reply as we follow Brohn down a small embankment and along a narrow foot-path leading to the busy square.

The area is wide and must be a mile deep with short, one and two-story buildings standing like blocky sentinels around its perimeter. The buildings are an odd combination of slick synth structures mixed in with old sandstone shops, bars, and some pretty unappealing-looking restaurants. I can also see a few clusters of moldy wooden crates under a giant tattered umbrella at what I think is supposed to be a makeshift café.

The patchy ground around the sidewalks, like the air itself, is a sickly and rutted mess. The hot sizzling air seems to have baked everything in the town to a crispy reddish-brown. Even the bustling people share the same look. Jammed into the massive square, most of them are covered nearly head-to-toe in scruffy boots, baggy jeans, and loose-fitting brown and yellow overcoats, but the exposed faces under the sea of cowboy hats are charbroiled and flaky-red.

Brohn leads us right into the square, where we find ourselves in the middle of overlapping cries of vendors selling their various wares. It's a sensory overload, almost too much to take in. Swarms of marble-sized flies buzz through the steaming air. Throughout the open market, there are tables piled high with scarves and wraps in a wild palette of colors and patterns. Metal racks lined up a hundred yards deep are filled with an array of blue jeans, earth-toned shirts, and long brown coats on hangers. People rifle through it all as sellers scramble after them, offering deals and picking discarded selections up from the ground. Other tables are lined with canvas sacks labeled by hand, the names of various seasonings and spices scrawled in black ink on off-white tags. A whole section of tables set up on one side of the square feature cases of pistols and endless racks of rifles.

Wedged in between two of those tables, a boy sits on a small stool with a large, oil-filled pot front of him. He flips brown and green shards of food high into the air, where they hover before landing back down in the pot with a splatter and sizzle of hot oil. To our left is a long table with cages filled with flapping and fluttering chickens. Billows of tiny white and brown feathers fill the air and mingle with the smells of feces and sweat.

Brohn reaches over and tugs my sleeve, leaning in close.

"Want to go say 'Hi' to some of your fellow poultry farm prisoners?"

I giggle, and a woman brushing past me gives me a nasty look before shuffling along to continue with her shopping.

Behind several of the long tables, vendors stand inside clear glass boxes. The boxes have a small, mesh-covered opening up near the vendors' faces and another opening down at table level, which is where they seem to be accepting big silver coins, lumps of black or gold pebbles, or, in some cases, small glass bottles of what looks like water, in exchange for their goods.

"I wonder if water is currency here," Rain muses, gesturing with her chin toward a woman who has maybe two dozen of those little bottles tucked into a leather belt around her waist. "If so, those tap-coins Vail and Roland gave us won't be of much use." The woman catches us looking at her and hisses at us to "Scratch off!"

At one of the tables, lined with bright red plastic gas cans, a man is screaming at a mousy-looking vendor. "You trying to cheat me?" the bigger man says. His bushy eyebrows clamp together in a scowl, and his long beard bristles as he stabs wildly with his finger to a spot somewhere on the other side of the market. "I can get a better price from Gusher, right over there!"

"Then you should go do that," the vendor says calmly. Not only does the smaller man not seem intimidated by the person shouting at him, he doesn't even really look up at the raving red-faced client who now has the side of his fist pressed up against the glass. "I'm offering the best price I can," the shop-keeper sighs. His breathy voice is barely audible from behind the glass and over the bubbling noise of the crowd. "Gusher'll tell you the same thing. Probably already has. Costs go up. Prices go up. It's called capitalism. I'd tell you to go look it up, but my guess is that reading isn't your strong suit."

In a flurry of his cape-like trench coat, the bearded man whips a gun from a holster just under his jacket and fires at the vendor. The explosion of gunfire startles everyone as the bullets ping off the glass, leaving nothing but smoky patches where they hit.

The vendor ducks, and most of the shoppers go scrambling for cover. A bunch of men around us drop to one knee and whip out their own guns, pointing them at the shooter, then at the vendor's table, then at each other. The vendor, still crouched behind his bullet-proof glass shield, whips out an old-style sawed-off shotgun of his own and aims it at the bearded man, who takes a step back but doesn't lower his gun.

I hit the ground with Brohn and Rain, and the three of us crawl under the nearest table.

When it's apparent that no one has the stomach for a full-on street massacre, the men all stand, holster their weapons, and go on about their business. Everyone else gets to their feet and goes back to their shopping and shouting, like nothing's happened. It's business as usual. No one seems too shaken by the extraordinary events.

No one, that is, except for me, Brohn, and Rain. The three of us stay crouched down even as the rest of the crowd returns to their shuffling along around us, many of them casting annoyed grunts in our direction or growling at us to stand up and get out of their way.

Scanning the area like baby mice about to emerge for the first from their burrow, we stand slowly and start walking again. This time, we stay a little closer to each other, our heads on a swivel and our bodies tense with anticipation of the next shoot-out.

We don't have to wait long.

About twenty feet away, two men—one with a threadbare jean-jacket, one bare-chested—get into a shoving match, with one claiming the dusty leather trench coat on the ground is his while the other swears he just bought it off the rack behind them. They pull their guns, each firing at the same time. A bullet rips through the bare-chested man's shoulder, and he staggers back, knocking down one of the racks of coats and falling into it in a bloody tangle. The man in the jean-jacket drops to his knees and pitches forward, his face slamming into the hard-packed ground as a thick pool of dark blood oozes from his head into the dirt. With the bare-chested man groaning in pain and sinking into the coats like they're quicksand, a quick-stepping roundish woman takes advantage of the jostling and shouting onlookers, scoops the dusty jacket up from the ground, and skitters away into the crowd as some of the bystanders laugh and cheer her on.

"Did you see that?" Brohn calls out to me over the din of the crowd. "It's like the Old West out here!"

Brohn, Rain and I are now shoulder-to-shoulder-to-shoulder, but it's quickly gotten so loud and crowded in the market that I feel like we might get swallowed up by the swarm, like three twigs lost in the Colorado rapids. "If it weren't for some of those synth-steel buildings," Brohn shouts, "and the newer model Sig Sauers and plasma pistols some of these people are carrying, this could easily be two hundred years ago."

Rain offers up a disdainful smirk. "Always nice to see human evolution take a giant step backward."

I remember what Hiller said back in the Processor about Brohn, Manthy, and me being what she called an "evolutionary upheaval, or some glitch in the genetic code." It occurs to me for the first time that the world and I might be moving in exact opposite directions. I point this out to Brohn and Rain as the three of us duck into a small alleyway to re-group and get our bearings.

"Sounds like a good scenario for us, anyhow," Brohn says with a relieved gasp, looking back out at the crowd of chaos we just slipped away from. "I don't think I'd want to be moving in the same direction as these people."

"At this rate," Rain says, her hands on her knees as she takes some deep breaths to slow her pounding heart, "they'll have devolved into something Medieval by the time we get out of here."

Rain's right. In looks and feel, not to mention the *violence as the first resort* vibe, this place really is like the gun culture of the Old West. Of course, what little I know about the Old West comes from a single book called *The History of Cowboys in Film*, which I read when I was about ten years old. I've never seen an actual film other than the videos projected onto the viz-screens back home, but I know what they are, and our cowboy book gave us a look into part of our country's violent past and the myths that sprang from it. The book was filled with pictures of the Old West, real and from the movies, that support Rain's theory.

Boots. Hats. Dusty roads. And, naturally, bloody street duels.

"There does seem to be some pretty serious vigilante justice going on," I pant. We haven't really been running, but my adrenaline is through the roof. I'm leaning against the smooth beige stones of the building's wall, silently grateful for the shade, the relative quiet, and being able to take the time I need for my heartbeat to drop back down from its jack-hammer rate.

"The only thing missing are horses," Brohn says through a crooked grin.

"Too bad," Rain says with an exaggerated sigh. "I'd love to be able to ride a real horse again."

We're gathered in a close clump in the alleyway now. I've lost any connection I had to Render, who's flown off to somewhere in the distance, though I'm not sure where or why. He might have been startled by the gunfire, or else bothered by the constant din of the market. Or he might also just be feeling hungry, adventurous, or at his wits' end.

I have to remind myself that he's gone through all the same turbulence we have. The Valta was his home, too, and now, like us, he's a homeless straggler struggling to survive.

"We need to find Vail's contact, get that part for the truck, and get out of here," Brohn says. "It's only a matter of time before we look at someone the wrong way and wind up with our bodies full of bullet holes."

Slipping back out of the alley and toward the edge of the busy market, we dodge and weave our way past hundreds of hostile looks and, frankly, some less than floral odors.

We're just negotiating our way through a gaggle of twittering women standing outside a bar when I hear Render issuing a series of urgent *kraas!* from somewhere up above. At first, I'm shocked to be able to hear him above this ear-splitting din, but his voice has become so ingrained in my brain I could probably pick it up from a mile away and over ten times this much noise. I grab Brohn and Rain by the backs of their jackets and point up to where Render is perched on the top edge of the building across the way. He beats his wings but doesn't take off. Instead, he bobs his head, gesturing with his beak at the doorway in front of us.

"Well," Rain says looking up at the nondescript building, "I guess Render's found our place."

"I guess," I say. "Though I don't know how he could possibly know for sure."

Brohn looks up, shielding his eyes against the sun with his hand and trying not to get run over by the pedestrians shoving their way past us. "With the information Vail gave us, plus whatever weird instincts your bird up there is developing lately, I'm willing to give him the benefit of the doubt."

"So, we go in?" I ask, but Rain is already striding toward the open door, so we don't exactly have a choice.

She leads us through the doorway and plunges right into the middle of a crowd of sweaty, jostling people. Like the market outside, this place is a noisy tangle of bobbing heads and flailing limbs. Only in here, cut off from the stale but open air, the funk of sweat and unwashed bodies presses down on us like a tangible weight, as does the oppressive pulse of the deafening music blasting our ears and vibrating through the floors.

I clamp my hand over my nose and try to keep up with Rain,

who's zigzagging her way toward the bar. She may only be five feet tall, but she marches forward like she's a fearless giant in a teeming world of baby elves. Brohn takes me by the hand as we do our best to keep up with her. The last thing we need now is to get separated in this strange, archaic place. As Rain weaves deftly through the crowd, I notice we're getting some curious stares along the way. It might be that we're teenagers in a room filled with adults. Or it could be that we seem to be the only ones without handguns slung in holsters around our waists or rifles strapped across our backs.

As I look down, I realize that it's most likely the way we're dressed that's drawing confused eyes. Most people in here look like the pictures of the cowboys from my old book. The three of us, on the other hand, are in the outfits Vail supplied us with back in Salt Lake City, where clothing styles seem to be far tidier and more conservative. Our combination of dark green camo cargo pants, black compression shirts, and pocketed combat vests is probably pretty confusing to this crowd. I'm sure we must look half-military, half-mountain climber, and all stranger.

But stares or no stares, we don't have a choice but to follow Rain on her quest.

Shouldering her way through the crowd of lurching dancers, Rain marches right up to the bar and edges over to the burly bartender, who's busy chatting in a relatively empty space with a bored-looking woman who's puffing lazily on a cigar. They're quite the pair: His thick shoulders and broad chest threaten to snap every stitch in his yellowing, used-to-be-white tuxedo shirt. The sleeves of his poor strained shirt are cuffed up to reveal cylindrical, wrist-less forearms like marble columns.

I raise an eyebrow when I see that he has tattoos similar to mine peeking out from around his elbows. The woman he's talking to is oddly pretty, with wide-set eyes and high cheek-bones on a creased bronze face. She's draped in layers of silk scarves, her long hair cascading in silver, blue, and black waves down to her waist. Her wrists are heavy with a colorful array of beaded bracelets. A pair of thigh-high black boots complete her odd ensemble, and I can't help wondering if she's a sorceress or a stripper.

"We're looking for Saucy," Rain shouts to the big man over the thunder of music, the clink of glasses, the screech of chairs against the wooden floor, and the general cacophony of the crowd behind us.

The man sneers at Rain and turns back to the strange cigar-smoking lady, who continues to stare off at her reflection in the spotted and fractured mirror behind the bar. Brohn leans forward to call out to the man. "Do you know where we can find Saucy?"

"Scratch off," the man growls and flicks his thumb back toward the door.

A wide-bodied man in a denim jacket shoulders his way past Brohn with a dismissive grunt and shouts across the bar for the other man to give him "a stoup of toxic." The bartender pours what I hope is beer into a big metal mug and pushes it toward the client, who growls a half-hearted "Thanks" before disappearing back into the crowd.

"Vail sent us," I shout to the bartender. "Vail and Roland?"

"Never heard of 'em," the man barks.

"Of course you haven't," the woman snaps at him. She's suddenly alert, like she just woke up from a trance. "We only keep you around for the important stuff, like stocking the bar and keeping mice out of the supply closet."

The man hangs his watermelon-sized head and steps away to busy himself at the other end of the bar.

"You're looking for me," the woman says, tapping herself on the chest as she turns our way. "I'm Saucy." She sucks hard on the wet end of her fat cigar and exhales a thick gray plume of smoke into the air. "Vail sent me a synch-comm yesterday. Said a bunch of gung-ho teenagers would be showing up, looking for a thermonic sensor cartridge and possibly directions to San Francisco. She called you a 'Conspiracy.'" Stone-faced, she looks from one of us to the other. "I'm assuming that's you, because teenagers and this place don't exactly mix, if you know what I'm sayin'."

"Yes, ma'am," Brohn says.

"Ma'am?" the woman chuckles. "You really aren't from around here, are you?"

"Reno?" I ask. "Or Salt Lake City?"

"Earth," she replies with a snort.

As I stare at her, still wondering what to make of the sarcastic, cigar-smoking, half-helpful, half-nasty stranger, she stands up and leans way over the bar to grab something from the other side. As she stretches over and down, her shirt and her layers of scarves lift up to reveal a large black bird tattooed on her lower back. It's got its wings spread wide, with a bunch of smaller black birds in various stages of flight behind it.

She heaves herself back up with a grunt, spins around, and slaps a fluorescent blue stick into my hand.

"There it is," she announces way more loudly than I think someone should who's helping out virtual strangers who happen to be on the run from secret government agents.

"This is the thermonic sensor cartridge?" I ask, practically in a whisper.

"It's not a stoup of toxic," Saucy shouts with a wrinkled nose and a crooked grin full of snark.

"What do we owe you?" Brohn asks, not wanting to look this particular gift horse too carefully in the mouth. He pats the pockets of his pants and vest. "We don't really have any..."

"She knows," Saucy says, looking at me with a hard stare that looks kind of flirtatious—but also slightly deadly. "And I suspect the rest of you do, too."

Suddenly I remember what Vail told us before we left. "You really...want Render's DNA?" I ask with a swallow. The thought of it makes me sick.

"Yes. Assuming Render is the raven I've been hearing so much about. Don't look so surprised, girlie! He's nearly as famous as you are. They may have herded us all into their little cattle camps and destroyed what's left of our society, but people still find ways to communicate. It's what separates us humans from idiots and inanimate objects."

"I just don't see how Render's DNA is going to help you—"

"...to save the world?" Saucy lets out a laugh. "You've seen what it's like out there. And hell, you've seen what it's like in here. Broken. All of it. I plan on doing my part to help rebuild it. And DNA, in case you missed this little tidbit during your self-schooling sessions back in your little mountain town, is the building block of life."

I look from Brohn to Rain, but their expressions are as confused-looking as mine must be. Still, this woman, eccentricities and idiosyncrasies aside, has provided the device and the information we need to get to our final destination. What harm could a little feather do?

I reach into my inside jacket pocket and pull out the long black feather Render let me extract from his chest before we set out for the city. I hand it to Saucy and say a silent prayer that he's not still irritated with me for the whole plucking process.

Saucy slides the feather under her nose like she's sampling an expensive cigar. She closes her eyes and inhales before slipping it into a glass test tube she's taken out of her inside jacket pocket.

Brohn raises an eyebrow and leans forward to ask, "So, are we even?"

"Even as Steven. Steady as Freddy. Listen, Vail tells me you're trying to catch on with the Insubordinates."

"Insubordinates?" I ask.

"The San Francisco underground. Holed up like rats in one of the few complete and cultivated cities left in the country. So you're off to expose the truth, fight the government's army, take down the evil dictators in charge, bring back our democracy, and save the world? Your basic teenage quest?"

"I'm not sure about all that. We..." Rain starts to say, but Saucy stops her with a raised hand.

"You do anything that helps take down President Krug, and I'll be happy. If you die along the way—and you'd hardly be the first—then all I'm out is the price of a thermonic sensor cartridge," she shouts, pointing to the bartender, "which Gus over there lifted for me anyway, so no skin off my nose."

Gus tips his head at Saucy and goes back to pulling on a lever to fill a huge metal mug of beer for a squinty-eyed man with a beat-up cowboy hat and a blond dreadlocked beard, who's seated at the other end of the bar.

"Thanks," Brohn says. "We really appreciate—"

Saucy raises her hand again and blows a contorting cloud of putrid smoke into the air. "Let's not do the whole gratitude, exchange of pleasantries thing. I'm here because I value an ideal above my personal safety, and I'm hurt enough to want revenge and crazy enough to think I can put something good back into the world. Sound familiar?"

The three of us nod in unison like kittens hypnotized by a dangling bangle.

"Before we go," I say, shaking off the trance, "your tattoo?"

"Which one? I've got twenty-two of them."

"The one on your back. The birds."

"The ravens?"

"So, they *are* ravens."

"What else would it be?"

"I don't know. Crows, maybe?"

"My dear Kress," Saucy says, "a bunch of crows would be a Murder. I'm a business-owner and a facilitator. Occasionally, I'm a pot-stirrer and a thermonic sensor cartridge supplier. But one thing I'm not is a murderer. Besides," she adds with a knowing wink, "you can't have a Conspiracy without a shared secret or two."

Before we have a chance to ask her what she means, she hops to her feet and strides into the crowd, the top of her head bobbing like a beach toy on the water, until she disappears from view through a door on the far side of the room.

"What the hell was that all about?" Rain asks. "What secret? And why does she want Render's DNA, anyhow?"

I shrug like I don't know and don't care, but the truth is, I think I might know, and I very *definitely* care.

"Come on," I say. "Let's head out."

We emerge into the open air from the reeking, noisy, and overcrowded bar. A man whistles at Rain as he passes. "Well aren't you a pretty little thing?" Ignoring him, we keep walking, leaving the man and all of our recent problems behind.

Or so we think.

20

OUT OF THE CORNER OF MY EYE, I SEE A HAND LATCH ONTO RAIN'S shoulder and whip her around.

The hand belongs to the stranger, who has a kind face but clearly unkind intentions. Unlike most of the other people we've seen here, his teeth are white and straight. He's smiling as if he's a kind uncle about to offer advice to his wayward niece. "When someone pays you a compliment, the polite thing to do is to show your gratitude."

"We don't want any trouble," Brohn says, stepping protectively between Rain and the man.

"Looks like what I want and what you *don't* want just aren't lining up today," the man says evenly, his smile morphing ominously into a curled-lip sneer. He's decent-looking with a slim build and overall pleasant features. His clothes and fedora are old but clean. Even his thin tie looks newly ironed. In this small but crowded city of big bravado, random gun violence, mysterious women, and large, menacing men, this guy seems oddly out of place. Like a banker in a bull-fighting ring.

He looks from me to Rain before turning his attention back to Brohn. "Looks like you're outnumbered. Perhaps you'll allow me to take one of these lovely young ladies off your hands?" He reaches over and runs his hand down Rain's straight black hair like he's sampling material for a new suit.

She rewards him with a straight punch to the face that sends him reeling.

A trickle of blood drips from his nose, and his eyes tear up, but he doesn't fall down. Instead, he straightens up and lunges right at Rain.

Any pretense of civility has disappeared from his eyes and has been replaced with red fury. He balls up his fist and goes to take a swing at Rain, but Brohn intercepts him with a quick, sharp jab to the jaw. The man staggers, and Brohn cocks his fist, ready to finish him off, but the man is faster and stronger than he looks. In a flash, he's whipped out a gun from a holster under his jacket. He charges at Brohn, the gun clamped in his hand with his arm fully extended. Startled, Brohn stumbles backward into me. Despite all evidence we've seen to the contrary, I'm hoping the gun is for show, just a bluff, but the man squeezes the trigger and a shot whizzes past my ear, right between me and Brohn.

The man looks like he might really try to kill us right here in the middle of the sidewalk, only to leave us as more casualties of Reno's insane vigilante justice.

But just as he's squeezing the trigger to take a second shot, a black flash whips down out of nowhere, a missile aimed squarely at the shooter's head.

It's Render, and he's in full protective mode. Leading with his sharp talons, he slashes at the man's face, raking his claws down his cheeks and neck. Startled, the man loses both his hat, and, more importantly, his grip on his gun, which clatters to the uneven wooden planks of the sidewalk. In a flurry of his powerful wings, Render launches himself back into the air, stabbing with his razor-sharp beak as he goes.

With one hand pressed against his eye, blood seeping through his fingers, the man leans down and picks up his gun. Spinning, staggering, and shrieking in agony, he fires wildly into the air.

I scream out to Render, but it turns out I don't need to worry. The guy doesn't come anywhere close to hitting him. Render banks steeply to the right and swoops around in the blink of an eye to renew his attack. The man drops his gun again and flails wildly, as the raven carves deep red trenches into his foe's hands and forearms.

Rattled now, the man stumbles back a full ten yards as Render circles around behind him, dragging his claws along the back and sides of the man's head and neck. The man shrieks. By now a crowd is gathering to watch him drop to his knees, his arms clamped over his head in pain and terror. Blindly, he crawls back toward us, fumbling for his gun, which Rain kicks away. In the same smooth motion, she delivers a punishing strike to the kneeling man's face with the heel of her hand. This time, there's no simple trickle of blood. Instead, his nose releases a full-blown river.

Three men, two with beards and one with a face full of buttery-yellow stubble, burst out of the bar. Moving as one, they draw their guns from holsters under their jackets and prepare to fire at Render who, satisfied that the first man is no longer a threat, is streaking into the sky. The three men must be friends with our enemy, because one of them stops to check on his wounds as the other two fire wildly up at Render, who is engaged in a skillful evasive maneuver. This isn't his first rodeo, and it's highly unlikely that a couple of half-drunk idiots are going to have any success against him with their pistols.

Still, I'm strongly considering lunging at the two shooters before they can get a bead on their target when Brohn locks his hand around my upper arm and points down a nearby alleyway just off the main road. "Kress, Render's fine! But we need to get out of here!"

I nod, and Rain and I race after him as he tears down the

alleyway. We're greeted by a maze of smaller alleys and laneways, all branching off in different directions. Overflowing garbage bins, towers of precariously-stacked wooden skids, and piles of jagged sheet metal line the already-narrow alleys and make it impossible to tell which direction might be the safest.

Two little boys push their heads through the rails of a second-floor balcony just above us.

"Don't mind us," one of the boys calls down. "We just want to watch you die!"

This sends both boys into peals of high-pitched laughter, hand-slapping, and shoulder-punching.

"Great," Brohn says. "Thanks."

"Forget them," Rain squeals. "Which way?"

Brohn gestures with his thumb back the way we came. "Any way but that one!"

When I spin back, I immediately see what he means. The three men have apparently given up on shooting Render or helping their bleeding friend, and are pursuing us at top speed down the alley. Their trench coats waft out behind them as they sprint toward us. Once they're close enough, they raise their weapons and start firing.

We duck and scramble away as bullets blast fist-sized holes into the brittle walls around us. Dodging around piles of garbage and scrapped building materials, we bolt down the alley to our left. It leads us to a small, cluttered courtyard, which branches off into three more alleyways. Brohn sprints down the middle lane this time, leading us to a low metal fence, which we clamber over with the three armed men kicking metal garbage bins aside behind us and closing in fast.

The last thing I recall is the crack of bullets filling the air around us. Then the world goes pure white, before fading to a deep, inky black. The walls of the narrow alley go fuzzy and then disappear along with Brohn, Rain, and everything else.

I'm sure I've been shot, and now I'm drifting off into a slow, blurry death.

It doesn't hurt as much as I thought it would, but I don't have time to figure out why as I fade into the nebulous vacuum of unconsciousness.

I DON'T KNOW how much time has passed, but when things start to return to focus, I'm greeted by Brohn's and Rain's smiling faces. Cardyn and Manthy are just behind them, leaning over their shoulders. I rub my eyes with the heels of my hands as the details of my surroundings continue to take shape.

After a deep breath and a painful squint, I take a long look around: My friends. The smooth concrete floor. The work-benches. The truck that brought us all here.

We're back in the garage.

"But how…?" I begin to ask.

"I told you I'd keep an eye on you," Brohn says as he helps me to my feet. I need to lean on him as I look around in a daze.

"Am I dreaming?"

Rain says, "I don't think so."

"Then I'm dead?"

Cardyn shakes his head and laughs. "I don't know what Heaven looks like, but I seriously doubt that it's a crummy garage in a desert just outside the Reno city limits."

"How did I, I mean…how did we get here? I don't remember anything after getting shot."

"First of all," Brohn says, "you didn't get shot. None of us did. Those idiots couldn't hit the broad side of a barn with a bazooka."

"Um, Brohn?" Rain says. I look over to see her eyeing the back of his shirt. "I'm not so sure about that."

Brohn spins around to reveal that his shirt has a hole in it, precisely the size of a bullet. He yanks it off, only to reveal a pink mark on his skin, no bigger than a pencil eraser.

"You were hit," I say, stupefied. "But how...?"

Brohn's fingers are on his lower back, feeling for a wound that doesn't exist. "I don't know," he tells me, his eyes wide with confusion. After a moment he pulls his shirt back on. "It must've been something else," he says dismissively, and I get the distinct impression that he doesn't want to talk about it. "I suppose I must have caught it on something."

"As for the rest of it," Rain tells me, apparently willing to accept Brohn's flimsy explanation for now, "you can thank Render for saving us."

"Render?"

"Apparently, he initiated your connection. Your eyes did that weird thing where they turn pure black, and before we knew it, you were ordering us to follow you. Your voice was pretty weird, Kress."

"Ordering you to...?"

"Military command-style," Brohn informs me, clearly impressed. "No doubts. No hesitation. You and Render together make an excellent General."

"You were zigging and zagging through those alleys like you'd lived there all your life," Rain says. "You led us into a creaky old building, up some stairs, down a hallway, onto the roof, down a fire escape, out an alleyway, past a bunch of soldiers, through the entire town, back to the desert, and right back here to the garage, without a single other shot being fired."

"I did all that?" My head is swimming as I try to access a memory, to recall any of it. But all I can see is blankness, like a white sheet of paper.

"We wouldn't be having this conversation if you hadn't."

"And it was Render leading the way?" I ask.

Brohn strokes his chin like he's deep in thought. "Well," he says, "unless there's another magical black bird you know and can connect with, then yes, I'd say it was probably him."

I rub my temples with my fingertips. My friends are still coming into focus, and I can make out some more of the detail of the garage around us.

The truck is there, of course. Two of its big side panels are off, exposing a complicated network of filaments and motherboards underneath. It's also up on jacks, and its two back wheels are off and leaning up against the garage wall. Brohn and Rain hook their hands under my arms and slowly lift me up from the chair where I've apparently been slumped for I don't know how long.

Cardyn says, "Welcome back to the land of the living!" while Manthy walks back over to the truck, quietly wiping her hands on a grease-stained towel.

I glance up at Cardyn and tip my head in Manthy's direction. "Has she been able to fix whatever was broken on that thing?"

"I think so. She hasn't exactly been chatty with me while you three were off on your adventure. But she seems to know what she's doing. Don't ask me how."

"And you gave her the thermonic sensor cartridge?"

"Brohn gave it to her. She seems to know what to do with it. Again—"

"I know," I say with a twisting smile. "Don't ask you how."

Cardyn beams at me and somehow manages to throw his arms around me, Brohn, and Rain at the same time in a giant bear-hug. "It was very nice of the three of you to not get killed."

"It was our pleasure," I mumble into his chest.

Rain laughs and says she's going to see if Manthy needs a hand with the truck repairs. Cardyn decides to tag along with her, leaving Brohn and me alone in front of one of the thick-legged wooden work benches.

My head is still a bit cloudy, and I must look woozy, because Brohn drags a chair over and encourages me to sit down.

"I'm okay," I tell him. "Actually, it feels good to stand up for a second. How long was I out?"

Brohn pushes some tools aside and hops up onto the work bench. "It took us twenty minutes or so just to get back out of town. Another twenty or thirty to make our way back to the garage. Then you were out for another hour or so after we tried to revive you."

"Revive me?"

"Cardyn thought you were in some kind of coma. Maybe sleep-walking or something."

"You say I was unconscious…or whatever I was…for another hour?"

"About. But you were breathing just fine. Normal pulse. You even had this cherubic little smile. Card said you looked like you were keeping a happy secret."

"I don't think *I'm* the one with the secret."

"You mean Render, right?"

"He can't initiate our connection. I mean, not like that. I never thought he could, at least."

"I'm going to go out on a limb and say that yes, I think he can. Not only that, I think maybe he's even more psychic than we thought."

I stare at Brohn for a second, trying to determine if he's teasing me. But he looks as serious as I've ever seen him. He pushes aside some more tools and pats the workbench, inviting me to join him. Overtaken by another wave of confusion, I do as he suggests.

Brohn stares over to where the others are fiddling and banging around with the truck.

"So listen, I've been thinking about something."

For a moment I wonder if he's talking about the mysterious hole in his shirt and welt on his back. But as he stares into my eyes, somehow I know what he's talking about. "You've been thinking about the dead soldiers and the girl from from the military base where we met Vail and Roland."

"Actually, yes. The ones you saw."

"The ones Render saw," I correct him.

Brohn shrugs. "I mean, what if he was seeing something from the past? Or maybe even from the future? The people you say he saw could have been killed days before we got there. Or a year ago. It's even possible they're going to be killed in those barracks today or tomorrow, or a year from now."

"Render's just a bird," I say. "A clever one. But he's not a fortune teller, Brohn."

"You also say he can't initiate your connection, and yet, here we are. All I'm saying is that whatever you have with him seems to be evolving into something bigger."

Ugh. There's that word again. *Evolving.* In my mind, it doesn't mean progress. It means being left behind while some strange ability I never asked for takes over and turns me into something other than myself.

I'm just getting ready to object to the whole idea when, over in the middle of the garage, the truck wheezes, sighs, and then bellows with great confidence to life.

Brohn and I jump a little and look over to where Manthy is holding up a handful of frayed green wires attached to a thin silver cylinder like she's just plucked a metal carrot from the ground. "The solar cell was fried," she announces loud enough for all of us to hear.

"And?" Brohn calls over to her.

"And it's okay. I installed the thermonic sensor cartridge you brought back and rerouted the signal to the drive-chain patch." I have no idea what she's talking about. But she seems to know, so that's good enough for me.

"And?" Brohn asks again.

Manthy wipes her hands on a grease-stained rag. "It works. It'll get us to San Francisco."

K. A. RILEY

Hearing the pronouncement that our vehicle has a clean bill of health, Cardyn and Rain start dancing around like little kids. Cardyn goes to give Manthy a hug, but he's met with a hand to his chest and a vicious glare, both of which stop him in his tracks.

Hoping to defuse the situation, Brohn and I hop down from the work bench and walk over to thank and congratulate Manthy, who looks at us like we're crazy before heading over to snap the access panels back into place on the side of the truck.

"I can't believe I'm saying this after everything that's happened, but it looks like things are working out," Rain practically sings. "All we have to do now is make it to San Francisco, find this elusive underground movement, reveal what we know, make use of what we've learned, and, you know, save the world."

"All without getting killed," Cardyn adds.

"Yes," I agree enthusiastically. "Staying alive is a vital part of this plan. Let's get out of here then, shall we?"

We all pile into the truck, Brohn eases behind the wheel, and we drive back out onto the road, happy to be done with this archaic and anarchic town, and happier still to be escaping with our lives.

21

ABOUT FOUR HOURS LATER, BROHN SLOWS THE TRUCK TO A STOP. Rain leans forward into the cab to ask him what's going on.

"There's no more road," Brohn says, pointing to the steep drop-off in front of us.

He's right. Our road has ended. Literally. The buckled pavement has come to an abrupt stop at a deep trench dug into the earth about twenty feet ahead. On the far side of the trench, maybe a hundred yards across, are some sections of fencing and old laser-wire. The barrier doesn't look particularly solid, though. Here and there, I can see a few huge gaps, and much of the fence looks pointless and rusted with age.

"I guess no one cares if people go in or out anymore," Rain observes.

"We'll have to go the rest of the way on foot," I say. "We should stash the truck somewhere first, though."

Brohn manages to pull in behind a broad rock formation just off the road, and we set about camouflaging the vehicle as best we can with scrub-brush and tangles of dried vines from a nearby cluster of struggling vegetation.

When the truck is as hidden as it's going to get, the five of us walk over to the edge of the trench and scan the distance to the other side.

"Looks passable," Rain declares as she drops to slide down the embankment.

We follow her down and cross the rocky span before making our way to the other side, where we clamber up, brush the red dust from our clothes and take a look around at San Francisco.

Or at least what we *think* is San Francisco.

It turns out that the so-called "complete and cultivated" city that was supposed to be our final destination is actually just a long stretch of rickety wooden and metal shelters, endless rows of domed orange tents, with open sewers cutting through the middle of it all. A mountain range of garbage—heaping and steaming under the hot sun—encircles the dying shantytown.

A few people straggle here and there in the spaces between the orange tents, walking slowly along the dirt footpaths. A few older folks—both men and women—have congregated in the shade under awnings built over some of the entranceways.

An enormous, half-built tower lurks way off in the distance. Tall metal spires jut out of its clunky red and brown base. It lords over the entire region like an angry ruler casting a venomous eye on his pathetic subjects.

"It's another one of those Arcologies," Rain says, squinting into the distance. "There's so much poverty here. I wonder if those things will be the cure?"

"More likely they're the cause," Brohn growls. He told me once that he hates inequality. He said that it always leads to more and more injustice, though I suspect that he got the idea from his father. It's not like we've ever known wealth. We grew up in a town full of children, fending for ourselves with scrap-metal and few supplies. Our entire lives have consisted of the purest form of equality: complete, pervasive, and abject poverty.

Before Brohn has time to launch into an angry oration, though, Card announces that he's hungry and is starting to wonder if any of the rancid garbage bobbing along in the open sewers has any nutritional value.

"Only if you think it's nutritious to vomit and die," I tell him.

"How about that?" he says, ignoring my tone and gesturing to something up ahead.

When we all look to where he's pointing, our eyes land on a small roadside shack standing on its own between two of the domed orange tents. The shack's sides are rusted corrugated metal, barely strong enough to hold up what looks like a cardboard roof covered in some kind of clear plastic tarp.

"I don't know if that's a restaurant," I reply. "It could be someone's house. Either way, I'm not really sure we should go barging in there." The memory of being chased and shot at in Reno just a few hours ago is still fresh, and it's an experience I don't care to repeat. Especially if it means losing hours in some weird coma-like state.

Card doesn't seem to care one way or the other. "I'll take my chances," he says.

Before the rest of us have time to agree or object, Cardyn is marching over to the wobbly little structure, clutching his stomach with both hands and grumbling about how hungry he is.

He leans over the wooden plank that apparently serves as a counter and sticks his head all the way into the opening.

"Hello? Anyone here? Especially anyone with something to eat?"

I slide up next to him and take a quick peek into the interior of the small shed. There are small, fat canvas sacks lined up like bird's eggs along a slanted shelf. A dozen or so glass jars of different sizes and shapes and filled with orange and red powder sit in a neat row on the shelf just below that. Something that looks like a cross between a giant salamander and a skinny racoon hangs dead by its back legs from a hook on the ceiling.

"Let me guess," a woman's voice calls out from right behind us. "Lost and hungry?"

Startled, we whip around.

The woman is frail, and she leans on a slightly bent ski pole for support. Her long white hair is braided on either side and hangs down nearly to her elbows. She looks us over with silver-gray eyes.

"Both," Cardyn says.

"Is this San Francisco?" Brohn asks, stepping forward and half-shoving Cardyn out of his way in the process.

The woman gives Brohn a good long stare before shaking her head. "Oakland. San Francisco is that way." She points with a bony finger to a spot we can't quite see off in the distance.

Cardyn shoves his way back in front of Brohn. "I don't suppose we could...um, get something to eat? Is this your place?"

The woman nods and grimaces before marching past us to head over to the side of the shed, where she unlocks a padlock and opens a rickety door in the side of the structure. She reappears inside, presses her elbows onto the wooden counter, and stares out at us.

"Got trade?" she asks, leaning forward and squinting at me.

"Excuse me?"

"Eggs? Plant-scans? Marks?"

"I think she means tap-coins. Payment," Rain advises.

"Oh." I dig into my bag and extract a handful of the tap-coins we got from Vail and Roland back in Salt Lake City. "We have these," I say, offering her a small handful of the coins and hoping it's not too little to be insulting.

The woman fondles the coins in her palm and laughs. "Mostly people trade now. The I.D.S. went off-line a few years ago."

"What is the I.D.S?" Brohn asks, probably recalling that Vail had mentioned it back in Salt Lake City.

"The Implant Disbursement System." The woman says it like it's a question she's stupefied to be asking. "You really don't know the I.D.S?"

We all shake our heads in unison, and she laughs again. "Definitely hungry and *very* definitely lost. I think I get the picture," she says with a wink.

"What picture is that?" Rain asks.

"The one without the Order in it," she says with another wink. She reaches down and pulls out a stack of dented aluminum cups, which she lines up one by one on the splintered wooden counter between us. Turning her back to us, she grabs a large metal pot by one of its handles and lifts it with a grunt from the small heating element it's sitting on. She pulls a big silver spoon down from a hook just above her head and pivots to face us once again. Dipping the spoon into the pot, she ladles a helping of not-so-savory-looking white chunks floating in purple water into each of the cups.

"Tow-Stew," she says, tipping her chin toward the line of cups. "Ever had it?"

"Ew," Cardyn says to me, his nose wrinkled. "I'm not eating anything made out of toes."

I give him a dirty look and hope our hostess didn't hear him. Last thing we need is for her to get annoyed with us and leave us to starve.

"She said toadstools," I whisper to Cardyn behind my hand. I turn to the woman, smiling appreciatively. "We used to have Amanita Bisporigera back in the Valta where we come from," I reply. "But we didn't eat them. They're poisonous. We did eat the Aspen Oyster Mushrooms sometimes, but they made some of us sick."

Now it's the woman's turn to stare, and I'm wondering if I accidentally insulted her or if maybe I have something on my face. I run a hand along my cheek and dab at the corner of my mouth just to be on the safe side.

"What are you on about?" she asks.

I look from Brohn and Rain to Cardyn and Manthy, but they all just shrug. "I was just saying about how we had certain toad-stools where we come from."

Now the woman laughs again. "Not '*toadstools.*' This is tofu stew. You know? Stew made from tofu. Tow-stew."

"Oh," I blush.

Cardyn chuckles and gives me an elbow to the arm. "I guess we were both wrong."

Our host introduces herself as Caramella. She gives us each a small wooden spoon, and we sample the stew, slowly at first and then with gusto. It turns out to be surprisingly tasty. Of course, after living on scraps of protein flakes and vitamin supplements the past few days, our standards have dipped pretty low.

Caramella points us to an orange tent, which is attached to a shack similar to hers just down the path. "You'll want to talk to Tread."

"Tread?"

"He's a good guy. The kind of good guy who can help some good people like yourselves do some even better things." She leans in close and whispers, "You're the Seventeens, right?"

We stare at each other in stunned silence.

"You know about the Seventeens?" Rain asks.

"I know about the five of you. That is to say, I've heard of you. Used to be eight of you, right?"

"That's right," Brohn snaps. I put my hand on his upper arm to remind him not to let his emotions take over. Anger comes fast whenever we're reminded of the two friends we lost in the Processor.

"Sorry," I tell Carmella. "Touchy subject."

"Understood. I've lost my share, too."

"I'm confused, though. How did you hear about us?"

"Word gets around," she says. "We've been hearing stories about you for a while now. Tread and I thought you were made up. An invention."

"Nope," Cardyn mumbles through a mouth overflowing with the tow-stew. "Although there seems to be a lot of that going around."

"What's that?"

"Invention."

"What he means," Rain explains, "is that for the last several months, everything we thought we were, we weren't. And everything we thought was happening, wasn't."

"And now you're looking for answers?"

"Yeah," Card burbles before swallowing down the ocean of soup in his overfilled mouth. "And revenge."

Manthy mumbles something about Cardyn being a pig. I don't know if he hears her, but he drags his sleeve across his mouth and manages to remove most of the soup from his face.

Caramella looks us over like a proud parent. "Well, you may be confused about a lot of things. But knowing what you want doesn't seem to be one of them."

We finish our tow-stew and thank her before heading down the way to see if this Tread person is really going to be a help or just another hindrance we'll need to deal with. As we make our way from Caramella's shack down to his, we get some odd stares and the occasional nod from the tired-looking old folks sitting in the orange tents along the way.

Over on a little flat patch of land, a dozen or so kids are happily kicking a clunky-looking lump of plastic around. Although the landscape looks ravaged, it's nice to see kids playing. It's something we haven't seen since we were at the camp with Adric and Celia. Something about it gives me a dash of hope for the future.

We stop to watch for a minute. The kids are wary of us at first, but when they see we're not soldiers and that we're unarmed, they seem to figure out we're not worth interrupting their game over and jump back into their frantic scrambling and squealing. After another minute or two, Rain strides ahead, and the rest of us follow.

"That was us," Brohn says with one last look at the scampering kids. "A long time ago. Do you remember playing like that?"

I tell him, "Not really."

"No," he says. "You never really did join in those dumb games, did you?"

"I wanted to," I confess. "But I also *didn't* want to."

Brohn nods and takes my hand as we continue down the makeshift path. "Surprisingly, I know exactly what you mean. Always up in the lab with your father. Or standing off to the side somewhere after he...left."

"I thought you never noticed me back then," I say with a smile. "I'm always amazed when you tell me you knew what I was up to."

"Well," he says, throwing his million-dollar grin my way, "I notice you now, Kress. I don't think I could ever stop noticing you."

I stride the rest of the way to Tread's place with my hand in Brohn's and a flutter of delight in my heart.

TREAD TURNS out to be a bear of a man, nearly as big around as he is tall. After sampling the meager fare that passes for food around here, as tasty as some of it is, I'm not sure how anyone could ever manage to get so big on so little. Yet he's a mountain of a man, perched as he is on a bench seat that's been torn out of an old car. He's dressed in what looks like a repurposed café awning and big yellow rubber boots that go all the way up to his lumpy knees, which resemble two heaping piles of sunburned mashed potatoes. His eyes sparkle such a luminous blue that they look wet.

Oddly enough, he smells really good. Like flowers or perfume or something. Considering there are open sewers running through the shantytown and heaps of soggy garbage steaming in the sun, any pleasant smell is an equally pleasant surprise.

When we introduce ourselves, Tread nods knowingly. I can't speak for the others, but his lack of questions or surprise at seeing us gives me the creeps. I feel like the five of us have somehow become the subject of required reading in a war-torn world where people are resigned to their fate and where gossip is currency.

I'm not so sure it's a good thing. The last thing I ever wanted was for San Francisco's entire population to anticipate our arrival.

Tread tells us that the city has become central to a resistance movement. "They call themselves the Insubordinates," he says.

"Right. We've heard of them," Rain says, taking the lead for our peculiar encounter with this giant, heavily-sweating man. "Our friend Vail mentioned them."

Tread wipes his forehead with a brown cloth, which he then rings out onto the ground in front of us. "They thought they could bring peace by protesting the war. Well, that just put a target on their backs as big around as Yosemite National Park. No one wanted to support a bunch of do-gooders who support the Order."

"They don't sound like they're supporting the Order. Just opposing the war. Besides, there *is* no Order—is there?"

"You say 'tomato,' I say 'traitor.' No way President Krug was going to let anyone stand between him and his war."

"But the war's a myth. An illusion. Isn't it?" Rain's voice is starting to lose a little of its former conviction, as if Tread is making her doubt her own mind.

"Every war is an illusion," he replies. "They're based on what you want versus what you can actually get people to believe. I'd tell you to forget about whatever your mission here is, but I'm guessing you didn't come all this way to turn around and go back to wherever you came from."

"That'd be a good guess," Cardyn quips.

"Actually," Rain says, "where we came from isn't there anymore."

Tread gives her a long look. "You too?"

Rain nods, and Tread eyes the five of us again. More closely now, like he's seeing us for the first time. Finally, he wipes his eyes and his chin quivers. "Seems like everyone's lost someone."

"Some of us have lost everyone," Brohn replies in a tone that hurts my heart. I want to tell him he still has me, but I know perfectly well that I can't replace any of the family he's lost.

Tread makes a sweeping motion with his thick arm and scans the shantytown around us. "I wasn't born here. Many of us weren't. We were brought here 'for our own protection.' Came from Reno, I'm assuming?"

I tell him, "Yes."

"Reno is just one of what Krug's people are calling the 'New Towns.' More like concentration camps if you ask me. Supposed to be safe havens from the Eastern Order and the war. Pure cat piss. They're prisons is what they are, and don't you dare think otherwise. It's a consolidation of power, a way for Krug to keep millions of us jammed into cities filled with guns and drugs so we'll kill each other while the Wealthies live it up in the Arcologies and continue to blame us for all the ills of the world. Every corrupt government since the beginning of time swears it's only burning down the enemy villages in order to save them."

"But you're not the enemy," Rain protests. "Neither are we. This is our country. Our government. They're supposed to protect us."

Tread smiles at her and shakes his head, which causes several of his chins to wobble. "You have the power to change things, to influence people. To rebel. That makes you the enemy. As for the rest of us, we're just the innocent civilians caught in the middle. From what I hear, the five of you plan on doing something about that."

"Damn right!" Cardyn proclaims.

Tread smiles his amusement but nods his approval. "Do you know how to get where you're going next?"

"Um, not exactly," I say.

"We have a general idea," Rain says, pushing her shoulders back confidently.

"A general idea will usually end up with you getting yourselves *specifically* killed. I've got an old digi-grid in the back. It'll smooth the way for you a bit, anyway."

Tread heaves himself up. He's so big, it's like he has to move in shifts. Limping and jiggling away, he disappears into what looks like a small storage room in the back of the shed and begins clanging and rifling around through a bunch of old metal cabinets.

I pull Brohn aside. "Do you think we can trust him?" I whisper into his ear.

"Not sure. But I know I can trust you. What do you think?"

I look up to see him staring deep into my eyes as if he's trying to read me. The problem is that all I'm thinking about now is how handsome he is. His thick, dark hair and bright blue eyes. The stubble on his jaw. His broad shoulders. And those strong arms that have held me and made me feel safer than I ever have in my life.

"Actually, right now, you're making it pretty hard to focus," I admit.

He lets out a laugh. "I have faith in you, Kress. You have better instincts than any of us. What does your gut say?"

"My gut tells me this guy needs to meet Render."

I swipe my left index finger along the tattoos on my right wrist. Practically before I've finished the action, Render swoops down and alights on the top of the orange tent just next to Tread's.

I tap into Render's mind, and he taps into mine. The feedback loop is sometimes faint, sometimes painful. But this time, it's clear and calm. He doesn't seem to fear Tread, which means I don't have any reason to, either. My instincts may be good, but they're always better when they're combined with his.

When I've severed the connection, I turn back to Brohn, giving my head a shake to clear out the last bits of leftover sensory overlap. "We're good," I say with a hearty thumb's up. "Render's not sensing any warning bells or anything."

"I don't think I'll ever get used to seeing your eyes do that," Brohn says, a funny, crooked smile on his lips.

Cardyn stands behind me and puts his chin on my shoulder. "Nice work, Snoopy."

I elbow him in the stomach.

Tread returns with his digi-graph, which he sets on the end of the bench before plopping down himself. He flicks his fingers over the silver sphere, and it opens up like a flower. Another flick, and a blue map appears. He points out over the unending field of derelict half-houses, impromptu shelters, and flat expanses of rubble and debris then back to the holo-display floating in the air in front of us.

"San Francisco is here, just across the Bay. But you won't be able to get over there. Government sealed it off over a year ago."

"Sealed it off? You mean barricaded the whole city?" Rain asks.

"Like what they did with us," Cardyn says.

Tread tilts his head to the side like a dog hearing a noise whose source it can't quite identify.

"We're from a town called the Valta," Cardyn explains. We were behind a military barricade for most of our lives."

Tread shakes his head and lets out a knowing sigh. "Yeah. I've heard about the Valta. Well, I'll give Krug this much: He doesn't do anything halfway."

"Neither do we," I say. "Now, about getting across this Bay...?"

Now Tread offers up a full belly-laugh. "You kids are something else, aren't you?" When none of us says anything, he looks around like he's making sure no one's eavesdropping. "Okay. I'll play along. Seems like the San Fran rebels got in too deep and now they don't know how to get back out. They figured they'd claim the city and start a revolution. The revolution would spread, and all would be right with the world."

"But it didn't work out that way," Brohn says.

"Of course it didn't. Ideals are great in theory. Having principles, 'fighting for what's right,' answering to a higher calling… That stuff works all the time in the old movies. But have you ever seen an ideal turn an evil man into a kind one? Or a greedy man into a giving one? Ever seen an ideal stop a bullet?"

"No," I say. "But we've seen what happens when fear stops good people from trying."

"Fair enough."

Brohn's getting impatient, or maybe the talk of stopping bullets is agitating him. "The checkpoints," he growls as he points to the floating blue image of the city. "Can you get us into the city or not? Because if you can, we'll owe you big. If you can't, we'll find someone who can. Then we'll owe *them* big."

Tread puts up his hands and says, "Whoa" like he's reining in a horse. "I'm definitely your man. I can get you in. At least, I know someone who can. His name is Kammet. Staff Sergeant Dennis Kammet. He does some work as a transport and supply-chain coordinator, but his main claim to fame is that he's the sneakiest, cleverest bastard I've ever met. He's in with the Insubordinates right under his commanders' noses." He lets out another great big belly laugh and turns his head to the side to spit over the back of his car bench. "Kammet passes intel to the Insubordinates. Lets them know when there's going to be a raid or increased security at checkpoints when they need to move around in the city. He'll get you in. What I can't do is promise you'll like what you find. Or that you'll even survive it."

He flicks at the image, causing it to rotate lazily in the air. "This is a collection of intel we've been gathering for over a year now. It's not complete, but neither is the government's San Fran operation. They've got D.C. locked up back East. Bunch of New Towns, too. Chicago. Cincinnati. Philadelphia. Charlotte. Atlanta. New Orleans. Everyone packed tighter than a constipated rhino. Out here, they've got a lot of guns...but also a lot of flaws in their system and, frankly, some pretty poorly trained soldiers."

He points with his thick finger to a bunch of spots on the blue schematic that are lit up red, and others that blink a shimmering fluorescent green.

"The checkpoints here and here," he says, "are very strong. Lots of cameras, guards, redundancy security protocols. The works. Here and here, on the other hand...these are new installations. Glitchy operating systems, patchy security, untrained guards. They're tightening things up, but it's a slow go. The Insubordinates have kept them occupied and disoriented with their little diversion raids."

"And you think we can get in through one of these places?"

"Frankly, I don't know *what* you can do. But you seem to have a pretty good set of survival skills between the five of you. Let's see what you'll be looking at." He presses his fingertips together over one of the green spots on the flickering hologram and flicks them open, causing the area to expand to reveal more detail. The new expanded image floats above the main schematic, and Tread brushes at it to make it turn and spin as he tells us what we're looking at. "This is updated as of yesterday, so it should be accurate. Two cameras. Both off-line. A searchlight that's currently being repaired because it's not very bright. Two guards. Frankly, they're also not very bright. And a security gate with a high-end motion-detector, a weapons deployment system, and a coded access panel..."

"That doesn't sound good," Cardyn whines.

"...all going in *tomorrow*," Tread finishes with a smile.

"Then this is their weak spot right now?" I ask, kneeling down to get a closer look at the expanded image. The detail is excellent. Though, as Tread warned, it's patchy with gaps and blacked-out sections in places. But it's better than what we had before, which, of course, was nothing.

"It's weak. Maybe not weak enough. But you have one advantage."

"Which is?"

"The checkpoints are designed to keep people on the inside from getting out. They don't spend a lot of time worrying about anybody from the outside trying to get in. Frankly, who wants to sneak *into* a lion's den?"

"We're past doing what we want to do," I say. "We're ready to do what we *need* to do. And right now, everything we've been through has led us here."

"Our lives have been all about questions," Rain explains. "It's time we finally got some answers."

"I can relate to that," Tread replies, raising one eyebrow as if he's impressed. "Okay, you'll need to go to this four-story building next door to Grace Cathedral."

"Are there guards? How do we get in?"

"No. No guards. Just a solid steel door at the bottom of a small set of concrete steps out back. You'll need a key to get in. You'll find it once you're there."

"Once we're there? What does it look like?"

"Trust me. You'll know it when you see it. Now listen, you don't have a pile of time. I wasn't kidding about those security installations going in tomorrow. Tomorrow *morning*, in fact. My buddy Kammet runs one of the shuttle-trucks back and forth across the bridge. I can get you a ride over. Other than that, all I can give you is information. The rest is up to you."

"Information is pretty valuable these days," I say as we get ready to go. "Is there anything we can do for you in return?"

"Find a way to save this village," he says. "Find a way to save it without burning it to the ground."

22

MAKING OUR WAY ON FOOT OUT OF THE OAKLAND SHANTYTOWN, we find the lot with the military supply and transport trucks, just like Tread described. Although we can hear the sound of talking and busyness on the far side of the lot, the side we approach from is unguarded, with only a low metal fence standing in our way.

"No sense in weighing the pros and cons," Brohn says as he puts his hands on the top of the fence and vaults over. He lands quietly, and the rest of us quickly follow suit, though no one executes the leap quite so easily as he does.

With Rain in the lead, we're hunched over and walking in a brisk single file between two rows of the big blocky vehicles when an arm appears from the open side of one of the trucks. For the second time today, a hand grabs Rain by the collar, and she's yanked clean off her feet and into the dark interior of the vehicle. Cardyn, who's just behind her, shrieks, and the rest of us race over to help.

The hand and arm, it turns out, belong to Dennis Kammet, the man Tread told us about.

"Sorry about the dramatic kidnapping," he says after a quick round of introductions. "But this is your ride, and we're leaving right now."

He lifts a panel up from the truck's floor by a large steel ring and ushers us down into the small compartment below. He drops the panel back down over us, and we hear him pulling a blanket or some kind of tarp over the top, so that even the thin lines of light around the edges of the panel are blocked out. The five of us find ourselves scrunched together in stifling heat and total darkness.

"Well," Cardyn whispers, "at least now the five of us know what a hand feels like inside of an oven mitt."

"More like inside an oven," Manthy mutters.

The truck lurches into gear and rumbles along a relatively smooth road for twenty minutes or so before finally slowing to a halt. The thundering clump of Kammet's boots above us stirs all kinds of dirt loose in the hidden compartment, and we stifle our hacking coughs as best we can. After a moment, Kammet pulls the tarp away and lifts the panel, filling our lives with light and air again. He reaches down to help unwedge us, one at a time, from the tiny space under the floorboards of the truck.

"Next stop is the San Francisco side," he says as I gulp a deep breath of relatively fresh air.

Once we get to the far side of the bridge, Kammet presses a button on the instrument panel in the truck's cab. When he gives us the go-ahead signal, we leap, one by one, from the slow-moving truck and tumble down a small grassy embankment where we brush off our clothes, get our bearings, and gather our wits.

"The guards are just over there," Rain says, pointing toward an outpost. "Ideas?"

Brohn turns to me. "Render?"

"Render."

I glide my fingertips along my tattoos and initiate the connection. The five of us crouch down behind some bushes near a clearing at the foot of a small hill. "There's going to be some noise," I warn the others.

We're barely settled in when, swooping down behind the embankment, Render hits the ground in the middle of the clearing and proceeds to beat his huge wings like he's trying to take off but can't. He kicks up an enormous cloud of dust in the process and thrashes around enough to vibrate the ground below our feet. His cries sound eerily human, and I'm proud to see how good he's getting at mimicry.

Startled by what sounds very much like a child in distress, one of the guards tells his partner to stay at the post while he goes to investigate.

"Too bad," I whisper. "I was hoping they'd both come over."

"It's okay," Brohn replies under his breath. "It just means we'll have to divide our attention between the two guards."

Rain puts three fingers up and points to a small footpath leading up to the checkpoint. I nod my understanding as she, Cardyn, and Manthy slip away, leaving me and Brohn ducked down behind a small cluster of trees.

In the clearing, Render is still crying his little heart out and spraying dust and black feathers into the air as he continues to writhe, limp, and roll around on the ground.

The lone guard clambers over the hill and slides down past the tree-line into the clearing. He looks baffled to discover that the cries he heard are coming from a big black bird who suddenly doesn't seem all that distressed. Render stops his whirlwind of motion, hops to his feet, and gives the guard what I swear is a mocking "Gotcha!" before flying away into the afternoon sky.

As the guard raises his head to watch the raven glide out over the treetops, Brohn sprints silently out from our hiding place, his feet barely seeming to touch the ground, and taps the man on the shoulder. The puzzled guard spins around only to be greeted by Brohn's muscular forearm, which strikes him full-force on the

224

bridge of the nose. The man staggers back and drops to his knees, blood plinking to the dry ground. Before he has a chance to recover or figure out what's happened to him, I slip around behind him and lock my arms around his neck in a rear choke-hold. He's already too dazed from Brohn's blow to offer much resistance. Within two seconds, his head lolls to the side. I release my grip, and he slumps over as gently as a heavily-drugged kitten.

Brohn and I exchange a hearty high-five and get ready to climb up over the small hill to see how our three friends are faring with their guard.

But before we can take more than two steps, Cardyn, Rain, and Manthy appear at the top of the hill and start making their way down toward us. Cardyn has guard number two slung over his shoulder. Wincing with the effort, he leans forward and drops the unconscious man to the ground. The guard's clothes are dirty and rumpled, and his face is a pulpy mess. He looks like he's been dragged head-first through a rock quarry.

"Whew!" Card gasps, his hands on his knees as he struggles for breath. "He's heavier than he looks."

"What'd you do to him?" I ask.

"Oh," Rain says sheepishly, holding up her bloody-knuckled fists. "Actually, that was me."

"Just you?" Brohn asks. "Looks like this guy got marched over by an entire platoon."

Rain shrugs. "I guess I had to vent some pent-up anger."

"Looks like about seventeen years' worth! I'm just glad you took it out on him and not on us."

With Manthy's help, we drag the two guards by their heels over to the small cluster of trees about a hundred yards or so from the checkpoint. We bind their hands, gag them, and try to tie them to a tree with the immobilizer cuffs they have on their belts. Even though we learned how to operate manacles like these as part of our training in the Processor, this kind is more sophisticated. At first, we can't figure out how to make the electro-cuffs work, but after a moment I realize that they're keyed to each guard's fingerprints. It's just a matter of pressing the guards' fingertips to the sensors on the cuffs to release the yellow energy-band. The band sizzles to life, and we snap them around the guards' wrists.

As soon as we've secured the two unconscious men, we march together back through the clearing, up the small hill, and over to the checkpoint.

With no guards left on duty and no working cameras or security protocols to worry about, we're able to slip easily past the gateway and into the city of San Francisco.

Unlike the quiet woods of the Valta, the militaristic set-up of the Processor, the congested streets of Reno, or the slums we just left behind in Oakland, this place looks the way I always imagined a healthy city should look.

The houses lining the hilly streets are colorful and clean. The roads are actually well-maintained, rather than pitted and pock-marked. People are shopping and strolling around through small parks of lush green grass, like they've never heard there's a war being fought outside the city's perimeter. There are even kids around, scampering and laughing. It would all seem totally normal, if you didn't count the soldiers on patrol or the glistening turquoise-colored mag-jeeps they're cruising around in.

Pleased with himself over his recent performance in helping to dispatch the two guards, Render is flying happily overhead. With our connection open, he sends me more images of the city. Every time we do this, the images get a little more vivid, a little more complete. It doesn't hurt or feel as disorienting as it used to. I feel like I have a live feed running straight to my brain now, rather than the interruption in all my other senses that used to occur.

Using the various landmarks supplied by Tread back in the

Oakland shantytown, we're able to navigate the maze of steep side streets and meandering alleys.

We sneak from building to building, dodging patrolling soldiers as we go. There aren't many of them, but they're heavily armed. The people walking by don't pay them much attention and just seem to keep their heads down and go on about their business.

"I'm not sure what's going on here," I say as we duck down a narrow alley.

"Maybe the residents are all prisoners," Brohn suggests. "Locked in the city like they locked us in the Valta for all those years."

Rain isn't so sure. "Maybe these are all government people. Employees or something. Or maybe the families of the soldiers."

"They don't seem like family to me," Cardyn points out. "Seems more like they're scared of the soldiers but sort of in denial. They don't look at them—have you noticed that? I wonder if we're going to wind up liberating these people or fighting against them by the time this is all over."

"Good question," I say. "Scary. But good."

"Listen," Rain says, "whatever happens, I think we'd be smart to keep our heads down and stay off the main roads as much as possible. If Hiller's people know we're still alive, they'll be on the lookout for us."

"Even here?" Card asks. "Even after all these months?"

"I wouldn't put anything past them," I say as I lead the others along. "Caramella and Tread had heard about us. It wouldn't surprise me if the enemy knows we've been making our way west."

Scampering down another long, narrow alley with Render chirping and *kraa*-ing from his perch on an old black fire-escape, we arrive at the back of the building Tread described to us. The enclosed area behind the building is small and cramped. It's also a dead-end, which means there's nowhere to go from here, except down a concrete stairway leading below ground level to a steel door. Three black incinerator bins, overflowing with garbage, are pressed up against a tall metal fence with coils of flickering blue laser-wire running along the top. A gutted mag-van sits in a clunky heap on an inactive hover pad. Even though it's still daytime, the sun struggles to make its way past the ring of tall buildings surrounding the small courtyard.

"This has got to be the place," I say.

Brohn cranes his neck to look up at the tall gray buildings around us and then back to the squat, four-story building we're preparing to enter. "I hope Tread's intel is as good as he says."

"We're about to find out."

"If things go wrong or if we get separated—," I start to say, but Rain cuts me off.

"Don't worry, Kress. Nothing bad'll happen."

"I agree. But just in case, let's arrange to meet right here. It's quiet and far enough from the main road that it seems pretty safe."

Everyone agrees, though no one wants to talk about the possibility of losing one another.

Single file, we walk down the concrete stairs to the metal door below. I try the door first, but it doesn't budge.

"Try the input panel," Cardyn suggests.

I take his advice and press my palm to the panel next to the door, but nothing happens.

"Feel like venting any more pent-up rage?" Card says jokingly to Rain.

"Sorry," she says. "my knuckles are still a little too raw right now. Brohn?"

"I can try."

Brohn runs his hand along the edge of the door. "Feels pretty strong," he says. He smashes his shoulder against it. The door shudders for a second, and a deep impression appears where

Brohn hit it. Other than that, though, it stays firmly in place. "No way. It's solid."

"I bet Terk could've knocked it down with one finger," Card boasts. We all nod in agreement, offering a silent salute to our long-gone giant friend.

"I can't imagine Tread would get us this far and wouldn't tell us how to get in," Rain complains.

"Maybe he did," I suggest.

"What do you mean?"

"He said we'd find the key once we got here."

Card looks around for a second. "I don't see any key. Maybe it's hidden somewhere?"

"Or maybe it's not hidden at all."

We all look at Manthy at the same time. She frowns at us. "Oh, come on now!"

"We need you, Manthy."

"I didn't ask to be able to do this."

"Render didn't ask to be able to fly, but he can, so he does."

"I hate all of you so much."

I put my hands on her shoulders and look her in the eyes. "And we'll always love you, too."

Manthy sighs and steps forward as we part way for her. She presses her cheek to the input panel like she's listening to it talk to her. Which, strangely enough, is what seems to be happening. She presses her hand to the wall by the door. Her fingers tremble, and she starts to sink to the ground. In a flash, Cardyn locks his arms under hers and catches her before she falls. He eases her down onto the bottom step.

"It hurts," she says. She's shaking now and starting to cry. Cardyn puts his arm around her, and she leans her head against his shoulder for a second before sitting back up and trying her best to stand. "No. I'm okay."

"But Manthy—"

"I said I'm fine." She's trying to sound harsh, but her voice is weak from the effort. "Anyway," she says with a nod toward the door, "it's open."

We look over and, just as she said, the red light on the panel indicator has clicked off, and the door has swung open a few inches.

With Manthy shaking off her dizziness, we ease our way inside. I lead the way with the others following close behind.

The building's basement is old and musty, and reeks of mold and decay. The stone walls of the long gray hallway are cracked and crumbling. Long conduits run overhead, and Brohn has to duck his head as we walk. All of a sudden, I'm having flashbacks to the Valta and the Processor, two places where we lived in what amounted to underground bunkers. I can see why Render gets so much joy out of living large parts of his life in the sky.

At the end of the hallway, we come to another door.

Brohn takes the lead. He pushes on the door, which doesn't budge at first, so he leans in harder with his shoulder.

"The closure must be rusted shut," Rain says.

Brohn steps back and examines the area around the door. "I think you're probably right."

Manthy has taken a very large step back.

"Don't worry," I tell her. "No tech on this one."

"Great," she says with a pouty scowl. "My life is getting better by the minute."

Insisting he can take the door down, Brohn takes a step back and charges forward, slamming his shoulder against the big slab of wood. There's a loud crack, which I think must be the sound of Brohn's bones breaking, but to my relief, he seems fine. The door, on the other hand, has splintered around its handle and a puff of black dust explodes upward from around the frame. Brohn gives the remnants of the door another push, and this time it creaks open like it's in pain.

"That was…impressive," I tell him with a wink.

"Yeah," he replies. "I've got to admit I'm even impressed with

1022

myself. I wasn't sure I had it in me."

"I'm beginning to suspect you have a lot more in you than you ever knew."

When Brohn shoves the door the rest of the way open, we can see a set of concrete stairs leading up.

"This better not be a trap," Rain says.

"If it is," Cardyn says, his voice echoing in the gloomy stairwell, "whoever's at the other end of it better hope they don't get you mad."

Rain laughs. She seems to be enjoying her new role as the enforcer of our Conspiracy. She's always been known among us as the resident brainiac, but now that she's got a healthy dose of brawn to go with it, she's turning into a perfect, pint-sized fighting package.

After a quick jog, we get to the top of the stairs and find another door, this one unlocked. It opens into a large, empty room with broken chandeliers hanging from the ceiling and a couple more smashed to pieces, covered in dust and cobwebs on the floor. On the far side of the room is an office of some kind behind a wall of glass. The ceiling in the space is high, with old, exposed girders running its length. It looks like we might be in a lobby of some kind.

"I think it must've been a hotel," Rain says.

"Maybe an office building?" I suggest.

"Whatever it was, it isn't that anymore," Cardyn says. "This place would need CPR just to get back to comatose."

Card's right. Some places we've seen seem to be clinging to something they once were. This place isn't even clinging to life. With layers of grime covering the walls and heaps of trash decaying in random piles all over the floor, it's given up on whatever it used to be.

We tread as quietly as we can into the dreary, open space.

Cardyn pinches his nose. "Smells like Death took a dump in here."

Manthy shakes her head at him. "Nice."

A wooden staircase with some of the steps missing, the rest looking like a series of mold-covered shards, rises up before us.

Just as Brohn starts moving toward the stairs, Manthy clamps her hands to her ears and lets out a choked shriek, sagging to a seat on the floor.

"Manthy!" Cardyn cries out. "What's wrong?"

When she doesn't answer, we all rush to her side.

"It hurts!"

"Let's go back."

"No. We need to keep going," she says, pulling herself to her feet. "Tread said we'd find answers here."

We try to press forward, climbing gingerly up the rotted steps, but Manthy gasps and drops to her knees again.

"Up there...," she says, pointing up to the second-floor landing. "It's coming from up there."

"What is?"

She shakes her head. "The pain."

I suggest that Rain and I go up ahead and leave Brohn and Cardyn to take care of her, but she snaps at me not to do that.

"I can manage," she growls. "Please, just let me."

I don't argue, but I have my doubts. Her voice is as shaky as her legs. If we run into trouble, I can't imagine she'll be much help at the moment.

But somehow, we manage to climb the rest of the way up the fractured staircase. We have to hold onto the gold railing hanging limply from the wall as we navigate around the big cracks and holes to avoid crashing through.

At the top, we step into a second-floor hallway with a series of doors on either side.

The first door on our left is white and bigger than the rest, so we take a chance and try the handle, which turns easily.

When the door swings gently open we step into the room, only to be greeted by a hellish scene.

23

THE MAIN ROOM IS LARGE, WITH SEVERAL OTHER OPEN ROOMS branching off on either side. Dingy, peeling red wallpaper and water stains cover white walls.

My eyes land on a woman lying against the far wall. What looks like artificial skin on her legs has been torn away, exposing frayed wiring and corroded gears. Her face is contorted in a grimace of permanent agony. Except for her slowly-blinking and unfocused eyes, she seems lifeless as a partially-assembled mannequin. I have to look twice just to be sure she's a real person and not a heap of discarded prosthetics.

Another woman sits slumped in a hovering mag-chair. Bundles of cables and thin, twisted shafts of metal snake out of her torso where her arms and legs should be. A man with large square panels missing from his skull lies motionless in a plush leather chair in the corner. Along the far wall and behind a thin white curtain, seven more people lie mostly motionless on old-style military cots. Coils of red, green, and silver wires connect them to a bank of clicking monitors lining the wall above them.

I gasp at the sight. Somehow, we've wandered into a room full of tortured souls and cyborgs gone horribly wrong, and all I want is to get away as fast as possible.

A voice from behind us startles us all into a simultaneous group-jump.

"I'm Caldwell," the unusually short man in a white lab coat tells us, extending his stubby open hand to each of us in turn. We're too stunned to shake it, but he doesn't seem to mind. "Tread's an old friend," he says through a welcoming smile as he taps a small comm-link tucked just behind his ear. "He told me to expect you."

Finally, Brohn steps forward and extends his hand. "Brohn."

Beaming brightly, Caldwell gives Brohn's hand a vigorous shake. "Good to know you."

"I'm Kress," I say before being greeted with the same wide smile and strong handshake.

Rain and Cardyn introduce themselves as well, but Manthy stands quietly behind me with her head down.

"Is she okay?"

"That's Manthy," I say apologetically. "And no. But she will be. She's having a bit of a...headache."

"Who are they?" Manthy whispers over my shoulder. "What's happened here?"

"These are the Modifieds," Caldwell explains. "I'm their care-taker. Part nurse. Part mechanic. There used to be more of us. But as you can see, it's not a job anyone would want to do for long."

"We've heard about the Modifieds," Rain says. "We didn't know for sure if they were real."

"Unfortunately, a lot of them probably wish they weren't."

"That's terrible."

Caldwell looks up at us and shrugs. "They wanted a better life. They wanted immortality. Instead they got the frailty of a compromised immune system, the glitchiness of a computer, and the inflexibility of a machine. Basically, the worst of three different worlds. Turns out the dream of binary and genetic compatibility was more of a nightmare."

Caldwell walks us around the room and introduces us to his patients, if I can even call them that. Many of them are lying on the army cots with no sheets or blankets. Some sit up and greet us as we pass, but their voices are breathy and weak.

"This is Marcelo and Retta," Caldwell tells us as we pass by two of the Modifieds who are sitting shoulder to shoulder on the floor, staring blankly up at the ceiling. "After Marcelo's procedure, he tried to 'fix' his brain with a hammer and a digi-driver. Retta here, who's his wife, by the way, was a gunnery-sergeant in President Krug's Patriot Army. She signed on for military-grade vision, complete with audio-enhancers and night and distance vision. Now she's blind and deaf. We do everything we can for them, but supplies and personnel are limited, and we're always in danger of getting raided if we stick our heads out too far."

"What about the Insubordinates?" I ask. "We were told we could find them here."

"These aren't them, are they?" Cardyn asks in a hoarse whisper. He's looking around at the Modifieds with an expression that's a mixture of compassion, sorrow, and steely determination to help.

Caldwell smiles and shakes his head. "No. Though the Insubordinates take care of the Modifieds, because no one else will. It's been a while since we've been raided, but people are still kind of skittish around here. You never know who you can trust."

"We get that," I tell him. "But we've come too far and been through too much to stop now. Can you take us to whoever's in charge?"

I expect Caldwell to balk at this, but he seems genuinely relieved. I swear I can see the tension melt out of his face and shoulders. "They'll be so happy you made it here," he sighs. "We've been waiting for you."

"Made it?" I ask.

"Here. To San Francisco. I get the feeling you're exactly what we need."

"Why do I get the feeling everyone around here knows more about us than we know about...anything?"

"The Insubordinates," Rain interjects. "You can take us to them?"

"You'll need to meet with the Major."

"The Major? Who's he?"

A slow smile spreads over Caldwell's lips. "You'll see."

24

CALDWELL LEADS US OUT OF THE ROOM AND UP ANOTHER SET OF slightly-less rickety stairs to a third-floor office.

After escorting us in, he taps the comm-link behind his ear. "Wait here. The Major's coming. I'm afraid I can't stay. I've got inventory to look after," he explains before disappearing back down the hallway.

The room is smaller than the one that housed the Modifieds. There are two synthetic couches and a few matching blue and white striped chairs surrounding a low table of shiny black glass that sits between them. Clean cabinets of white panels and glass line one of the walls. I can't speak for the others, but when I picture whoever the "Major" is, I'm expecting a barrel-chested, stubble-jawed man with an arsenal of guns strapped to his back and maybe some horrific battle scars on his face.

The person who walks into the room, however, causes our mouths to drop open.

The 5' 3" grinning, thin-limbed person in slightly baggy khaki cargo pants and a lime-green hoodie doesn't look anything like the burly, cigar-smoking leader of an underground resistance movement I expected. More like a newborn, spindly-legged foal.

With tears brightening his blue eyes, Brohn cries out "Wisp!" and leaps at her. He gathers the girl up in his arms and spins her around. "*You're* the Major?"

Wisp's long ponytail whips around behind her and settles onto her shoulder as she laughs heartily in her brother's arms, hugging him back. When he finally sets her down, he stares at her with his eyes as wide as dinner plates. He's got his hands on her shoulders like he's afraid she'll vanish into the ether if he lets go.

I can't help but laugh. If his smile gets any bigger, the corners of his mouth look like they might make their way around his entire head and meet at the back.

Cardyn, Rain, Manthy, and I rush over and join him and Wisp in a suffocating group hug. All at once, the walls we've put up for the sake of survival come crashing down, and we're laughing, crying, and locking our arms around each other's shoulders and waists. It's a hug I wish would last forever, but Wisp finally manages to unlock herself from our combined vice-grip and bring us back to reality.

"Okay, okay," she squeals. "Talk about getting killed with kindness! I've made it this far. I'd hate to get crushed to death after all that by the five of you."

Laughing and crying, everyone takes a small step back, not wanting to distance ourselves too far from this little, impossible miracle called "Wisp." A miracle we never thought we'd see again.

Brohn has dropped one hand to his side, but the other is still planted firmly on his little sister's shoulder.

"But how…?" is all he can manage through his happy tears.

Rain finishes asking the question we all want to ask. "We saw the Valta. It was leveled. There was nothing…no one left."

Wisp's eyes fill with tears, but she wipes them away with back of her hand. She lays her other hand on Brohn's wrist and manages a feeble smile. "Let's just say, you didn't exactly leave us in the best hands. The new Sixteens were a joke, only not the funny kind. So I stepped up."

"Stepped up?" I ask.

Wisp hangs her head before looking back up at the five of us. "The Recruiters came again just a few months after they came for you. Way too early. Caught us off guard. Most of us knew right away they were up to no good. We'd already started to doubt what we were seeing on the viz-screens. Well, some of us did, anyway. It wasn't even news anymore, just a bunch of revolting propaganda put out by Krug's new Patriot Party. But the Sixteens of the 2043 Cohort were still gung-ho about the war. Spence, Vella, Talia…all of them. They were always so competitive with your Cohort. They figured if the war wasn't over by now, you must've failed, so it was their job to turn the conflict in our favor. But a lot of us were starting to feel skeptical. Suspicious, even. Things just weren't adding up."

"Adding up?" Brohn asks, finally dropping his hand from Wisp's shoulder.

"I don't know how to explain it. There was something in the air. We just sensed something wasn't right. When I noticed that some of the war footage was the exact same as footage they broadcast a couple of years ago, and I mean *exactly* the same, all those suspicions kicked into high gear. I tried warning the Sixteens, but they didn't buy it. They said it was probably just a glitch in the viz-cast or that maybe I'd only imagined it. But I was sure. When the Recruiters showed up, the Sixteens figured they'd been called up early to contribute to the war effort. They rushed out to give the Recruiters a big welcome, but the rest of us stayed back in the school or else dashed off to try to hide in the woods. Sure enough, the Recruiters went after us."

Wisp pauses. Her voice suddenly drops off a cliff to a near whisper, like she's forgotten how to talk for a second.

"Those Recruiters…they killed us. Slaughtered us all." Her eyes fill with tears again, but there's some strength or defiance inside her that refuses to let them fall. "We ran, hid, fought…did whatever we could. But there were too many of them. And we didn't have weapons…"

"It's okay," Brohn says, his voice as soothing and reassuring as a soft, warm blanket on a cold night. "Did anyone else…?"

Wisp drops her head and doesn't say a word. She doesn't have to.

So now we know. They're gone. They're really all gone. Everyone but her. Everyone we knew, loved, protected, and cared about. The Neos and Juvens. The Sixteens. The friends we laughed and cried with, struggled to survive with…all gone. I look at Brohn, Cardyn, Rain, Manthy, and Wisp. If Adric and Celia are taking care of Kella as promised, that makes seven survivors, including me, from a town that doesn't even exist anymore.

"I shouldn't have survived," she says. "I shouldn't even be here."

"You're strong," Brohn says. "You're clever. It doesn't surprise me that you did."

"That's not what I mean. I mean I should have died with our friends. It's not fair that I made it out and they didn't. I feel like me being here…it disrespects their memories somehow."

Brohn tells her he's sorry but she's wrong. "Your being here is exactly what every one of them would have wanted. If you had died back there…well, there'd be no one here to honor their memories at all."

Wisp sighs, reaches up to give Brohn's cheek a gentle pat, and calls us over to the cluster of furniture around the low, oval-shaped teleconference table. We all sit down, our images reflected in the black glass table between us, and she finishes telling us about her escape from the Valta. "I knew about Kress's hiding place down the ravine on the far side of the plateau where she used to go with Cardyn and that bird of hers."

"Render," I say.

"Right. Render. What ever happened to him? He disappeared soon after you left with the Recruiters."

Cardyn chuckles. "Oh, he managed to track us down."

Rain tips her chin toward the ceiling. "He's flying around out there somewhere right now."

"Got us through a lot of tough times these past few months," Brohn says. "Honestly, we wouldn't be here without him, and we would never have found you." He looks over at me and gives me a wink and a silent thanks. "We owe him a lot."

"Then I definitely need to thank him. Seems I have a lot of thanking to do. I only survived because I had help—"

Behind Wisp, a young woman with her arms clamped around a clipboard appears in the doorway. Her eyes are down, and she taps lightly on the door frame with her knuckles to get Wisp's attention.

Wisp excuses herself and turns toward the woman. "Is this about the inventory?"

The woman nods. She looks to be in her twenties or early thirties, but she has the meek nervousness of an intimidated ten-year-old.

"Tell Pim to have his team take inventory of the rations in Shelter Two and Three and leave the weapons count to Holly. And have Orion fix those receiving pads in the comm-links. We'll meet in H.Q. Central at twenty-one-hundred to review logistics."

The woman nods again and gives us all a half-smile before turning around and disappearing from the doorway.

"That's Sabine," Wisp explains, turning back toward us. "She's quiet as a mouse. She never sleeps, and she gets more done in an hour than anyone else around here gets done in a week. I would have introduced you, but she's a little skittish about meeting new people."

Brohn looks several levels beyond impressed with his little sister. I don't blame him. The last time we saw Wisp, she was being tossed around by one of the Recruiters like he was a pit-bull with a squeaky chew-toy. Now she's sitting here, apparently in command of an improvised, ragtag army and doling out commands like a veteran field general.

"You're really in charge of people here?" Rain asks, her voice filled with admiration and with what sounds like a hint of jealousy. "You didn't even train. You didn't get recruited."

Wisp gives Rain a dismissive shrug. "I don't like to think of it as being in charge. There are a lot of folks here who are angry, desperate, or in need of guidance. I just help to nudge them along. Turns out that living like we did in the Valta gave us certain survival skills a lot of people around here don't really have. It's one thing to know an injustice is happening, but it's another thing to be able to do something about it."

"So what happened to you after the Recruiters left?" I ask. "After...?"

Wisp gives me a knowing look. "At first, I didn't know what to do. I considered just throwing myself off the nearest cliff and ending it all. But I couldn't do that when I didn't know what had happened to all of you. So I gathered whatever supplies I could carry and headed west. I made it nearly three days on foot when I felt I couldn't take another step. That's when I got lucky, and someone threw a bag over my head, tossed me into the back of a refrigerator truck, and started beating the hell out of me."

"Yikes," Cardyn exclaims. "Really?"

"Oh, it was as real as it gets."

"And that was 'lucky'? I'd hate to hear what you consider *un*lucky."

"Could've been worse," Wisp says, tilting her head and pointing to a jagged scar running down the side of her neck.

Brohn's face goes into a contortion of confusion and fury. "Who did that to you?"

Wisp holds up a hand to both of the boys. "They were on the run. Like me. They'd escaped from somewhere down south. They didn't know who I was. They said they thought I was with the Eastern Order. Of course, when they heard me and saw me, they realized there probably aren't too many thirteen-year-old, hundred-pound girls from the Eastern Order wandering around alone through bombed-out towns and strips of desert. So, I explained my situation and latched on with them. They knew people in San Francisco, brought me along, and eventually got me here." Wisp makes a sweeping gesture with her hand. "You're sitting in the heart of the rebellion. This old building was once an office for immigration lawyers before they all got shut down. It was called Fields, Evans, and Style after the legal team who owned it. Now we just call it 'Style.'"

Wisp goes on to explain her time with the Insubordinates and how they took her in, nursed her back to health, and eventually turned to her for leadership. "They didn't know what they were doing. It was all just fear and in-fighting. They were too scared to even admit they were scared. A few of them came from towns like ours. Others had escaped from the few big cities left, like Salt Lake and Reno."

"We know Reno," Rain pipes in. "Unfortunately."

"And, from what I've heard, they're just getting worse," Wisp says. "What do you know about the Order?"

"That they're a hoax," Rain snaps. "At least, that's what it sounds like."

Wisp raises an eyebrow in mild surprise but then nods as if this were the most expected and obvious answer in the world.

"There are a bunch of people out there who've been suspicious about this so-called war for a long time. There are even a few who have figured out something close to the truth. But there are only a handful of us who know for sure, and most of them are right here in this building where we've been setting up headquarters."

"Headquarters? For what? What exactly is it you do here?"

Wisp slips out of her hoodie and lays it over the arm of the couch. "We investigate. We plan. We inform. And, eventually, we'll fight."

I can't believe that Wisp—our little Wisp from the Valta—has turned out to be such a bad-ass. She's still small and baby-faced, but she exudes an aura that's tough-as-nails. It reminds me of her brother, this hidden, secret strength inside her. Only, coming from her small frame, it seems even more surprising.

She stands, crosses the room, and taps a panel on the wall. A small door whooshes open to reveal a refrigerator lined with tall, cylindrical vials of ion-water. She tosses one to each of us as she walks back to sit on the couch. She laughs as she tells us that the Insubordinates who saved her and the ones she's been gathering still call her "Wisp."

But the truth is, it hardly seems a suitable name anymore. She's got to be a good three or four inches shorter than me and she's slender from top to bottom. But seeing her from any kind of distance, the way she moves like a jungle cat, her lean muscles rippling under her black tank-top, her eyes flashing fire as she tells her story, I'd guess she's at least seven feet tall, strong as a horse, and big across as a barn.

"You really came out here and set all this up on your own, huh?" Brohn asks as he beams with brotherly pride.

Wisp laughs and taps a comm-link she has just behind her ear. She holds up a "just a minute" finger to us, listens for a second, and nods. "Things may have just turned in our favor," she says to the person on the other end of the conversation. She laughs and says, "Copy that," before tapping her comm-link off and flicking her thumb toward the doorway. "In answer to your question, I hardly did this on my own. I had help. My lieutenant and right-hand man is just coming down the hallway now. He's the one who told us the truth about the Order, the Processors, and Krug's N.P.P. That's his New Patriot Party. He's the one who helped get us set up. He helped me do the best I could with the others while we waited and hoped you'd find your way here."

With that, she turns toward the doorway. "Ah. Here he is now."

For the second time in fifteen minutes, we're stunned into silence by a familiar face.

Wisp's lieutenant strides in, and she stands up to welcome him before turning back to us.

"I think you know Granden."

25

I SIT UP STRAIGHT, STUNNED AT THE SIGHT OF THE MAN I BOTH hoped and feared I'd see again someday.

Granden pauses and runs his fingers through his tidy, light brown hair and makes a couple of micro-adjustments to his belt and shirt collar like he's preparing to walk into a fancy dinner party. He gives us a half-wave as he steps fully into the room.

He's dressed in civilian clothes, which is a strange sight and a look I've never seen on him before. When I knew him, he was almost always decked out in his black and green military uniform. Most of the time, he had an array of weapons on him, a bunch of pistols, knives, or rifles for our training sessions. Now, he's outfitted in the combination of loose, weathered black jeans and the tailored white button-shirts we saw people wearing back in Salt Lake City. His boots are those retro-fitted synth-cloth kind made to look like leather, and his black pea-coat is just long enough to cover the holster and the slick golden Sig Sauer .320 slung around his waist.

I don't know whether to hug him, thank him, or kill him. He may have helped us in the end, but he was also part of a whole network of lies told by a team of government agents dedicated to weeding out special kids to help them keep those lies going. At least according to Hiller. The sight of him makes me realize just how little the other Seventeens and I have pieced together, how much was guess-work, and how much might be completely wrong. It's like I've been working on an impossible puzzle all these months, and the potential answer key just walked into the room.

So what do you say to the man who trained you, lied to you, aided in your physical and psychological torture, and maybe saved your life?

I can tell the others are just as conflicted as I am. Despite Granden's warm smile and his promise that he's "really one of the good guys," Brohn leaps up in a territorial show of defiance. Rain jumps up to stand next to him. Cardyn stands with them, his fists on his hips, and scowls at Granden. Manthy doesn't stand up, but she crosses her arms tight, gives Granden one vicious, evil-eyed stare, and then turns her gaze to the floor. I decide to join Brohn, Rain, and Cardyn. I'm just standing up when Wisp waves for all of us to sit back down, but we don't.

"Seriously," she says with a pleasant laugh. "At ease. We're all on the same side here. I know you've been through some crazy times together. But those days are behind you. Time to look forward."

"You don't know what he did to us in there," Brohn growls as he stabs an accusing finger in Granden's direction.

"Actually, I do. Mr. Granden here has been very forthcoming about his role in the Processor, about its inner-workings and its mission, and more importantly, about the Eastern Order itself."

"We already know," Cardyn says from his cross-armed pout. "The Order's made up. It never existed."

"That's true," Wisp says. "Partly. You got some of the story. Let Mr. Granden tell you the rest."

"Convince us we should trust him," Rain snarls in full battle mode.

"He got you out of there," Wisp says, looking at us from one to the next. "And he helped you get here. Obviously, you got his message back in the Valta. Nothing has been more important to me in all of this than you, Brohn. I started to tell you that I only survived because I had help. Well, you're looking at the help I had. He was the one who found me when the Recruiters were sweeping the woods for survivors. He told me to stay where I was and not make any noise and not to worry. And then he disappeared and so did the Recruiters. Thanks to Granden, I can stand here, alive and well, and tell you all this in person."

The tension in the room drops a level, and the four of us who are standing sit back down on the couch with Manthy. Brohn hasn't unclenched his fists or his jaw, though. And Rain still looks like she wants to see just how long Granden can keep up that angelic smile while she holds his head under molten lava. While it's true that Granden didn't seem to revel in torturing us the way Hiller, Trench, Kellerson, and Chucker did back in the Processor, his face—his very presence—calls to mind Terk, Karmine, Kella, and a whole host of memories I've spent a long time trying desperately to forget.

Apparently sensing the dwindling remnants of our hostility, Granden gives us a gentle nod and clears his throat. "It's good to…see you again. And yes, I'm glad you got my message and that you trusted it enough to follow it."

He's addressing all of us, but he holds his gaze on me the longest. He wrings his hands like he's nervous, which I guess makes sense. It wasn't that long ago that he was in charge of us with a few dozen armed soldiers plus Hiller around to help keep us in line. Now, we're free. Which means we're free to get up and leave or else free to leap over the glass table and across the small space between us and make him pay for his part in what they did to us. Either way, any hold he had on us is gone.

Granden looks over at Wisp who nods her approval for him

to go on. "It sounds like Hiller told you the truth…," he says at last.

"But not all of it, right?" Brohn interrupts.

"No, Brohn. Not all of it. Not the history of it. Not how it all happened and what led up to you being recruited every year."

"So what happened? What did she leave out?"

Granden sighs and takes another long look at us. It's not a patronizing look or even one of friendly recognition. It's more like he's relieved to be able to unburden himself. He takes a deep breath and seems to relax. He sits down on the arm of the couch next to Wisp. He puts one foot on the floor and the other one up on the couch with his forearm draped over his knee, like this is the most casual and normal moment in the world.

"As you know," he says after a brief pause, "the Freedom Wars started in 2028. The same year as the failed Telemachus mission to Mars. Most of you would have been around two years old." He looks at us again as if expecting us to debate him on this point, but we all just sit and wait for him to continue. He shifts his gaze from Wisp to us and goes on. "Legitimate concerns like climate change, mass immigration, and rampant gun violence were manipulated by a few fear-mongers to stir up a wave of panic. A handful of corrupt people at the top of the government decided to ride that wave all the way to unlimited power and wealth. They called themselves the Patriot Party."

"We know about the Patriot Party," Rain says, her voice laced with impatience. "That's Krug's party."

"They're the *only* party, Rain. The others are just for show. Window-dressing. One of the many ways Krug keeps up the illusion of democracy. Those soldiers you see everywhere…the ones patrolling around outside, the ones you got to know so well in the Processor, that's the Patriot Army. We used to know them by names like 'Homeland Security' and the 'National Guard.' Krug's got the other military branches deployed overseas: Iran. North Korea. The New Congolese Republic. The Patriot Party is their cover. Their legitimacy. The Patriot *Army* is their insurance against dissent."

"So the Eastern Order...?" Rain starts to say, but Granden gives her a dismissive wave of his hand.

"Is nothing. A ghost story. In 2032, your town was one of many attacked by an enemy you were told was the Eastern Order. What you didn't know at the time was that there never was an Eastern Order. Not exactly, anyway. There never was an invading army. The Eastern Order was invented as a cover for all kinds of greed and atrocities committed by President Krug and his Patriot Party. If you're looking for an enemy, they're it."

Brohn's cheek pulses under his clenched jaw. "So you're saying it was Krug's people, this Patriot Army, who bombed the Valta?"

"Under instructions from Krug and his Patriot Party. Yes. Back East, they brought in an underground group of bio-geneticists called the Deenays to analyze and assess the possibility of incorporating certain gifted individuals into their plans. The goal was terrifying in its simplicity. Krug and his Patriot Party were determined to spread fear to enable them to keep their wealth while creating a permanent underclass and staying in power for, well, forever. The goal was total power and absolute wealth for a few and a life of poverty, fear, in-fighting, and slavery for everyone else. That's what the Arcologies are for. For every one of those monstrosities that goes up, another individual gets rich and another ten million are consigned to the shanty-towns decaying in their shadow."

"We saw one of the Arcologies on the way here," Cardyn concedes. "In Oakland. It must suck to have to look outside every day from your pile of garbage and see a nice big tower you can never hope to get into."

"It's no accident, Cardyn. 'Divide and conquer' used to be a cliché. Now, it's a way of life."

Rain's mouth hangs open. "Then what we saw on the viz-screens was the military killing our own people?"

"That was the ugly genius of it," Granden says. He sounds impressed and depressed at the same time. "It was Krug's master plan. The Order wound up being anyone you decided *needed* to be your enemy. If a new family moved into a neighborhood, the residents feared it was the Order. When thirty women in St. Louis chained themselves to a government installation to protest the use of nuclear weapons against the Congolese rebels, the women were accused of being members of the Order. When Canadian immigrants flooded into Minnesota and the Dakotas to escape the deadly effects of climate change sweeping through the southern provinces, they became the Order, and flying squads of vigilantes were formed in towns all along the border to take them down. Since Krug and the Patriot Party controlled the media, there was no way to question any of it. So it went on and on. All across the country until it was nothing but 'us against them' everywhere you went."

"Except that the 'them' was us," I say.

Granden frowns. "Exactly. It became a world of made up enemies who had to be exterminated at all costs."

"Why us, though? Why the Seventeens?"

Granden stands up and paces in small steps next to the table between us. Even though he towers over Wisp who's still sitting relaxed and cross-legged on the couch, he continues to glance over at her for approval as he talks.

He says, "The Seventeens..." and scans the tiled ceiling like it somehow has all the answers. "The Seventeens started with the Deenays' DEMo Program. That stands for DNA Evolution and Modification. You see, Krug and the Patriots weren't satisfied with just regular political power. They wanted total domination over the future of humanity. And you were the key. You're too young to remember the big wave of superhero movies of the late 20th and early 21st centuries. Well, that wasn't just fiction.

K. A. RILEY

Certain people seemed to be developing actual superhuman abilities. Not the red cape flying kind of stuff. A lot of it tended to be
a kind of techno-human connectedness no one had anticipated.
Everyone thought technology would improve humanity. What
they didn't realize is that digital technologies weren't just something invented by humans for the benefit of humans."

"Then what were they?" Manthy asks.

"They were a natural next step of human evolution. Digital
code was just another way of writing the human genetic code.
Computers weren't learning how to be human like everyone
thought and feared might happen. Instead, humans were evolving, so the theory goes, to incorporate binary processing into our
human brains. You've seen some of the results downstairs."

"You mean the Modifieds," Manthy says through a menacing
scowl.

"That's right, Manthy. There used to be more, but their
mortality rates were, well, close to one-hundred percent. We take
care of the rest as best we can. It turns out that the potential for
binary-DNA sequencing kicked in full-force when the pituitary
gland in some teenagers caused certain DNA strands to take
what the geneticists called a 'techno-evolutionary detour.' It
turns out that some of you have evolved without *needing* to be
modified."

"And that's why the Seventeens?" I ask.

"Pretty much. No one knew for sure why it seemed to only
affect people exactly your age. Up in their labs, some of the
Deenays guessed it was because you were far enough away from
the pollution and urban decay to allow for the evolution. Some of
them suspected it was the altitude. Or sunspots. Or depletions in
the ozone layer of the atmosphere. A couple of them even
suggested that maybe you were all aliens sent here to study and
mimic us before you decided to invade and destroy us. No one
took that theory seriously, though. In the end, it started to look
like it had something to do with the geography of the earth, itself.

The locations tended to be clustered around the 40th parallels North. No one knows why. Maybe a geo-thermal phenomenon. Maybe bio-magnetic. Some actually said it wasn't anything at all. That the so-called evolution was a hoax, a myth, something dreamed up by Krug who they figured had gone completely insane."

"But it turned out to be true," Manthy mumbles. She sounds sad, like a little kid coming to terms with the death of a beloved family pet.

Granden points to her and then to Brohn and finally to me. "And you're the proof. The three of you. You're not the only ones, either. They found others."

"Others like us?"

"So there *are* others," Rain says.

"Yes. Krug pushed for the program in secret. Got all kinds of bills and laws passed that funded the Deenays' experiments. If you were a weapon, he was going to be sure you were under his control. He was paranoid. Still is. Hiller was charged with setting the whole thing up. The idea was to set up Processors all over the country. They were multi-purpose: identify those with special abilities, recruit the pliant ones to work on behalf of the government, weed out the ones who might pose a threat, and brainwash or modify the rest into compliance."

Cardyn squints at Granden. "And by 'weed out,' you mean…?"

"Kill us," Rain finishes.

Granden gives Rain and Cardyn a grim nod. "Once the tests identified you as having special abilities, if you were also determined to be Noncompliant, you were tagged as too dangerous to be kept alive."

I feel like I'm going to cry, but I swallow hard and manage to keep my composure. "I don't understand why we spent all that time being trained in the Processor if we were just going to be…."

"It was all for Krug's benefit, not yours. There were others like your friend Terk who got maimed as part of the so-called training as guinea pigs for the Modified Program. You, Brohn, and Manthy were what they call Emergents, which means you got scheduled for termination. Manthy because she represented a potential Asset for the government, but her temperament was deemed far too dangerous to risk taking a chance on. She showed all the signs of a free-thinker, someone who would never surrender her will for a cause like theirs. A textbook Noncompliant."

"And what about the rest of us?"

"Only Karmine and Kella were to be spared originally. There were really only three categories: Noncompliants, Assets, and Emergents."

We all must be giving Granden the same confused look because he stops abruptly.

"I think you may be overloading them," Wisp says. She gives Granden's knee a motherly tap before turning her attention to us. "I know this is a lot to throw at you. But it really wasn't all that complicated. The Deenays discovered that some kids were developing potential abilities. Krug figured he could exploit those abilities. Processors were built, and the Patriot Party put the Recruitment Program into place. Certain towns like ours were attacked and then sealed off. All access and knowledge of the outside world was strictly controlled through the viz-screens. Krug and the Deenays created three designations: Noncompliants, Assets, and Emergents. Assets were those who bought into the war and could be incorporated into Krug's Patriot Army. Emergents were the ones with potential abilities who got sent to the Deenays for study or to be converted into Modifieds. Noncompliants were all the ones who couldn't be turned. They were killed. No matter which category you fell into, though, there were only two outcomes: become a slave or become a corpse."

"And the Eastern Order?" I ask.

"That was a distraction," Granden says, plopping back down

onto the arm of the couch and picking up again with his explanation. "The Eastern Order was the hand the magician waves so you won't see what he's doing with his other hand. Once the threat was established..."

"It caught on," Rain finishes for him. "Like wildfire."

Granden says, "Yes. Although more like a virus. This wasn't something you could put out with a little water. The nation was consumed with the Order. You've seen it on the viz-screens. Okay, some of it was staged. But a lot of what you saw was real. Terrified neighbors killed each other while the Deenays continued with their experiments, and Krug sat back, accumulated more power, and laughed himself all the way to political immortality. In the Processor, Karmine and Kella were flagged as potential Assets. But you and your little feathered friend out there compromised those plans. So, you were all scheduled to be terminated." Granden locks his eyes on mine. "You for what you thought was a simple neuro-link between you and Render—"

"What is it really?" I ask. I want him to go on with his explanation, but I have a desperate need to know what Render and I really are to each other. "Cardyn calls it 'telempathy.'"

Granden beams a wide smile and points at Cardyn. "Not bad," he says. "That's about as close a term as I can imagine to describe your connection. Technically, it's called an Interspecies Neuro-Tech Rapport, or, an INTR-link. That was your father's term for it. He was a key architect in the Modified program. Of course, he didn't know the extent of what he was working on and had no idea he was helping Krug and the Deenays to put what they hoped would be a stranglehold on absolute power for a long time to come. When your father found out what they were up to, he fled with you, your mother, and your brother to the Valta. He thought you'd all be safe there. No one knew where he was, and the Valta was the last place on earth Krug would go looking. Or so he thought. He underestimated his importance to them. He was the key to their success. That's why he did what he did."

"What do you mean? What did he do?"

Taking a deep breath, Granden looks from me to Wisp then back to me. "He took all the knowledge he had, condensed it into a few small micro-circuits, hid the program, and then he returned to his laboratory back east, and destroyed what was left of his lab. Then, he…disappeared."

"Disappeared?"

Granden crosses the space between us and kneels down in front of me. "I'm sorry, Kress. I really am. Krug isn't in the habit of letting people stick around who've crossed him."

Granden leans forward and runs his fingertips along my tattoos, just as he did all those months ago back in the Processor. "Kress, your father hid his program inside of you. The micro-circuitry in your tattoos contains all his secrets. His program is the key to Krug and the Deenays' success, but it also makes you the key to bringing them down. Your father sacrificed himself for you. For all of us, really."

"You're telling me the circuitry in my arm doesn't have anything to do with my connection to Render?"

"Exactly. He didn't give you a gift. He just helped to release one you already had."

Suddenly, I can't catch my breath. I feel like I'm underwater and swimming as hard as I can to the surface that just keeps getting farther away.

"How—how do you know all this?" I finally mange to ask.

"I was on the inside for a long time."

"The inside?"

"Of the Patriots. You're not the only one who lost a father."

"What—your father disappeared, too?"

"Well, his soul did. A long time ago."

Granden calls out for a holo-display. "News feed. Cycle one."

The glimmering image that materializes above the black glass table between us is a familiar one. Growing up in the Valta, it's a face we saw countless times on the viz-screens. A face with chapped lips and crooked yellow teeth under a head of slicked-back hair.

"President Krug."

Granden puts his hand on my shoulder. "Kress, your father lived to fight evil. Mine lives to spread it."

26

"Your father is...?"

"President Krug. Yes."

"That's why Granden was assigned to the Processor," Wisp tells us. "Apparently, you were the most promising of all the Seventeens in the three different towns currently under lockdown."

"Three?" I ask.

"Three so far," Granden responds. "There are more planned. Not just here, but in other parts of the world as well."

"Here," Wisp says. "We've been talking for a long time. Let us show you what we mean. We have an entire room just down the hall we call 'Intel Central.' It's where we work to uncover everything Krug doesn't want anyone to find out. Follow me."

Wisp stands up and invites the rest of us to do the same. I thought that getting some answers would make me feel lighter somehow, more liberated. Turns out it's the opposite. My legs feel tired and sore. My head is throbbing and spinning at the same time. I can't focus or figure out if I should be angry about the past or worried about the future. Brohn must be going through something similar because he lets out an aching groan as he stands and begins to walk toward the door with everyone else. Rain follows just behind him. Cardyn and Manthy bring up the rear.

Wisp and Granden lead all of us out of the room and down the hall. "It's so good to see you all," Wisp beams as we walk along the dark corridor. "Just having you here…it's all I've dreamed about for ages."

"Us, too," Brohn exclaims.

Walking up next to me, Manthy mumbles that her head is hurting again.

"Can you give me a second?" I ask Wisp. She looks from me to Manthy and nods her understanding.

"I'm okay," Manthy insists, although her fingertips pressed to her temple say otherwise.

"It's happening when she gets around digi-tech," Cardyn observes.

"This room where you're taking us," Brohn asks, "any chance it's tech-heavy?"

"Unfortunately," Wisp says, "it's about as high-tech as we get." Her voice is soft and oddly matronly for a teenage girl and leader of an underground resistance movement. She asks Manthy if she would rather wait back in the other room. "I can call down one of the Insubordinates to stay with you in the lounge and keep you company."

"No thank you," Manthy says with a slow shake of her head. "I just needed a second to get used to it."

"It's like waves in her brain," I explain to Wisp. "This connection she has. It takes some getting used to."

"I can't say I completely understand," Wisp says with bright eyes and a sympathetic smile. "But I'm looking forward to talking with you more about it."

"Are you sure about going in?" I ask Manthy.

She nods and slips her hand into mine, and we follow Wisp into the room. Unlike the first room with its comfy couches and chairs and mostly open space, this one is filled wall to wall and ceiling to ceiling with holo-monitors, viz-screens, mag-pads, and a whole bank of holographic input panels floating above a long glass console. The darkness of the windowless room is pierced by the hazy glow of the shifting images on a semi-circle of spherical monitors that surround a person sitting in a hover-chair, facing away from us. The person is busy fiddling with some of the floating screens, spinning the glass basketball-sized monitors, and watching images zip through the air and pass from screen to screen.

"So this is Intel Central," Wisp says with a wave of her hand. Her voice is laced with pride. "Thanks to Mr. Granden and Olivia here, we have some of the most sophisticated civilian-level tech available, with eyes in a lot of places. We're doing our best to watch the watchers."

"Olivia?" Brohn asks.

"Oh. Of course. You haven't met Olivia yet. She's a Modified."

"Not one of those people from downstairs?" Cardyn whispers to Wisp from behind his hand.

Wisp puts a finger to her temple. "No. She's one of the rare ones who didn't go completely...you know. Here. I'll introduce you."

Wisp taps the person on the shoulder. The woman who spins around in the floating chair barely looks human. Her scarred and angular face hosts a network of embedded circuitry with small gold microchips protruding in a neat row along her jawline. She has the strangest eyes, pixilated black and white, like round chessboards. Her bald head is dotted with a half-dozen silver patches shaped like distorted puzzle pieces. Her round, legless torso ends in a band of silver and blue lights that seems to connect her to the hovering chair. What's left of her body is packed into a shiny black compression top with white markings, not that much different than my tattoos, woven into its surface.

It's a startling image. I'm not sure at first if it's beautiful or horrifying.

There's no question about her voice, however. That's hypnotic and as lovely as a song.

"I'm Olivia," she purrs with a sweet smile and just the slightest hint of something tinny, almost mechanical, behind her resonant voice. "And yes," she says to Cardyn, "I'm a Modified." She looks at our group of stunned faces and laughs. "Don't worry. I don't bite. Often."

"You don't bite at all," Wisp chuckles.

Olivia swings her pixilated eyes down along her body and back to us. "I'll spare you the embarrassment of asking. This all started out with a few implants here and there, and a few more after a training accident," she practically sings, her voice lilting as it comes at us in slightly echoing but gentle waves.

"Olivia was part of the training crew for the Telemachus mission to Mars," Granden explains.

Olivia nods. "After the first round of surgeries, I could run half the tech at NASA and most of the appliances in my house with a few taps on my implants. But pretty soon, it wasn't enough. I didn't just want to control the tech. I wanted to be able to communicate with it. For real, I mean. Not just the illusion of communication we've gotten used to. Anyway, it turned into a kind of addiction. That, plus an unfortunate six months as a human lab-rat in the Deenays' facilities back East, led to this."

She holds up her arms and shows us the bundles of fiber optic filaments where her hands and the ends of her forearms used to be. The thin colorful threads glisten and dance like jellyfish tendrils in the sharp light cast by the glass holo-monitors, info-spheres, and viz-screens around us.

At Wisp's request, Olivia spins back to the holo-displays and calls up the information Wisp promised to give us. The dozens of tendrils bursting from her forearms snake in and out of tiny ports in the arm of her hover-chair and on the bank of monitors around her.

A floating, rotating 3-D map of the earth appears in vibrant greens, browns, and blues with three silver circles hovering over three spots on the schematic.

"Can you enlarge it?" Wisp asks Olivia.

She says, "No problem," and, although she doesn't move, the image zooms in close over one of the three spinning silver circles to reveal eight cube-shaped buildings around a large green court-yard underneath.

"I'm sure you recognize these," Granden says.

"Processors," Manthy mutters.

"Three towns. Three Processors. Three Halos," Granden says simply, pointing one at a time to the three different spots over-laid on the slowly-spinning globe of light and color. "This one is in a small town south of Chicago. This one is just outside of Phil-adelphia. This one here you know well. It's in the middle of a place called Fort Leonard Wood, not too far from St. Louis, Missouri. This one is where we met and where I trained you for three months. There are other Processors planned for other towns that are currently on military lockdown near Madrid, Ankara, Beijing. The point is, you are either the start of a global system of recruitment and experimentation, or else you're going to help put an end to it. Once my father found out how poten-tially important some of you from the Valta were to his dream of a global network of weaponized teenagers, he said he wanted me to oversee you personally. Insisted on it, actually. The truth is, he's been getting more and more paranoid. More crazy, really. I was the only one he trusted. Or so he said. Sometimes I think he suspected I might turn on him, and so he sent me off with Hiller just to get me out of the way."

Rain slips her jacket off and ties it around her waist. "Does he know what happened? I mean about our escape and your helping us?"

Granden shakes his head. "He thinks I'm dead. He was told I died during your attempted escape. There were some others working on the inside with me. They made sure my body was found, identified, brought back to Washington D.C., and given a proper burial fit for the son of the great President Krug."

"Wonderful," Rain says. "So now the psychotic president of a corrupt government and figurehead of a bunch of mad scientists thinks we killed his son."

Granden chuckles and corrects Rain. "They're mad *geneticists*, technically. And don't worry. Krug thinks you died during the escape as well."

Rain slides her black hair back behind her ears and smooths it down with both hands, a sure sign she's impatient and frustrated, bordering on angry. "So what do we do now? We're outnumbered, and it sounds like most people who would be on our side don't even know there's a cause worth fighting for."

"That's true, Rain. Olivia is our first step in surveillance and education. She's been able to tap into certain communication networks. With her help, we're hoping to gather as much of the truth as possible and then spread it around to as many people as are willing to listen. We're hoping, this time, the virus that spreads will be one of truth instead of lies. If we can replace the illusion of the Eastern Order with the reality of Krug and the Patriot Party, we can get people to start fighting a real enemy instead of each other."

"To do this, eventually, we're going to need to educate as many people as possible," Wisp adds. "Knowledge. That's the key to freedom. We'll need to expose the lies and free the others like you, the ones who are still in those other operational Processors. There are as many as a dozen other Seventeens with abilities who are scattered throughout the two other existing Processors that Olivia has tracked down. Krug wants to turn those Seventeens into weapons. We can't let that happen."

"You said, 'eventually,'" I point out. "What do we do in the meantime?"

"We do what anyone does in a fight. We fight."

"Fighting sounds more like an *idea* than an actual plan," Brohn says to Wisp.

"I agree."

"What do you propose?"

"Well, first of all, we were hoping you'd find your way here."

"Which we did."

"Which you did. After that, we thought we might persuade you to help us, you know, save the world."

"Oh, is that all?" Cardyn chimes in. "No problem. After all, there are a whole *five* of us!"

Granden, Wisp, and Olivia exchange a look and a laugh.

Wisp steps forward. "Believe it or not and like it or not, you five may be our best hope at turning this thing around. The others look to me for leadership, which is fine. Being the Major, I can handle. But there's no one here who can do what the five of you can do. Olivia can get us a certain amount of intel, but it's limited, and the Patriots are learning how to secure their systems."

Cardyn sulks. "But only Kress, Manthy, and possibly Brohn have super powers."

Manthy punches Cardyn hard on the arm. "Getting headaches every time I walk by a computer isn't a super power, Jerk."

"There may be more to all of you than you know," Wisp says, and I swear I'm going to be blinded by the mysterious twinkle in her eye.

"We do have a plan," Granden assures us.

Wisp gives a long look around the room. "We start here. In this very building. As you know, we're taking care of the Modifieds downstairs. You met Sabine back in the Lounge where we were before. She used to be on the San Francisco city council, until she objected too many times to the wrong people. Now she helps me coordinate logistics. This room, as you know, is Tech Central. The fourth floor just above us is sleeping quarters. With your help, we're going to finish turning the entire top floor into a training facility." As Wisp talks, Olivia is able to focus on and illuminate the corresponding parts of the holo-schematics on one the floating spheres around her. She zooms in from an overview of San Francisco down to a street view that shows the Style Building in chalky gray-scale with its top floor lit up in vibrant red.

Wisp points to the third floor. "We're here. In one week, there's a control hand-off. The Patriot Army will be vulnerable." She flicks her finger at three more spots on the map, which are lit up in electric blue. If we hit them here, here, and here—that's their Munitions Depot, their Communications Central, and their Command Headquarters—we can disrupt their entire chain of command, commandeer a good chunk of their weapons, sever their supply lines, and cut their ability to communicate with the outside. That gives us control of San Francisco."

"Wow," Cardyn sighs. "That sounds like a really good plan. Just excellent. But things tend to get a bit more complicated when there's an entire army dedicated to making sure excellent plans fail and we all end up dead."

"We're ready for whatever anyone can throw at us," Rain boasts. "We can do this. Granden knows what we've been through. He helped train us. He knows what we can do."

Wisp and Granden both nod, but it's Wisp who finally speaks. "I don't doubt what you can do or how much you can contribute to the cause. But there are only five of you. As Cardyn pointed out, that's hardly an army."

"But you said there were others. Other Insubordinates."

"There are. There are a couple hundred of us. But only about forty or fifty or so in this building at any given time. The rest of us are scattered around the city, hidden away in little pockets here and there. Some have managed to blend into the general population. No matter where they are, though, they lack training and leadership."

Card raises a hand timidly. "Then why don't we train and lead them?"

"Spoken like a true warrior," Wisp says. "Exactly what I had in mind myself."

"What do you suggest?" I ask.

"I've been giving it some thought. It's manageable if we break it down. Here. Rain and I will handle strategy. You and Manthy will team up with Olivia to handle surveillance. Along with Render, of course. We can do all that from this room. Brohn and Cardyn will get the top floor set up and head up the training."

"What kind of training, exactly?" I ask.

"You got drilled in all kinds of psychological tests and in armed and unarmed combat. The Insubordinates don't have anywhere close to the experience you have. Brohn has the physical skills needed, and, from what Granden tells me, Cardyn is good at communicating with people in a way they can easily understand. Granden is the perfect person to help coordinate it all," Wisp says. "After all, he trained you. Who better than him to help you to train the others?"

I look over to Granden who gives Wisp a squint and a slow half-hearted nod. "I had over three months with the Seventeens," he says. "We have just under a week now. I'm not promising any miracles."

"I'm not praying for any," Wisp says. "Just a little effort and some general competence. We have the will and the resources. What we don't have is time. In one week, our chances of pulling this off will go from slim to none."

"It's really that dire?" Rain asks.

Wisp and Granden exchange a quick glace before Granden clears his throat and turns toward Rain. "In one week, the Patriot Army will bring in reinforcements, just like Wisp says. But there's more." He shifts his gaze from Rain to the rest of us almost apologetically, like he can't bear to look any of us in the eye. "In one week, those new troops will be accompanying none other than President Krug himself."

Cardyn sounds incredulous. "Krug will be here? In San Francisco? President Krug? The one responsible for all of...this?"

Wisp and Granden nod their heads in unison like synchronized swimmers gearing up for their big finale. "He's heard about the Insubordinates," Wisp says. "He's here to put out any fires before they can really get going."

Brohn rubs his chin. "Then we'd better make sure we've got a real bonfire going when it comes time to greet him. One he can't ever hope to put out."

Wisp looks up at her big brother with a smile of pure pride spread across her face. "Our thinking exactly."

She thanks Olivia for her help and starts to head out of the room. "We start first thing in the morning. For now, time to get some sleep."

We say our goodbyes to Olivia and follow Wisp and Granden out the room, down the hall, and up a flight of stairs. At the top landing, Wisp takes us past a series of rooms. "These are our dorms. It's where we sleep in between dodging the Patriot Army, gathering intel, and trying to stay alive just one day longer. I hate to pull you into this. I really do. If it's any consolation, the beds are deceptively comfortable. Enjoy them while you can. Starting tomorrow, we're going to be dealing with some pretty serious *dis*comfort."

Wisp taps a small button on a bracelet on her wrist, and the door to the room swings open.

2 7

THE BEDS ARE LITTLE MORE THAN LOW, WHITE-SHEETED AND metal-framed army cots set up with military precision in a straight line against the near wall of the clean, high-ceilinged room. The far wall contains a tall dresser with two vertical doors and eight smaller drawers, a viz-screen of glimmering black glass, and a door-less entryway leading to a shower room decorated with a checkerboard pattern of white and yellow tiles. There's just enough sun from the only window to give the room an angelic halo effect with beams of light from the rapidly fading evening sun illuminating the tiny dancing particles of dust skittering around throughout the open space.

"Anyway," Wisp says with a sweep of her hand. "The rest of us are already set up in rooms along the hall. This room is all yours. Get some sleep. You've been through a lot."

"With a lot more to come," Granden adds grimly.

Wisp gives each of us a tight hug before leaving with Granden right behind her.

The five of us stand in hushed awe of the room for a full minute and stare until Rain breaks the silence.

"Beds!" she squeals as she dashes over to the nearest cot and hurls herself into it. The bed squeaks and sags as she lands. She bounces and rolls around, gathering the white sheets in a tangle around her until she's little more than a soft cotton burrito with a beaming face and a head of long black hair splayed out in every direction.

Cardyn is quick to follow her, and he spreads his arms wide and swan-dives, face first, into the second bed. He bounces high into the air, twists around, lands on his back, and kicks his feet up in a spasm of pure glee.

Brohn, Manthy, and I are bit more reserved. Laughing at our friends' uninhibited joy, we cross the room and plop down one at a time onto the next three beds.

It's been an exhausting adventure getting here. I'm tired all over. Eyes. Brain. Muscles. Bones. I'm a human yawn.

"What's wrong with this picture?" Brohn asks, his nose turned up in a disgusted scrunch.

"Besides the fact that you're clearly entrenched in an alpha male suppression of a powerful and well-deserved desire to giggle yourself silly?" Cardyn asks.

Brohn holds up a tightly clenched fist. "I'm suppressing something all right, Card, but it's not the giggles. No. Don't you see? The beds are in a row."

We know instantly what he means, and we spring into action. Just like we did back in the Valta, in the Processor, in the desert cave, and every other time we've had the opportunity, we drag the beds into a rough star-shape with the heads together to form a kind of spoked wheel with a communal circle in the middle.

After kicking off our boots, we each take a seat at the end of our bed. Rain and I sit cross-legged. Brohn sits with his long legs, muscular even through his pocketed pants, over the edge of his bed with his arms angled out behind him and his stocking feet planted firmly on the ground. Cardyn is on his stomach, facing the rest of us with his legs kicked up into the air, his feet twirling and tapping together like a giddy red-headed eight-year-old girl at her first sleepover. Manthy, as always, is lying on her back, her head at the far end of the bed, so we get the best view and smell possible of her stinky bare feet.

We're just sighing and settling in when Manthy clamps her eyes shut and presses her fingertips to her temples. "Still feels like elephants are tap-dancing in my head."

"That's the drawback of connecting," I remind her. "Doesn't matter if you're connecting with digi-tech or with a clever bird. It's like you told me once: it's a matter of sharing, not taking over. Whether we realize it or want it or not, we always give away a part of ourselves when we connect with someone—or something —else."

"I never thought I'd like either of those things," Manthy says, sitting up abruptly with an ironic smile of realization spreading out on her face.

"What's that?"

"Sharing and giving away a part of myself." She blushes as she looks over at Brohn, Cardyn, and Rain before turning her attention back to me and finally to the floor. "I guess I was always...I don't know...afraid of..."

"Of...?" I ask.

"Of being vulnerable. It never occurred to me that being vulnerable *with* someone is better than trying to be powerful all alone."

I reach across to Manthy's bed and give her smelly foot a gentle squeeze. She doesn't recoil, tell me to back off, or give me a dirty look. Instead, she just falls back into her sheets, her hands folded behind her head, and stares up at the ceiling.

Brohn drops back onto his elbows and looks up at the tiled ceiling, too. "I still don't know how you guys do that. The whole connecting thing, I mean."

"We'll tell you as soon as we figure it out ourselves," I laugh. "It does get easier," I add, turning back to Manthy. "As long as we think of it as a partnership, not a parlor trick. And as long as we remember that being able to *do* something incredible doesn't necessarily *make* us someone incredible. Although, in your case, I'd definitely say you've got a lot of both going on."

Manthy looks over at me out of the corner of her eyes and smiles again, something I don't think I'll ever get used to. The girl who used to walk around in the shadows with her head down now seems taller, more adult, more alive. She pulls her thick brown hair out of its tidy ponytail and is sporting what has to be the prettiest smile I've ever seen in my life. I'm happy for her. I'm happy for how far she's come and for the amazing person she's turned into. No. That's not it, exactly. She's always been amazing. I guess if I'm being honest, I'm happy with myself for finally recognizing her amazingness.

"You do realize," Cardyn says evenly, his giddy smile devolving into a somber frown, "we can't possibly pull this off. I mean, I've been thinking about this since we got here. There's us five. Rain and I can't do anything special, and Brohn, well, we don't totally know about you yet. Wisp, who, okay I'll grant you, is pretty bad-ass. Granden. We know what he can do. Fifty untrained and scared-poopless Insubordinates. Olivia who's awesome in theory but useless if the power goes out. And a roomful of Modifieds who don't even know where or probably even *who* they are anymore." Cardyn stops for a second and then starts counting off on his fingers. "And we're supposed to take down a Munitions Depot, Communications Central, the Patriot Army Command Headquarters, and liberate the entire city of San Francisco?"

"In a week," I remind him.

"I have an idea," Cardyn exclaims, his finger in the air. "Why don't we just cut out the middle-man and kill ourselves, so the

Patriot Army doesn't have to worry about wasting five of their precious bullets?"

Brohn gives Cardyn a dirty look and a guttural grunt. "Cardyn's brilliant alternative plan aside, I'm usually not the wide-eyed optimist of our little group. But the odds of us having made it this far at all are pretty astronomical. Technically, we should have been killed in the Valta. Then in the Processor. Then on the road. Or by Adric and Celia. Or in that little military base in the middle of the desert. Or in Reno. Or Oakland. Or sneaking into this city. The point is, we probably shouldn't be here, but we are. Maybe there's room for one more long-shot in our future. I say we roll the dice and take our chances. What's the back-up plan? Surrender and join Kella, Karmine, and Terk as casualties of a pointless war?"

Manthy sits up and corrects him. "Kella's not a casualty. She's going to be just fine."

I admire her optimism, but I don't share it enough to agree with her out loud.

"No," Rain says to Cardyn, stretching her arms and then arching her back like a cat. "Brohn's right. No matter how we weigh the options, it still comes down to fight or die or live the rest of our lives as lab-rats or slaves. It's not a complicated equation."

Cardyn is just starting to resign himself to Rain's unimpeachable truth when we're interrupted by a sudden knocking and a voice that sounds like someone calling out, "Hello in there!" with a mouthful of caramel-covered marbles. We sit up, snap our heads around, and look at the door, but when the voice cries out again, it's clearly coming from the opposite side of the room. Actually, it's coming from the window. We look over and see the small black feathered face we've come to know as family. Render taps on the glass with his beak and cries out *kraa!* as I clamber over Cardyn's bed and leap over to open the window for him.

With me giggling hysterically and stumbling backward as I

raise the window, Render bursts into the room in an explosion of dust and feathers. We all laugh and cough into the cloud as he alights on the tall cherry-wood chest of drawers against the far wall. He struts along the top of the armoire like a rock-star on a stage before fluttering up onto the decorative scroll-shaped ornament at the top. He preens the feathers under one of his wings and ruffles his hackles.

"Nice to have our Conspiracy all together again and settled in one place," I say, rolling back into my bed.

Tipping his beak toward the ceiling, Render *kraas* his agreement, and we all laugh again.

"Is he going to stay in here with us?" Rain asks, a nearly-impossible-to-detect tremor of apprehension in her voice.

"Don't worry," I assure her. "I won't have him peck your lips off in the middle of the night."

We all share another good laugh. It's nice to be wiping tears of joy from eyes for a change instead of tears of sorrow.

"Did you ever figure out those visions of his?" Brohn asks almost absently, like he doesn't really care one way or the other.

Rain scratches her head. "Visions?"

"From the military base," Brohn says. "Remember? The soldiers. The dead girl."

"Yeah!" Cardyn chirps. "You mentioned something about that in the truck on the way to Reno."

I shake my head. "I don't know if the images I saw through Render were past or future. All I know—and I can guarantee you this—is they were real. Very real."

"I can't speak for anyone else," Cardyn says at last through a lion-like yawn. "But that is a heavier thought than I'm prepared to bear right now. I'm tired, and if what Wisp says is true, we have a very big week ahead of us, and we'll likely be dead before it's all over."

"I'm with you," Manthy says, turning over onto her side and

curling up into a cozy ball under her sheets. "Except for the being dead part. That, you can do on your own."

Rain asks me if I'm sure her lips are safe from Render. I grin and assure her they are. She gives me a thumb's up before fluffing up her pillow and disappearing under her sheets.

The five of us are quiet for a long time. Even Render has settled into sleep on the top of the armoire with his head tucked against his wing. Everyone's breath melts into a seamless purr. Except Brohn's. I hear him roll toward me in his cot, which is next to mine.

"You awake?" he asks quietly.

I whisper, "Yes."

"Worried?"

"This is going to be a challenge," I mutter into the near-dark.

"The training?"

"The being apart. Wisp wants me connected with Render and doing surveillance with Olivia and Manthy. You'll be busy upstairs with Cardyn, trying to turn a bunch of scared revolutionaries into an actual, functional army."

Brohn slides off his cot and slips onto mine, putting an arm around my waist and pressing a kiss to my forehead.

In so many ways we've grown up. We've lost our innocence. Yet we've still never done anything more than kiss. It's as if we're holding on to this last fragile strand of our youth as long as we can. We're protecting ourselves from too much perilous closeness, because we've already lost so much that we can't bear the thought of losing ourselves in each other.

"We'll still have nights together," he whispers. "It's not nearly enough, I know. But this isn't the end, you realize."

"Of the war? I know," I smile and stare into his bright blue eyes. "It's just the beginning."

"No. I meant us," he says with a gentle shake of his head. He takes my hand, intertwining his fingers with mine. "This isn't where we end, Kress. We've always had to fight against the weight of this tragic past dragging behind after us. But now, we have a future. For the first time, I really believe that. You and I have something to look forward to."

Even as I tell him I agree, I fall into a soft sleep, my hand still holding onto his.

End of Book 2

NOW AVAILABLE: REBELLION

The third book in the Resistance Trilogy, *Rebellion*, is coming in May 2019!

Aided by the Modifieds, led by Wisp in the Command Center and by Kress in the field, the Insubordinates wage a counter-offensive against the Patriot Army in an effort to liberate the city of San Francisco...

A NEW SERIES BY K. A. RILEY:

SEEKER'S WORLD

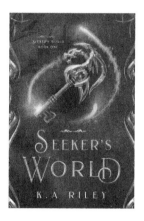

On her seventeenth birthday, Vega Sloane receives a series of strange and puzzling gifts. Among them is a key shaped like a dragon. The question is: What exactly is it meant to open?

All of a sudden, the peaceful town where Vega grew up is crawling with shadows, strange beings and unlikely allies.

Vega soon discovers that many of the ancient stories she once considered myths and legends are true, and that a magical world exists beyond her own...one that only the chosen few can see. It's a world where cruel beings stalk the lands and magic lives on the air, where the Blood-born prove their worth in an ancient academy that trains those born with special powers.

ALSO BY K. A. RILEY

Resistance Trilogy

Recruitment

Render

Rebellion

Emergents Trilogy

Survival

Sacrifice (Coming in November 2019)

Synthesis (Coming in 2020)

Transcendent Trilogy (Coming Soon!)

Travelers

Transfigured

Terminus

Seeker's World Series

Seeker's World

Seeker's Quest

Seeker's Fate

Athena's Law Series

Book One: *Rise of the Inciters*

Book Two: *Into an Unholy Land*

Book Three: *No Man's Land*

For updates on upcoming release dates, Blog entries, and exclusive excerpts from upcoming books and more:

https://karileywrites.org

Made in the USA
Coppell, TX
01 April 2021